THE NEW NEIGHBOR

THE NEW NEIGHBOR

RAY GARTON

OPEN ROAD
INTEGRATED MEDIA
NEW YORK

ISBN 978-1-4976-4276-8

This edition published in 2014 by Open Road Integrated Media, Inc.
345 Hudson Street
New York, NY 10014
www.openroadmedia.com

Acknowledgments

My thanks to the following people for their invaluable help: My wonderful wife Dawn, Steven Spruill, Karen Leonard, Steve Rubin, Brian and Tanya Hodges, Richard Curtis, John R. Douglas, Damian Wild, Rhonda Blackmon Walton, Cindi Loftus, and my terribly entertaining Facebook friends.

*This book is for
my friends
Latrice and Ken Innes
Thank you*

Global Inquisitor

Manic Mom Chainsaws Husband and Son In Crazed Attack

Chicago, Ill.

A mild-mannered housewife became a manic mom and took a chainsaw to her family until her desperate, bleeding husband blew her away with a shotgun!

35-year-old Marie Prosky, a housewife in the Chicago suburb of Arlington Heights, turned into a bloodthirsty butcher one afternoon, fired up her husband's chainsaw and used it to split open the skull of her sixteen-year-old son Gordon. The terrorized teen died instantly, but not his father, who bravely stood up to the buzzing butcher.

37-year-old Ronald Prosky, a reporter for a prominent Chicago newspaper, was seriously injured. The wicked wife used the chainsaw to cut into her husband's face and slice off one of his hands.

In spite of his injuries and loss of blood, Prosky was able to get to the shotgun and blow his wife to kingdom come!

While the gutsy gunman teetered on the edge of death in a nearby hospital, local police officials tried to piece the case together in search of answers, but are still unable to give a reason for Mrs. Prosky's bloodthirsty buzzing....

One Year Later

IT was under the light of a fat, bright moon on a dead summer night, while her husband Mitch slept off a fifth of cheap whiskey, that Connie Padgett sneaked out of their stubby bullet-like trailer with a small suitcase packed with the few things she could not leave behind. Her feet clanked on the three rattly metal steps below the trailer's door, then crunched in gravel as she closed the door carefully, silently. She limped painfully because, a couple of days ago, Mitch had thrown her against the night stand and she'd bruised her hip.

Through the trailer's window Connie could see the shimmer of their small black-and-white television, playing for its unconscious viewer, who was sprawled on the sofa breathing noisily through his mouth. As she turned and looked around her, she saw the same glow – sometimes gray, sometimes a hazy blend of colors – coming from nearly every trailer in the court, like frightened ghosts trying desperately to escape their small box-like prisons.

Connie walked past Mitch's rusty, battered Chevy pickup to the edge of the narrow graveled road that ran down the center of the Cherry Tree Trailer Court and looked around for the last time. At twenty-three, she'd spent the last two years at Cherry Tree, watching the Kansas flatland that surrounded it grow flatter and seemingly more vast while Mitch lost one job after another. The gap between jobs grew a bit longer each time and was filled with a bit more drinking and progressively chillier silences. In two short years that now seemed a lifetime, Connie had come to this: sneaking away with a single suitcase of personal belongings, wondering why she had ever married him in the first place.

He'd been different back then, two years ago; he'd been charming and warm and full of enthusiasm. The plan had been that he would work until they could afford to send her back to school, at which time she would finish her education and begin teaching. But it didn't work out that way. One job after another failed; he began drinking; he stopped looking for work, until they were finally so broke that she had no idea how he could afford the booze he brought home every night, let alone the gas it took to get him to the store. And, of course, along with the booze came the screaming fights, the swinging fists. It seemed inevitable and she had not been surprised.

But she hadn't expected what began to happen six months ago.

They got a new neighbor, a beautiful woman who turned the head of every man in the trailer court, including – maybe especially – Mitch's. During the day, he did favors for her; he worked on her car, repaired broken appliances and even painted a cabinet for her – with his own paint. In the evenings he drank, of course; he sat in front of the television with a bottle and a glass, looked angry and snapped at Connie, said horrible, hurtful things and sometimes struck her or threw her around the trailer. All of that was bad enough, but late at night he did something else that Connie thought was even worse. He went for walks. Of course, he couldn't stand up without swaying, but around eleven or so each night, he struggled off the sofa, slurred something about needing some fresh air, and went outside. He was always gone for hours. She had her suspicions, but wasn't certain until she followed him out one night.

He went over to her trailer. Connie had watched as the entire trailer rocked with their rutting. It was one thing that he was having an affair, but Mitch hadn't touched Connie in months. That was when she decided to leave.

She walked down the narrow road that ran through the trailer court, trying not to look at the trailer in which her husband's lover lived, but unable to keep from glancing across the way to the candle burning in the trailer's window. It was there every night, its flame winking in the darkness. Although Connie was ashamed of the thought, she often wished the candle would burn the trailer to the ground.

Looking at her watch, Connie realized she was early; she'd called a cab about two hours ago and it wouldn't arrive for about another ten minutes, so she took her time walking away from her home, glancing over her shoulder at her trailer now and then, half hoping Mitch would stick his head out the door and ask where she was going, maybe beg her to come back; maybe even tell her that he really did love her and promise that things would change. She had no idea what she would do if that were to happen, but she couldn't help wishing, hoping that the last two years of her life had not been wasted.

She walked slowly, watching that candle in the woman's window. There was a shapeless heap on her front porch: one of the two Dobermans. She kept the other one inside, walked both of them twice each day and treated them like royalty. They were named Cain and Abel and Connie couldn't help feeling that there was something sinister about those dogs. Watching them walk on each side of the woman every day reminded Connie of every evil queen and wicked stepmother she'd read about in fairytales as a child.

Something moved.

Connie stopped. The dog on the woman's porch lifted its head, ears stiff, and gave a low, throaty growl. On the opposite side of the trailer Connie spotted movement in the darkness. Bushes rustled and footsteps crunched over the ground.

A short squat figure emerged from the dark edge of the road. It looked to Connie like a dwarf. She stepped back into the shadows and hugged her bag to her stomach, holding her breath as the figure crept around the woman's trailer toward the porch and the Doberman, limping awkwardly into a pool of light from the window next door.

Connie dropped her bag when she saw his face. He turned to her suddenly, so she could see him fully, and she shrank back, horrified.

The Doberman stood, growling, and the man moved quickly. A long gleaming blade appeared in his hand with a metallic hiss and he waved at Connie, rasping, "Go! Get away from here! Now!" Then he rounded the trailer and lunged for the dog as the porch light came on and the door opened.

"Oh, my God," Connie whimpered, bending to grope for her bag. Clutching it, she stood and glanced once more at the trailer across the road as the glinting blade swept down and the dog made a long guttural sound that made Connie feel sick. Then the man cried out as the dog fell off the porch and the woman – Mitch's lover – appeared in the doorway, growling, "You!" with surprised recognition.

Connie ran toward the trailer court's entrance, praying that the cab would be waiting for her, but seeing clearly that it wasn't. She ran away, heading for the road and deciding to wave down the first car that came along, when –

– the man's voice ripped through the night as he screamed, "No! Die! You should die!"

The woman laughed and there was another sound. It was a sound Connie had never heard before, but she knew it was not human. Halfway to the road, she tried to run faster without falling because now there were footsteps behind her, also running, and the man was screaming, "No, I killed it! I killed it!"

Gravel crackled like frying bacon beneath the tires of the cab as it pulled to the shoulder in front of the trailer court. Connie laughed with relief as she gasped for breath, waving at the driver, crying, "Open the d-duh-door! Open the door!"

"You the one who called?" the driver asked through the window.

"Yes! Please! Open the –"

She stumbled and fell forward and her bag skidded over the gravel away from her, but she scurried to her feet instantly, ignored the bag as she threw herself toward the cab, tore the door open and fell into the back seat. She screamed when she turned to pull the door closed and saw the man right behind her. He pushed into the cab, slammed the door and shouted, "Drive! Drive now!" But the man wasn't the worst of it. The real reason for her scream was the black thing following him. It rocketed toward the cab, two or three feet off the ground, flapping broad wings that seemed to be made of dead skin. And the sound it made ...

Connie wanted to vomit.

Uttering a babble of curses, the driver put the car in gear and threw gravel behind them as he drove away.

"Faster!" the man said. "Faster!"

Connie felt numb, drugged, detached from her body, and stared open-mouthed at the man's face, not wanting to believe what she was seeing. Looking down, she saw the blade and, even worse, the hand that held it.The hand wasn't real.

"Don't worry," the man gasped, his chest heaving. "I won't hurt you. I came to help you." He reached out to touch her arm and she pulled back, pressing herself to the opposite door. He put his hand back in his lap and whispered, "You can never go back there again. Ever."

Last Weekend

A QUIET rustle passed through the congregation as Pastor Jeremy Quillerman stepped up to the pulpit. He was in his mid-fifties, with a round belly that pressed against the powder-blue shirt beneath the coat of his dark-gray suit. He walked with a limp, the origin of which was a mystery to everyone at the Christian Fellowship Non-Denominational Church. His right hand had small mangled nubs where his last three fingers used to be. The remaining thumb and forefinger latched over his bible like fleshy hooks as he placed it on the pulpit and smiled at his congregation. His face was soft, gentle, lined with the creases of countless smiles. His silver-streaked black hair was cut short, carefully combed and thinning on top. His thick mustache was dark but had a white stripe below each nostril.

The gentleness of his face, however, was offset by his eyes. The left eye was glass and, as a result, was wider than the right and bulged slightly. From the inside corner of the eye a pale scar, smooth and slightly glossy, crawled up over the bridge of his nose and up the center of his forehead, stopping just short of his receding hairline. The right eye was both hard and sad, as if it had seen too many things that were at once horrifying and heartbreaking.

Pastor Quillerman began his sermon the way he always did: as if he were having a quiet conversation with a dear friend.

"What is evil?" he asked. "Where do you suppose it nests? Is it easy to recognize? Will we always know it when we see it so we can steer clear? Or has the master of deception fooled us with a perfectly executed shell game and led us to believe that evil is lurking just around the corner or right behind us ... when it is, in reality, directly under our noses?"

The Pritchards were sitting halfway back from the front
in the left column of pews, George with his arm around Jen,
who had turned sixteen yesterday and who fidgeted beside
her seventeen-year-old brother Robby.

"In I Peter 5:8," Pastor Quillerman said, "and I'm reading
from the New International Reader's Version here, Peter
says, 'Control yourselves. Be on your guard. Your enemy
the devil is like a roaring lion. He prowls around looking
for someone to chew up and swallow.'"

Some of the Pritchards' neighbors were in the church,
too. Mr. and Mrs. LaBianco were seated in their usual
place: front pew, right column, on the aisle. And behind
them were the Weylands, Paul and his wife Denise and their
teenage daughters, Caryl and Stephanie.

"Now what, you may ask," the pastor went on, "does self
control have to do with being on guard against evil? Isn't it
enough simply to watch out for evil? Isn't it enough for us
to be constantly on the alert for its traps? Well, my friends,
that way of thinking happens to be one of its traps."

Sheri MacNeil sat in the very back pew with her son
Christopher. She always sat there, just in case the toddler
decided to start up a fuss or needed to go to the bathroom.

"Just as a child molester or a murderer almost never looks
like a child molester or murderer, evil is seldom obvious. In
the past, evil has been depicted as a red demon with horns
and a tail. We've become more sophisticated today, but I'm
afraid we still expect it to show itself, to look like evil. It's
natural. I find myself doing it all the time. We all want
something solid and specific to watch for. But when we
spend all of our time trying to do away with things that
might look questionable, sometimes we completely miss the
most insidious forms of evil that are right before us ... or, my
friends, or ... that are growing inside us."

Robby's best friend Dylan Garry was seated with his
mother in the opposite column of pews – Mr. Garry never
came to church – and the two boys made subtle, snide faces
at one another across the center aisle.

"Just as god lives in each of us – just as the kingdom of

heaven is within us, as Jesus said – we also have seeds of evil inside us," Pastor Quillerman said. "All those seeds need is a little nurturing, a little care, in order to blossom. Or sometimes, all they need is a little neglect – like weeds in a garden. We so often look outward for the things we need, for the answers to our questions, the solutions to our problems. More often than not, we would save a lot of time by looking inward. The novelist Steven Spruill once said, 'We are, all of us, all of the things we have ever been.' And that's a lot. We have within us so much to draw on, to learn from. But we tend to neglect it while we search outside ourselves.

"In Matthew 7:5, we are told, 'First take the piece of wood out of your own eye. Then you will be able to see clearly to take the bit of sawdust out of your friend's eye.' Look to yourself first – you may be guilty of the very thing you're accusing your friend of, and that makes you a hypocrite. Evil is like that. Before we can recognize it in front of us, we have to be able to recognize it inside of us. Because like everything else ... it's there. That's where self control comes in. If we cannot manage our own weaknesses and problems, we have no business passing judgment on others for theirs."

Jen played tic-tac-toe with herself on a scrap of paper and George's head began to nod. Karen poked her elbow in his ribs and his head popped up; after a while, though, it began, ever so slightly at first, to nod again.

The pastor said, "Evil never looks like evil. It looks innocent and harmless ... attractive ... even alluring. And sometimes ... sometimes ... it looks like the face we see when we look in the mirror."

Chapter 1

The Arrival

ROBBY Pritchard was masturbating when he first saw her. He was supposed to be doing his homework, and had intended to do it when he came to his room earlier. But his mind took no time at all to wander from his English literature textbook to thoughts of his English lit teacher, Miss Weiss.

Miss Weiss was young; this was her first teaching job. In fact, she was the youngest teacher Robby had ever had and he found this distracting. Not simply because she was young, but because she was beautiful. Tall, with dark-brown hair, long legs and tits that were ... well, she put Debbie Petievich to shame and Debbie Petievich – captain of the cheerleaders, chairman of the entertainment committee and the most sought after date at Enterprise High School – was no slouch. Maybe it was because Miss Weiss was older and in a position of authority that made her so much more desirable; maybe it was because Debbie Petievich, aside from her "sexualism and gorgeosity" as Dylan Gary put is, was such a bitch. Whatever the reason, Robby knew he was not alone; Miss Weiss had eclipsed Debbie Petievich in the minds of a lot of the guys at Enterprise.

On the evening of the new neighbor's arrival, Miss Weiss had also eclipsed English lit homework in Robby's mind. After his initial attempt to concentrate on his homework failed, he gave in and closed the book on his desk. The more he thought about her – fantasized, really, because he'd never actually seen her in the nude – the more aroused he

became and the more difficult it was to remain focused on
his work.

He turned his chair to face the computer monitor on
his L-shaped desk and went to porn site he'd book marked.
The screen filled with thumbnails of naked women engaged
in sex with men, other women, or themselves, in couples,
threesomes and groups. He chose a video, and as it opened,
he got up and locked his bedroom door, then removed his
shoes and jeans.

He knew his mom was loading the dinner dishes into the
washer and Dad was helping Jen with her homework, so no
one would bother him for a while. He started slowly as he
watched the video – a beautiful young brunette masturbating
with a vibrating dildo. It was a self-shot amateur video; the
woman was on her sofa, the camera apparently resting on
the coffee table. She smiled at him as she moved the dildo
with her left hand and fingered her clit with her right.

A car door slammed and there was a mild clatter outside,
but it could have been across town as far as he was concerned.
He stroked himself a little faster as he watched the brunette
– no more than nineteen, probably making the video for a
boyfriend.

Outside, the sounds continued and Robby's curiosity
stirred in a distracted sort of way as his hand moved faster.

A few long minutes passed unnoticed.

There were only the girl on the screen, the sensation of
his hand –

– and the noise outside.

After a while, something crashed.

Robby did not stop, but he turned from the monitor to
the shaded window. To satisfy his curiosity so he could
continue uninterrupted, he rolled his chair over to the
window, pulled the shade aside and looked out into the night.

There were lights on in the house across the street. It
had been empty and for sale for nearly six months, since the
Huitts had moved to the east coast, but now there was a car
in the drive with a U-Haul trailer behind it and a few boxes
on the ground. The trailer's doors had just been slammed

– he realized that was the crash he'd heard – and a woman stood by the trailer now, slapping her hands together to brush them off. Then she bent forward slightly to dust off her thighs.

Robby's hand continued to stroke and he knew he was close. He was about to drop the shade and go back to the monitor because he wanted to see the girl in the video squirm and wince as she reached orgasm, but –

– the woman across the street stood and turned, one hand on her hip, the other brushing aside a long strand of hair and –

– she looked at him.

Through the darkness of the clear, cold night, from across the street, she looked into his window and directly into his eyes.

Embarrassed and ashamed, Robby flinched, already trembling and grasping on the very edge of his orgasm. He jerked the vinyl shade back into place with his free hand, but his movement was too sudden, too strong, and the shade slipped from his hand and shot upward, rolling up above the window and –

– she was still watching him, staring, not absently, but with interest, as if perhaps she were watching some suspicious goings on at the house across the street, like a break-in or a domestic squabble in the yard, and –

– Robby wanted to duck below the window, feeling certain she could tell what he was doing even though he knew better, but he couldn't take his eyes from her, even as his hand moved faster and faster and his chest heaved and a small moan rose up in his throat. He couldn't take his eyes from her pale face, from her eyes, because it seemed odd that he could see them so clearly from that distance, and –

– in the glow of the streetlight, he saw her eyes narrow and crinkle slightly as her interest turned to amusement, and she smirked, then her narrow face opened in a smile directed at him and –

– that was when Robby came.

* * * *

"That's right," George Pritchard said encouragingly to his sixteen-year-old daughter, looking at the math problem she'd worked out in her notebook. "I think you've got it, Jen."

She bit her lower lip, frowning at the numbers. "It's hard," she muttered.

"I know, but you're catching on. It's going to get easier, I promise."

"Then I'll graduate and never use this information again, right?" she asked with a smirk.

"Something like that," he said as he stood from the dining room table and went into the kitchen, where the dishwasher was rumbling and harrumphing and his wife Karen was seated at the small desk in the corner licking envelopes. "What're you doing, hon?"

"Getting the bills ready to send tomorrow," she said.

He got a beer from the refrigerator, popped the can open and took a drink, leaning against the counter and watching his wife.

She looked tired as she addressed another envelope, sealed it, and put it on the stack, then started on another. Her shoulders sagged and her blonde hair was mussed; her movements were mechanical and her mind seemed to be on other things.

Karen was his second wife. His first – Robby's mother – had been run down by a drunk driver while crossing the street fifteen years ago and he'd vowed then never to remarry. It had been a wonderful marriage in every way. Of course, it had only lasted four years and might very well have soured with time, but those four years with Laura had been happy ones, with never a fight or a harsh word exchanged, with an openness that George had never experienced before, and a sex life that did not fade a fraction during their marriage but instead grew more exciting and creative. He talked about his first marriage little, if at all, because he found that no one believed that a marriage, even one so brief, could be so good.

But after three years of raising Robby on his own and having no social life whatsoever, outside of his work as general manager of a local FM radio station, George began to grow lonely. He hadn't slept well since Laura's death. For a while, it was because he missed having her beside him in bed, but as time passed, it was simply because he was alone in bed. Then, when Robby had to have his tonsils removed, George met Karen.

She was a nurse in the pediatrics ward at Redding Medical Center and seemed to sense that, although the tonsillectomy was a minor and routine operation, George was worried. One loss had been almost more than he could bear and he feared any possible complications. Karen was friendly and reassuring, but she seemed reluctant when George tried to engage her in more personal conversation, especially when he asked her out to dinner. He was not discouraged, though.

After Robby was discharged, George could not stop thinking about her. She was physically attractive – a soft face with a slightly upturned nose and lovely blue eyes that were at once warm and vulnerable, cautious, as if they had seen their share of pain and disappointment, perhaps more. But she also had about her a soothing calm, an assuredness and strength that seemed to outweigh the shadows of pain in her eyes, and that attracted George as much as her physical beauty.

He dropped by the hospital to visit with her during her lunch break and tried to get her telephone number. When that failed, he sent flowers with another invitation to dinner and his telephone number. Four days later, she called and, with obvious reluctance, agreed to go out with him.

On their first date, Karen told him about Jen, then six-years-old, and said she'd been reluctant to date because she wanted to give all the time she could to her daughter; raising a child alone was difficult and Karen wanted to make sure she had plenty of time available to make up for any mistakes she might make before it was too late. George said he understood perfectly and had no intention of coming between Karen and her daughter.

Their relationship proceeded slowly. There were no fireworks, but George enjoyed her company, warmed up to her easily, and with time, came to care for her a great deal, even love her. Jen seemed to like him and, when she met Rob, they hit it off nicely.

It was some time before George and Karen made love, but when they did, it was tender and loving, although not especially passionate.

Karen's first marriage had not been a good one and she was reluctant to marry again. She feared she would not be able to fill Laura's shoes, neither as George's wife nor Robby's mother. But George reassured her in his calming way that she had nothing to worry about.

After they were married, George frequently had to remind himself not to compare his relationship with Karen to his previous marriage. Sexually, Laura had been playful, imaginative, eager to please, and always ready to try something new. She often met him at the front door after work in a new piece of lingerie and they made love in every room in the house before having Rob. They'd viewed sex the way a child viewed recess at school – a time to play, to have fun.

Karen seemed to need no variety. She was always willing, but never enthused.

They usually stuck to one position and had sex on a regular, although not too frequent, basis. She always wrinkled her brow at the mention of sex toys and the one time he'd bought her some lingerie – he'd spent the afternoon shopping for just the right pieces – she'd declined to wear them. "It's too cold to wear that skimpy stuff," she said. "I don't have the kind of body you need to wear those things," she said, and each time he brought up the subject after that, she had a new reason for not wearing them.

But she was a good woman, intelligent and fair, warm and giving, and George decided he could live with that.

They had been married ten years. George was not

unhappy. He was not ecstatic, either. But he tried hard not to think about Laura very much. Instead, he told himself that, for four years, he'd had something that most people never experience in a lifetime. He was content. And he loved Karen; in ten years, that love had become worn and soft, like an old recliner that had patches and lumps but was still the most comfortable seat in the house.

George put his beer on the counter and went to Karen's side, put a hand on the back of her neck and squeezed gently as he bent down and nuzzled her hair, kissed the top of her head.

She looked up at him and smiled weakly.

"You look tired," he said.

"Bad day. We lost a little girl this morning."

In the past, George would have asked why she hadn't told him sooner, why she hadn't talked about it if it bothered her, but that had become tiresome. He'd learned to live with the fact that Karen was not very open about things that bothered her – even things that made her happy – and that if something was on her mind, she would tell him in her own time, if at all.

"AIDS," she went on. "We knew it was coming, but ... she was a sweet kid. It hit everybody hard."

"Sorry," he said, leaning down to kiss her on the mouth.

She gave him another smile, warmer than the last, then handed him the stack of envelopes. "You want to put these by the door? They have to go out in the morning."

As George started out of the kitchen with the envelopes, the doorbell rang. Figuring it was probably Al or Lynda Crane, their neighbors, he put the envelopes down on the small table in the entry way, opened the door.

He froze halfway into his smile, giving his face an odd look of surprise. Then he blinked, cleared his throat, and returned the smile to his face intact. "Yes?"

"I'm sorry to bother you," she said, her breath appearing in a small cloud of mist before her face, "but I'm moving into the house across the street and I have no heat. Yours was the closest house with a chimney and I was wondering if

I could borrow some firewood. Just for tonight. I'll replace it first thing tomorrow."

George blinked again, several rapid blinks in succession, because an unexpected and unbidden – even unwanted – image of Laura materialized in his mind suddenly.

She is above him, straddling his legs as he lies in bed on his back, both of them naked and she smiles as she holds up a white plastic Hitachi Magic Wand vibrator and says, "Surprise! I bought this today," turns it on, and places the head against the bottom side of his cock and his head rolls back as he moans with pleasure.

George coughed again, turning his head away from the woman at the door, mostly to hide the red warmth he felt flooding into his cheeks. He felt embarrassed by the wildly inappropriate thought, but he also felt guilty, as if he'd betrayed someone – Laura or Karen, he wasn't sure – because the voice of the beautiful woman at the door made him feel exactly the same way that vibrator had when Laura pressed it against his cock.

"Sure, we've got plenty of firewood," he said with a forced smile. "How much do you need?"

"Oh, just enough for tonight, that's all."

She wore tight jeans and a heavy red and black plaid shirt and she stood with shoulders slightly hunched and her arms folded just beneath her breasts, as if to ward off the cold.

"Come on in," George said. He stepped back to let her pass, then closed the door behind her. "You know, if you like, we've got an electric heater you could use."

"Thanks a lot, but I don't have any electricity yet. I came earlier than I'd expected and didn't have the power turned on."

"Ah, I see. Well." George slipped his fingers into the back pockets of his tan slacks, feeling an awkwardness he hadn't experienced since high school. "Um, my name's George Pritchard."

She smiled and held out a hand. "Lorelle Dupree."

George took her hand and she squeezed firmly; in spite of

the cold outside, her hand felt warm – probably, he decided, from being tucked beneath her arm.

Her hair, which fell over her shoulders in thick waves, was a deep red, the color of redwood, and her almond-shaped eyes were a brown so dark they were almost black. In spite of the healthy fullness of her hair, her face seemed drawn, pale, as if she were ill. Perhaps it was because she wore no makeup, but the skin beneath her eyes seemed to sag in dark half-moons and her cheekbones hung over darkened hollows. But despite the appearance of illness, she was beautiful, with lips that looked smooth as rose petals and a long elegant neck that sloped gracefully into her sweatshirt.

George realized he had been holding her hand looking at her for too long – several slow seconds too long – and he pulled his hand back rather abruptly.

"Well," he said, "the firewood's out in the garage. I can get a basketful for you." He was about to suggest that he carry it over for her, but thought better of it. She seemed friendly enough, but he did not enjoy the discomfort she stirred in him, the awkwardness –

– The wanting, he thought suddenly, surprising himself, I don't like the wanting –

– and, instead, he said, "I'll have my son carry it over for you."

He heard Karen's footsteps behind him and turned to see her smiling at the woman.

"Hi," she said, then turned to George with a subtle questioning look in her eyes.

"This is our new neighbor," he said, "Lorelle Dupree. She doesn't have any electricity and needs some firewood for the night."

Karen shook Lorelle's hand and said, "You must've bought the Huitt place across the street."

"Not exactly. I'm renting. I wasn't planning to move in until next week, but my plans changed, so now I'm over there in the cold and dark."

Karen turned to George. "Well, why don't you get Robby

to take some wood over for her." Then to Lorelle: "And we have some kerosene lanterns, if you need them."

"Oh, that would be great."

There was a moment then in which Lorelle and Karen smiled silently at one another – it lasted long enough for George to look from one to the other twice – as if they had met before and were trying to remember where and when.

George turned to go to Robby's bedroom and said, "I'll go get Rob – " but stopped when he saw Robby peering sheepishly around the corner of the hallway entrance. "Oh, here he is," George said. "Robby, this is Lorelle Dupree. She moved into the Huitt place."

Robby did not move; he remained hidden, with only a fraction of his face leaning past the corner.

George cocked a brow. "Robby?"

Stepping out of the hall, the tall, lanky boy bowed his head and looked at their guest as if peering over bifocals, and folded his hands before him.

George frowned. Robby looked as if he were being punished.

"Nice to meet you, Robby," Lorelle said, offering her hand again.

It took a moment, but Robby finally returned the gesture and nodded silently.

There was a tension in the room that made George want to squirm, to leave. He glanced at Karen, then Robby, feeling guilty for his surprisingly strong attraction to Lorelle and wondering if they sensed it, if it was showing on his face. He slapped Robby on the back and said, "C'mon, Rob, let's go out in the garage and get some wood for Miss Dupree. She needs heat."

As he and Robby headed for the kitchen and the entrance to the garage, and as Karen said to Lorelle, "I'll get the lanterns," George thought about his words and silently told himself with a smirk, What am I saying? She's got plenty of heat.

George was relieved to enter the cold garage with Robby and sighed as he closed the door behind them.

* * * *

"Are you in high school, Robby?" Lorelle asked.
"Yeah."
"What year?"
"Senior."
"Ah. So how's it going? Are you doing okay?"
"Yeah."

Robby hugged the basket of wood to his chest as they crossed the street; kerosene sloshed in the two lanterns Miss Dupree carried, one in each hand. He felt like a walking raisin, shriveled with humiliation. He'd wanted to scream at his dad for sending him on this errand with the woman who had watched him through his bedroom window as he came into his hand, and he wanted nothing more than to do as he'd been asked as quickly as possible and go back home.

No ... no, that wasn't entirely true. As his arm brushed the woman beside him, he realized there was something else he wanted even more. But that was about as likely as lying naked on a bear rug in front of a fire with Miss Weiss. Besides, Miss Dupree did not look well, so even if, by some wild act of God, she would want to do something with him, she probably wouldn't feel like it.

His undershorts were moist from his session only minutes ago. His cock felt limp, but not sated. It was still extremely sensitive from the attention it had received and threatened to grow hard again, in need of more. Although at least a foot of space separated them, Robby could feel Miss Dupree, as if he were standing within the heat of a blazing fire in the fireplace, and as the house across the street grew closer, Robby became more uncomfortable.

When they reached the house, she went in first and closed the door behind him, then led him into the blackness toward a glow that came from the living room. Although Robby had been in the house before and was well acquainted with its layout, he felt he had entered unfamiliar surroundings.

"Did you know the people who lived here before?" she asked.
"Uh-huh."

"Then you've probably been in here before."

"Uh-huh."

"Just set that down here," she said, putting down the lanterns and waving toward the hearth. "God, it's cold in here."

He put the basket on the hearth beside the fat flashlight she'd left shining there and stepped back, stuffing his hands into his jeans pockets. His leg bumped something warm and soft and he turned to find two stern golden eyes looking up at him. Thin black lips quivered back over long fangs for just an instant and Robby staggered back, blurting, "God!"

Miss Dupree hunkered down and began stacking wood atop a bunch of crumpled newspapers she'd already put in the fireplace. "Oh, that's Gomorrah. Say hello, Gomorrah."

The dog stepped forward and nudged Robby's hand with a cold nose.

"Where's Sodom?" she asked her pet. "Go find Sodom."

Gomorrah gave an abrupt, low bark and another dog emerged from the darkness, walking slowly, its slanted predatory eyes looking directly up at Robby. The dogs were enormous and almost identical – only the stark black and gray markings on their thick white fur differed.

"Wolves?" Robby asked nervously.

"Malamutes. Gorgeous, aren't they?"

"Fed them lately?"

"Oh, they look pretty vicious, but they're really pussycats." She stood and brushed her hands together, adding, "Unless I tell them not to be."

The glow of the flashlight made her already pale skin look ivory white. She stood, took the flashlight, and disappeared into the dark for a moment, casting a dancing glow on the walls and ceiling. She returned with a cigarette lighter and lit the newspaper, then touched the lighter's flame to the lantern wicks. Sitting on the hearth, she faced Robby and smiled. The top three buttons of her shirt were unfastened and the growing firelight crept down her chest, causing a V-shaped shadow between her breasts, which jostled with each movement of her arms, shifting the shadow back and forth liquidly.

"So, what kind of town have I moved into?" she asked.

"Where are you from, Miss Dupree?"

"The Bay Area. And please call me Lorelle."

"This is kind of a ... a hick town, I guess you'd call it."

"Redding?"

"Yeah, sort of. Lots of country music radio stations. Not much night life, unless you like hanging around in the Taco Bell parking lot after midnight on the weekends." Robby stood by the hearth, fidgeting as he spoke.

She patted the hearth and said, "Sit. You're my first houseguest; I can at least make you comfortable." Robby sat on the hearth and Sodom and Gomorrah curled up on the floor in front of them. "Would you like something to drink? I've got some Pepsi in an ice chest. Not exactly a cold weather beverage, but –"

"No, thank you."

"What do you do for fun, Robby?"

He shrugged, looking into the fire. Robby wanted to bite his lip, as if to punish himself for being unable to relax beside her ... but he couldn't do it.

"Do you have a girlfriend?"

His face grew so hot, he was afraid it would burst into flames. "N-no."

"Really? I'm surprised. Don't you have –"

"What do you do for a living, Miss Dupree?" he asked suddenly, finally looking at her.

"Lorelle."

"Okay. Lorelle. What do you do?"

"I'm an artist. I make jewelry, mostly. But I haven't been doing much this year. I made a couple of big sales last year and they've carried me through." She stood and took the lantern to a corner of the room and carried a bundle from there, dropping it in front of the fireplace. After she unfastened a couple of snaps, the bundle unrolled over the floor with a whisper.

A sleeping bag.

"See?" She stepped in front of Robby, bent toward him, took his left hand and lifted it, palm up, then placed her other hand over it. She wore a ring on each finger and, when their hands touched, she curled her fingers under, lightly brushing her nails over Robby's palm.

His back stiffened and he pressed his lips together hard, trying to brace himself against the tingling shudder of delight that passed through him, as if a swarm of moths were fluttering over his naked body.

Although he couldn't make out the rings in detail, their stones shimmered in the firelight as she moved her fingers slightly against his hand, opening her fingers again, then pulling her nails back down over his wrist, his palm.

"They're very pretty," he said, but it came out as a hoarse whisper. Lifting his eyes to look at her, he stopped halfway.

The unbuttoned V at the top of her shirt hung open and the fire's glow turned her chest a deep bronze. Tiny shards of light reflected from the rings danced over her smooth throat. And over her breasts.

Robby's tongue turned to sandpaper and seemed to scrape loudly as he passed it slowly over his lower lip.

"Was that you I saw in the window this evening, Robby?" Lorelle whispered.

He swallowed cotton as he looked up at her.

"It was, wasn't it?" She cocked her head, lifted a brow. "What were you doing?"

"I-I-I –" He dropped her hand, turned away from her and stood clumsily. " – should go. I should go now." The dogs stood, too, so suddenly that Robby thought, for a crazy second, that they were going to attack.

Lorelle made a quiet sound as he brushed past her. A laugh? Was that it?

"My furniture arrives tomorrow afternoon," she said, following him through the darkness with a lantern. "I could use a hand moving in. You know, arranging things, moving them around. Would you mind?"

"I-I don't know. I've got homework."

"I'd pay you for it, of course. With dinner. How's that sound? I'll make something special. What do you like?"

At the door, she stepped in front of him.

"Or better yet," she said softly, "I'll make something for you, a piece of jewelry. Or you can pick something out of the stuff I've got. Something to go around your neck, maybe?" She stroked a finger across his throat, then along the edge of his collar and –

– Robby almost sighed, almost whimpered, but clamped his throat shut as –

– she pressed her warm palm to his chest for a moment, a long, silent moment, and –

– Robby leaned his back against the doorjamb as the crotch of his jeans began to tighten against his growing erection, as –

– her hand fell away and she smiled a simple, friendly smile and said, "I think everyone should own at least one piece of fine jewelry, don't you?"

Robby coughed, nodded, and reached for the doorknob.

"Will you come? After school?" she asked.

"Maybe," he said, going outside. The biting chill was a relief.

"Tell your parents I said thanks again."

"Yeah, sure." He stuffed his hands in his pockets as he crossed the street. At his front door, he turned back, just for an instant.

She stood in her doorway, glowing lantern in hand, and smiled.

The shadows from the wavering flame cut deep into her pale face, opening black, bloodless lacerations that immediately closed again, then opened somewhere else. From the darkness behind her, four slanted eyes shimmered a dull yellow.

As Lorelle waved at him, Robby hurried into the house, then ducked down the hall to his room before anyone could see him, before anyone could notice the moistening bulge in his pants.

Chapter 2

Dark Thoughts

KAREN Pritchard lay on her side in bed, her back to George, but she couldn't sleep. She frowned at the digital clock on her night stand and watched the time click by in square red numbers as she wondered what it had been about Lorelle Dupree that had made her so uncomfortable.

No, uncomfortable was not the right word; unsettled was more accurate. After the woman left, Karen had gone back into the kitchen to unload the dishwasher and had dropped three glasses and a saucer, then tried to put a frying pan in the cupboard above the counter with the plates and bowls. Just as she caught herself in the silly mistake, George had walked in for another beer and she was afraid he'd wonder what was wrong, but he didn't even notice, just got his beer and left.

Did she look familiar? Was that it? Or was it because Karen had caught George eyeing her?

That was doubtful. Infidelity was something that had never concerned her, not with George. He was so ... devoted. Sometimes that seemed unlikely to her. They had a good home and were a reasonably happy – at least content – family, but when it came to sex, she knew George could do better. He had every reason to look for a lover outside of their marriage. There were even times when Karen realized she wouldn't blame him if he did. A couple of times, she'd even wished he would, thinking that perhaps it would take some pressure off her, as long as it was just sex he was looking for and nothing else. Early on in their marriage she'd expected him to do that, but, as far as she knew, he never had; so, she figured if he hadn't by now, he probably wouldn't.

"Sex," her mother had told her when Karen was in high school, "is something you do to have babies and keep your man. If you like it, that's great. If you don't – and believe me, honey, most women don't – you learn to live with it. That's all the sex education anybody needs." She'd said it as they watched the news on television one night, during a report on the controversy surrounding the importance – or danger, depending on how you looked at it – of teaching sex education in schools.

A few years later, when she shared that bit of motherly advice with Denise Hubert, her college roommate, Denise had thought she was joking. When she realized Karen was not, Denise was appalled.

"You didn't believe her, did you?" Denise asked.

"Why? Isn't it true?"

"Of course not! Everybody enjoys it!"

Although she did not voice her response at the time, Karen had thought, Not everybody.

Against the advice of her mother, Karen had one boyfriend in high school. (If she'd followed her mother's advice, she would have stayed away from men entirely.) Karen was not unattractive in high school, nor was she unpopular. She was studious and got impeccable grades and was active in school politics. But she was not a very good dancer and attended very few parties and only went out with groups, never on dates with boys. At least, not until Michael came along.

Karen did not particularly like Michael, but he liked her. He asked her out often and sat next to her in classes whenever possible. He was a popular boy, a jock, the kind of boy who made girls sigh and roll their eyes dreamily. Every girl Karen knew expressed shock at her indifference and, after enough of them told her to "go for it," she decided it was probably the thing to do and followed their advice, rejecting her mothers.

After a movie, then burgers and fries at the Pack-Out – all

of which Karen enjoyed so much she wished she'd done it sooner – he drove her up Hilltop Drive to the water tower. It was a favorite parking spot among the local teenagers. He parked at the edge of the bluffs that overlooked Redding.

Karen had never been to the bluffs, although she'd been invited. She knew there was only one reason for going there and had never been invited by someone she wanted to make out with. She wasn't sure she wanted to make out at all. She wasn't terribly enthused about going there with Michael, either, but she knew it was expected so she did not protest.

He had a joint and a bottle of Jack Daniels. She turned down both at first, but finally gave in when he started to get angry. Other cars came and went around them and the lights of Redding flickered below. Michael did not take long to make a move and she went along with it, rather enjoying the kissing and the way his hands felt on her. But that lasted only for a few minutes. Then he started handling her roughly, feeling her all over, panting as he clumsily pressed himself against her and pried her mouth open with his tongue. She tried to push him away at first, but remembered how quickly he'd gotten angry when she refused to smoke the joint or drink any of his booze. She decided not to risk angering him any more. After a while, he took his hands off of her and seemed to struggle with something for a moment, then grabbed her hand roughly and pressed it to his lap where he'd opened his pants. He closed her hand around something fat and hard and sticky and Karen gasped, pulling away from him.

"Stroke it," he said, putting his hands on her again and holding her close.

She took her hand away and pulled back a second time, gawking at his erection.

"C'mon," he panted "stroke it."

"Nuh-no."

"What?"

She just shook her head, still watching his cock as it twitched now and then, almost as if it were trying to break free of him, pull itself loose and just fall off so it could move about on its own.

"Well then –" Michael put his hand behind her head and pulled her face down into his lap. " – suck it."

With her face less than an inch from his rigid penis, Karen gasped and inhaled his damp musk odor, then clamped her mouth shut and just stared at it for a moment.

She'd never seen one before, except for the drawn illustrations in the medical book on her mother's shelf. In fact, she'd been exposed to very few men while growing up. Her father had left them when she was very small (later, she learned he'd run off with the woman who ran the soda fountain in Woolworth's, which explained the bitter way Karen's mother spoke of him all those years later and right up until her death) and she had no brothers. In grammar school, none of the girls seemed interested in boys, until high school, when all of that changed. But it hadn't changed for Karen. Not much, anyway. She was not uncomfortable with them, even enjoyed the company of a couple of unusually intelligent and interesting boys on campus. But this ...

It was ugly. Fat and stubby and lumpy with veins and topped with a puffy mushroom cap that had a glistening slit at the top, like an opening made with a single stroke of a razor blade, bleeding a clear thick fluid. And it kept twitching, impatient and restless.

"Come on!" Michael hissed. "Stroke it! Suck it or lick it, just do something!"

But she only stared at it, not even wanting to touch it.

His breath was hot against her ear as he whispered, "We'll go steady. Would you like that? Going steady? Huh?" He reached under her top and kneaded one breast with his hand. "We'll go steady ... if you'll just suck my cock."

We'll go steady ...

Karen thought about that as she stared at Michael's cock, so close that her nose was almost touching its moist head, which looked obscenely large, like a fleshy doorknob. Going steady with Michael would undeniably have its benefits, not the least of which would be the delight of being the envy of every girl on campus.

But was it worth this?

She touched it, cautiously at first, then wrapped her fingers around the hard shaft. He squirmed at her touch and his breathing became more frantic as she began moving her hand up and down. Carefully, just to see what it would be like, she opened her mouth, stuck her tongue out and touched the tip of it to his cock and –

– Michael squeezed the back of her neck and shoved her head down hard, at the same time thrusting his erection into her mouth. She gagged, clenched her eyes shut and struggled helplessly under his hold.

After a few moments, her struggles stopped and she allowed Michael to lift her head up and down, up and down, as if she were a puppet, until he exploded in her mouth and clogged her throat with semen. She quickly spun around, threw the car door opened and emptied her half-digested burger and fries onto the ground outside.

"Jesus Christ," he grumbled, starting the car after he fastened his pants, "did you have to throw up?"

She took a handkerchief from her purse and wiped her mouth, stomach still lurching, then whispered, "I'm sorry. I ... won't ... do it ... again."

Michael and Karen went steady for nearly four months and, during that time, Karen was the envy of every girl on campus. And, although they made many trips back to the bluffs, she never vomited again. She came close several times, but would not let herself. Neither did she enjoy the things they did up there. There were a few moments of pleasure when Michael touched her in just the right place and in just the right way, but they were always accidental and all too brief. She kept returning to the bluffs with Michael only because she rather enjoyed going steady with him.

That was when she began to believe her mother was right.

There had been other men since Michael, but not many, and none of them had lasted long. They soon grew tired of her indifference in bed, tired of her unwillingness to go along with their every sexual whim.

George was different. He was far gentler than any of the others, more giving, as concerned about her pleasure as his own. After their third time together, he'd become serious and said, "Tell me honestly, Karen – am I doing anything wrong? Are you ... do you enjoy being with me?"

"Yes," she whispered, cuddling next to him. "Why?"

"Well, you just don't ... seem to, sometimes."

"I'm sorry. It's not that I don't enjoy it. I just don't ... show it much I guess."

He didn't seem entirely convinced.

Karen said, "I've never enjoyed making love this much. Never."

It wasn't a lie. Making love with George was better than it had ever been with any other man. But then ... that wasn't saying much. She felt no great need to make love, and when they did, she did not feel the bursts of ecstasy she'd always read and heard she was supposed to feel; there were no explosions of light in her head, no screaming orgasms

It had nothing to do with George, of course. She wasn't sure what the problem was exactly. But part of it was the penis. Veined and lumpy, with that smell – like the smell of an old root cellar that hadn't been aired out for a long time – and they all had that sneering, slobbering slit at the tip, all trembled impatiently, selfish, stiff with anger, far more capable of taking pleasure than giving it. And at the end of it all, at the completion of their frantic drive for release, they all did what Karen had done that first time with Michael, something for which she'd always hated herself just a little – they vomited.

Forty-five minutes had clicked by on the digital clock by the time Karen realized her mind was wandering and she should get to sleep.

She wanted to roll over, snuggle up to George, but something kept her from it. Something that would not go away. Something that made her think:

What was it about –

* * * *

– Lorelle Dupree, George thought, lying awake beside Karen. He'd been going over their meeting at the door again and again, reliving it, listening to her voice. Feeling it. Thinking about the memory it had revived – the secret, velvety memory he'd kept tucked away like a cherished gift from a long-lost friend.

He examined that memory again, holding it this way and that, and realized that it was different. Something had changed, something he could not seem to change back.

Now, when he remembered lying in bed, overwhelmed by the sensations ricocheting through his body, it was not his late wife who pressed the vibrator to his cock, it was –

* * * *

" – Lorelle Dupree," Robby breathed in the dark of his bedroom.

His erection would not go away, no matter how hard he tried to distract or relieve himself.

Neither would the physical echo of Lorelle Dupree's finger on his throat and her hand on his chest, just over his pounding heart.

He lay there for most of the night, staring at his ceiling and occasionally saying her name, before finally falling asleep.

Chapter 3

Anxiety

ROBBY walked home from school the next day; he was tired from lack of sleep and thought the exercise and late-October cold would help revive him. As he turned off of Mistletoe Lane and onto his own street, he saw Jessie – the Garrys' big golden retriever – bounding toward him, her pink tongue dangling from her yellow-toothed grin. Sebastian, the Weyland's calico cat, was licking his paws contentedly beside the road, and panicked, darting out of Jessie's way an instant before being trampled by the dog's mitt-like paws.

"Hey, Jess!" Robby called halfheartedly as Jessie danced around him. He heard a door thump shut and looked across the street to see Mrs. LaBianco waddling down her front steps toward her car, jangling her keys as she waved at him and said hello. He waved back and smiled, feeling a twinge of pity for the woman. Just a few years ago, she was a very sweet, attractive middle-aged woman, thin and shapely, with only a few streaks of gray in her dark hair to give away her years. Then she began to balloon, putting on a tremendous amount of weight in a very short time, until she'd become the hulking woman who now wore only muumuus and kept her thinning hair in a sloppy bun in the back. She was still sweet, but now she was pathetic, too.

Two small children – a boy and girl – shot out of Sheri MacNeil's driveway on tricycles, giggling and making high-pitched squealing tire sounds. The boy, Sheri MacNeil's son Christopher, grinned at Robby and shouted, "We're racing!" A year-and-a-half ago Sheri's husband had left her to raise four-year-old Christopher on her own, and the neighborhood had sort of taken her under its wing. The neighborhood children spent a good deal of time at Sheri's house playing with Christopher and she seemed to enjoy watching over them. As he passed her house, Robby saw Sheri through her kitchen window and waved as he walked on toward his house.

Beyond his own house, and on the opposite side of the street, Robby saw Paul Weyland, short and bullet-shaped with his rust-colored hair in a crew cut. He was opening his garage when he spotted Robby. He waved with a meaty hand, but no smile disturbed his stern, rocky features. Robby had spoken to Weyland's daughters, Caryl and Stephanie, only a couple of times. They were pleasant, pretty girls, but, like their mother – whom Robby seldom saw without Mr. Weyland – their shyness and timidity gave the impression that they were constantly afraid their father would appear at any second and start shouting at them. Paul Weyland left no doubt that he was the head of his household.

The Pritchards lived on the north end of Deerfield Avenue, which came to a dead end at a small patch of wooded land. On the other side of that was Highway 44. It was a small, friendly-looking neighborhood, but it wasn't as friendly as it used to be. When Robby was a boy, there were no strangers on Deerfield. Everyone on the street knew everyone else; they watched out for one another's children and pets and if a family went on vacation, they knew their house and belongings were in good hands. Every spring, everyone cleaned out their garages and closets and held a neighborhood rummage sale. But, over the years, people moved out and new people moved in and kept to themselves, and the sense of community bled out of the neighborhood. Now, there were people on the street with whom Robby hadn't had so much as a conversation. People just didn't seem very friendly anymore.

Except for Lorelle Dupree. She seemed very friendly.

Dylan could talk about nothing else on the school bus that

morning. On his way to the end of the street, he'd spotted Lorelle through her front window – she had no curtains yet – wearing a short kimono that Dylan had claimed was open in front.

"I saw her tits!" he'd hissed. "I saw 'em! They were ... they were ... well, I think god made 'em personally. You know, like with his own hands. None of that assembly line creation with her, uh-uh. You think she likes younger men?"

Normally, Robby would have told Dylan about his encounter with Lorelle the night before. Talking about girls was their favorite pastime, although, much to his chagrin, Robby, unlike most of his peers, had precious little experience with them, and Dylan, a snaggle-toothed boy with glasses that slid down his nose and a soft roundness to his face that suggested a possible weight problem later in life, had even less. Somehow, though, he didn't feel right talking about it. Now, in the light of day, he knew that nothing had happened at Lorelle's outside of his imagination. So he'd gotten a look down her shirt and she'd touched him a couple of times in a friendly way – big deal. But there was something private about his visit with Lorelle, something almost sacred, made even more so by how he'd felt at the time and what he'd done when he got home. So he said nothing on the bus. But for the rest of the day, he found himself thinking about what Dylan had said, about what he had seen. And Robby found himself feeling envious.

There was a moving van parked in front of her house and two hefty men in green jumpsuits were carrying a sofa across the front lawn, but Lorelle was nowhere in sight.

Robby stopped at the mailbox to check the mail – his mother usually forgot to do it when she got home from work – then headed up the front walk with a handful of sweepstakes offers and sales flyers.

"Robby!"

He stopped, waited a beat before turning, and saw Lorelle waving at him from her front porch. She wore a black sweatshirt with a baggy pouch in front and an old

pair of jeans with a hole over her left thigh, revealing bare
flesh, her hair in a pony tail.

"Are you going to give me a hand this afternoon?" she
asked.

"Um, well ... "

"My power's on and I bought steaks for dinner. How
about it?"

"Well, um ... " He had a lot of homework –

– You've blown off your homework for a lot less, he
thought –

– and he knew being alone with her would make him a
nervous wreck, even though he knew nothing would happen.
Maybe he could take Dylan along –

– You want to be alone with her and you know it.

"Yeah," he finally called to her as the mail slipped from
his hand and scattered on the walk, "I'll be over in about ...
an hour, or so." He gathered the mail, then turned toward
the house.

Jen peered out her bedroom window at him, her face a
vague, gauzy mask behind the screen.

A fat, smoke-colored cloud glided by overhead, blocking
the sunlight for a long moment.

Robby started for the front door and forced himself not
to look back at the sound of Lorelle's voice.

"I'll see you then," she called as he went inside.

* * * *

Peering down the hall from her bedroom door, Jen
watched Robby come inside. With his head sagging forward
and hands shoved deep into the pockets of his down jacket,
he looked thoughtful and troubled, maybe even a little sad.
He turned to come down the hall and Jen pulled back so he
couldn't see her, then closed her door softly.

Robby's room was next to hers and she listened to him
close the door, take off his jacket, then flop onto his squeaky
bed with a sigh.

Jen returned to her desk and picked up her pen. She

was writing a letter to Diana Strait, her best friend. Diana had moved to Seattle seven months ago and they wrote one another regularly.

Things had not been quite the same since Diana had gone. Now she spent time with the twins down the street. And she saw Diana's friends, although somehow, they seemed to remain Diana's friends even in her absence.

Jen and Diana had become acquainted by accident one day two years ago when they'd both been put on detention together – Jen for not dressing for PE and Diana for mouthing off to a teacher – and had become friends instantly. Jen automatically became a member of the clique of half a dozen or so girls that Diana moved in, a group popular enough to raise Jen's standing in the eyes of her peers – and a group that never would have accepted her without Diana's insistence. All of the girls in Diana's clique were very studious and got good grades. Jen got fairly good grades, too, but not in the same way. For Jen, a B was a struggle, an A was an all-out war she had to fight with the books and tests. For that reason, she was unable to go out with the girls every day after school, or get together for a group date in the evening – what Diana called a "date orgy" – with half a dozen guys. Jen was, as Diana's friends so often pointed out, no fun, but Diana was always happy to help her with her homework so Jen didn't have to stay home all the time.

She never got to know any of those girls as well as Diana, and when Diana moved, her friends allotted Jen greetings in the hall and the occasional lunch, but little more.

So Jen was left with the twins and a good deal more undisturbed time in which to do her homework. But for Jen, that homework – like making friends – was miserably hard. Sometimes she could break a sweat hunched over her books, especially if there was a test the next day. She was not lacking intelligence or study skills, but she suffered from what she had decided was some kind of phobia. Just as some people panicked or became hysterical when they saw spiders or snakes or looked down from high places, Jen froze up at an open schoolbook, a blank notebook page or the beginning of a test. She could write a letter comfortably and with no problem because she knew it didn't have to be perfect, but numbers made her gut clench with fear and the prospect of stringing words together into a coherent sentence – and spelling them correctly – when writing a paper numbed her into a cold paralysis. She fought it diligently and managed to get fair grades, but it took a couple of hours or so to do an assignment that would take up only thirty minutes for other students – a student like Robby.

Jen envied the ease with which her brother got so many A's. And he spent less time than most on his assignments, breezed through homework, never had a nervous moment before a test. He had lots of free time on his hands to give Jen a little help with her homework. But he never did. There were a lot of things he didn't do.

When her mom married George – Jen had been calling him Dad since he'd adopted her right after the marriage – Jen liked the idea of having a big brother. She looked forward to the two of them getting to know one another and growing up together, being close the way Jen always thought brothers and sisters were supposed to be. But it didn't work out that way.

Jen knew a lot of girls whose brothers were relentlessly cruel to them and she was glad Robby wasn't one of those. But she also knew girls whose brothers were their friends and confidants and she wished Robby was one of those. Unfortunately, he was somewhere in between.

Sometimes she felt like she wasn't growing up with Robby, but rather growing up next door to him. She'd been trying since they'd first met to get to know him, really know him, the way the kids at school and the teachers and neighbors never could. But she was beginning to think it was impossible.

He wasn't exactly cold, just preoccupied or – no, it was indifference. His distance did not seem intentional, it was just ... Robby. Jen kept trying to bridge that distance. She'd talked about it with Tara – one of the twins – but all she said was, "You've got a crush on him."

"I do not!" Jen always replied.

"Sounds like it to me."

Both Tara and her brother Dana taunted her about it, but of course it wasn't true.

Not ... exactly.

Maybe she'd had a small crush on him when she was little, but she'd outgrown that. Well ... mostly.

Completely, she thought, her pen poised over an unfinished sentence in Diana's letter.

Back when Jen had a little crush on him, she had managed once to get a peek at the Robby no one else ever saw. It was by accident, and she'd never forgotten it.

It was on a summer afternoon six years ago when Jen had sneaked up on Robby's bedroom window. Robby had been putting together a model at his desk facing the half-open window. She'd intended to jump up with a shout and give Robby a scare, but as she crept through the bushes and hunkered below his window, she heard his bedsprings squeaking slightly and decided to listen a moment before popping up. When she heard him breathing heavily, she knew he wasn't working on his model anymore. Instead of jumping, she peered carefully over the edge of his window and her eyes grew twice their size because –

– Robby was lying on his bed with his legs hanging over the edge, knees spread, pants bunched around his ankles, and his ... his thing – at least, that was how she thought of it back than – was sticking straight up! Robby held it in his fist, running his hand up and down, up and down, faster and faster.

Jen watched, amazed, and watching something so private, so secret, stirred a strange excitement inside her. She'd never seen a boy's thing before, and she'd certainly never seen a boy doing this to his thing. She hadn't even known that boys did ... whatever this was.

Robby squirmed on his bed as he continued to play with himself, and then something fascinating happened: milk squirted from his thing. At least, it had looked like milk to her then; she knew better now. Robby groaned, panted, moved his hand faster, slurping it through the white fluid. Then he calmed, slowly relaxed, and became still.

Jen couldn't stop thinking about it for weeks. Whatever it was, she became enamored of it and was terribly tempted to ask Robby about it – why he did it, how it felt, and maybe, just maybe, if she could watch up close while he did it again. She never did, of course, and now the very idea that she'd thought such a thing made her slap a hand over her eyes and groan with embarrassment.

But still, every once in a while, the memory haunted her, rose up in her mind like a ghost and danced behind her eyes. It used to give her a little tingle of excitement when she thought about it, but now the tingle was deeper, lower ... and a little scary.

In her bedroom, Jen heard Robby's door open. She stepped into the hall quickly and he stopped, turned to her.

"I saw you talking to the new neighbor," she said. "What's she like?"

Robby raised his eyebrows, shrugged and said, "She's, um ... nice," then lifted a hand and said, "See ya."

She watched him go down the hall, then back to her bedroom with a sigh.

* * * *

George took a shower when he got home from work. He'd gotten little sleep the night before, overslept, and only had time for a quick wash before leaving the house; he'd felt dirty all day. After drying off, he glanced out the bathroom window to see Robby going across the street.

Wrapped in his terrycloth robe, George went to his bedroom, tossed his robe on the bed, and –

– something stung his bare right foot and spat a long wet hiss from under the bed.

"Son of a bitch!" George barked, hopping a few times on his left foot as his right began to bleed in four long thin stripes that ran from his outer ankle to the knuckle of his big toes.

Karen's Manx cat, Monroe, peered up at him from the dusty darkness under the bed. Hatred burned in the cat's black and yellow eyes as it bared its needle-like fangs and hissed again, then snarled and backed out of sight.

George swept one of his slippers off the floor, dropped to one knee and slapped at the bottom of the bed, grumbling. "You miserable goddamned –" But the cat dashed out from under the bed on the other side and George heard the heavy thump of its paws as it ran for the door. He looked up in time to see Monroe's jiggling tailless ass – and, worst of all, his dirty bare rectum – disappear from the room. Swearing again, George threw the slipper down and sat on the bed to rub his slashed foot, muttering, "Nine years. Nine goddamned years."

That was how long he'd put up with the only animal he'd ever encountered that he actually hated. He didn't like admitting that to himself because he was an animal lover. But the cat had hated him first. Monroe had been a tiny kitten when George and Karen married. The cat hadn't liked him then and seemed to hate him more with each passing year. George never knew where the animal was hiding or when it was going to attack him next. Each time, the temptation to give Monroe a swift kick was great, but George always resisted, knowing that if he actually hurt the cat, Karen would be furious, probably even hysterical. Sometimes he thought she cared more deeply about that vicious, neurotic cat than she did for him.

After dressing and shaving, he went down to the kitchen and asked Karen, "Where'd Robby go?"

"Across the street to help that woman arrange her furniture and unpack."

"Oh. And Jen?"

"At Al and Lynda's."

Al and Lynda Crane had twins Jen's age – a boy and girl – and if she wasn't at their house playing or eating with them, they were at hers.

"Aren't they going to eat?"

"Jen's eating with the twins and I guess that woman's

going to cook dinner for Robby." She removed two plates from the cupboard and set them down in front of the fat white Oster food processor.

"Oh?" George stepped behind her and wrapped his arms around her waist. "Then we're alone this evening?" After the thoughts he'd had while trying to sleep the night before, he'd felt horny all day.

The microwave beeped and Karen pulled away from him to take out the food.

Figures, George thought, a little surprised by the bitterness he suddenly felt. "What's for dinner?"

"Chicken."

He watched as she dished up the chicken and vegetables. She was frowning, as if she were angry about something.

"You're staring," she said. "What's wrong?"

"You looked upset, is all."

"Oh. Well, I'm just ... don't you think it's strange, George?"

"What?"

"That woman –"

"She has a name, you know."

" – asking Robby over like that. Cooking dinner for him."

"What's strange about that? She needed the help and she wanted to do something for him in return. That's all."

Still frowning, she shook her head. "I don't know."

"What, you think she's going to seduce him?"

"I just ... thought it was strange," she muttered. "That's all."

George took his dinner in the living room and turned on the news. Through a two-inch opening in the curtains over the front window, he could see the lights in Lorelle Dupree's windows across the street. Two silhouettes moved back and forth inside.

With a smirk, George wondered if maybe Karen was right. Robby wasn't a bad looking kid. He was no jock, but he wasn't a geek, either. For all George knew, maybe Lorelle Dupree was the Mrs. Robinson type, the kind of woman who liked to break in young men. He closed his eyes and imagined her with his son, both of them naked.

He imagined the sounds Robby would make as Lorelle introduced him to things about which he'd only fantasized, and he wondered if Robby would be as overwhelmed as he had been the first time. As the image crystallized, became vivid, George's smile dissolved. He turned to the television again as Karen came into the room with her dinner and sat across from him on the sofa.

She wore a simple blue shirt-dress, no stockings, barefoot, makeup washed off. Yet she looked no less attractive than she had that morning, freshly made up and dressed, on her way to work. She watched the television without looking at him and he watched her, trying to relax and get that feeling back, that feeling of ... ease. He wanted to put down his plate and go to her, nuzzle her neck and curl up on the sofa with her. But he knew better.

Monroe was coming.

The cat crept out from under the end table, lifted his bulk onto the sofa and placed his front paws on her thigh to peek over the edge of her dinner plate. She smiled as Monroe touched his nose to each piece of food on the plate.

George turned away from his wife as he winced disgustedly, then looked again to see Karen passing a hand over Monroe's orange fur as the cat curled up on her lap. George remembered when he and Karen used to eat dinner together, sitting close, touching one another, often exchanging smiles. He had been replaced by the cat. They used to lie on the floor together, too, curled up on pillows to watch television. Now she curled up with Monroe, and George didn't dare get too close to the cat for fear of being clawed. It was something he'd always tolerated, but over the years, it had become more and more difficult.

As Monroe began to purr, George's eyes returned to the opening of the curtains, to the shadows moving in the windows across the street, and his brows slowly huddled together, rippling his forehead.

If Karen was right and Lorelle Dupree was planning to seduce Robby, George had to admit that he was envious.

No, he thought, as his dinner grew cold, not envious. Jealous.

"Mind if I change the channel?" Karen asked.

George turned away from the window slowly, frown diminishing, and sighed, giving her the best smile he could without looking at the cat. Before biting into his chicken, he said, "No, hon. Whatever you want."

Chapter 4

First Time

A S Sodom and Gomorrah sniffed around the furniture, inspecting their new surroundings, Lorelle stepped back against the wall, put her hands on her hips and carefully scanned the living room. "What do you think, Robby?"

"Yeah," he said with a nod, "I think it's fine." They'd already moved the living room furniture around four times – not to mention arranging the dining room and bedroom furniture and assembling the large desk in the spare room after lugging it in from the garage – and Robby was tired. So was Lorelle, who was still pale and appeared weary.

Lorelle moved to his side and put an arm around his shoulder. "So do I. Now I just need to put up some curtains and hang some plants and it'll be home."

They'd been so busy the last ninety minutes that Robby had no time to feel self-conscious. Now he had to force himself not to squirm nervously under the gentle weight of her arm and the warm touch of her hand just below his right shoulder. A strand of her hair brushed his cheek and he caught a faint whiff of her dark, musky perfume.

"There's just one thing missing," she said, nodding toward the big wooden crate in the middle of the floor and said, "I'll be right back," then hurried out of the room.

They had been working around it all evening and Lorelle had refused to tell Robby what was inside, insisting it was to be a surprise. The crate was six feet long and stood about five feet high and when he tried to slide it out of his way while moving the sofa earlier, he realized it was very heavy.

Robby flopped onto the sofa with a sigh and watched the flames blazing in the fireplace. The dogs curled up at his feet and he idly scratched Sodom's head, enjoying the aroma of steaks and garlic bread from the kitchen. A few minutes later, the dogs pricked up their ears, then stood as Lorelle returned with a hammer. Using the clawed end, she pried away one side of the crate and a gout of thickly-packed shredded newspaper and fine wood shavings whispered to the floor like guts, revealing a coal-black hand with tensely clawed fingers, so smooth that it reflected the glow of the fire.

The dogs wagged their tails enthusiastically as they watched Lorelle disassemble the rest of the crate.

"What is that?" Robby asked, standing.

"You'll see." She pulled out more paper and Robby helped her remove and stack the sides of the crate.

His mouth fell open as he stared at the black onyx sculpture that grew out of the pile of shredded paper, feeling a little embarrassed at the tingle of excitement that passed through him. He walked halfway around the sculpture, then walked back and turned to Lorelle.

"Did you do this?" he asked. It came out, unintentionally, as a whisper.

Her mouth curled into a half-smile and she nodded. "Do you like it?"

Robby looked at the sculpture again and nodded slowly. "I ... yeah, it's ... well, it's ... "

"It's the only thing I've ever done that I couldn't bear to sell."

Sitting stiffly, as if at attention, the dogs watched the sculpture as if expecting it to do something. Gomorrah swept his tongue over his black lips.

Robby walked all the way around it this time. Shaking his head slightly, marveling at the sculpture's detail and trying not to blush. He failed, and was relieved when Lorelle clicked off the overhead light, leaving only the glow of the fire and the soft light coming in from the dining room.

"I think it looks better like this," she said quietly. "Don't you?"

He could only nod. In the shadows, Robby half expected the two onyx figures to move, to breathe. He looked from one to the other, staring at them silently for a long time.

"You can touch it if you want. Robby. That's what I made it for." Her voice was soft as a feather.

But he didn't. Not yet. He just looked at it. Watched it.

It was a man and woman, both naked, lying atop a twelve-inch-tall rectangular base, and although they were not quite life-size, they appeared so real, so alive, that it did not matter.

The man had the kind of body for which any man – including Robby – would sell his soul. It carried not an ounce of fat, but was not built with pumped up muscles like a professional body builder's. It reminded Robby of an illustration of the ideal male musculature in his nutrition and health textbook because it was impeccably proportioned, as if the man had not been born as an infant but newly created as an adult, sculpted out of flesh and bone. The woman gave the exact same impression but she was more interesting.

Robby was accustomed to being attracted to slim women with large firm breasts that perked upward, small tight asses and slender legs that tapered down to narrow delicate ankles. Movies, television and magazines like the ones stacked in his closet had populated his fantasies with women who perfectly met those standards. The woman in Lorelle's sculpture did not, but it didn't matter. In fact, she was somehow more alluring than any of the beautiful naked women he'd seen on the internet.

Her breasts were heavy but nicely rounded; they did not sag but were pendulous and were so real that he would not have been surprised if they had shifted slightly. Her ass was thrust carelessly upward and was not tight and muscular; it seemed to be made of two smoothly rounded three-quarter moons separated by a shallow crevice that curved downward between her kneeling legs to a fleshy mound with a fine coating of hair. And she had wings.

The man lay on his back and his erect penis, long and fat and smooth, curved upward slightly. Muscular body tense with ecstasy, his left hand clutched the woman's shoulder while his right clawed at the air. His shoulder-length hair was pooled around his head and his face was twisted into a mask of agonized pleasure – eyes tightly shut, lips torn back over clenched teeth, cords of muscle pulled taut beneath the skin of his neck. The woman straddled his legs and leaned forward, hard nipples almost touching his thighs, her fist wrapped tightly around the base of his cock, left arm stretched taut, nails clawing his right nipple. The bat-like wings that sprang from her back just below her shoulders resembled an angel's, but instead of feathers, they were covered with scales, and each fold came to a needle-sharp point. They seemed about to spread open to prepare for flight. Her head was turned slightly to one side and delicate, perfectly curved strands of her hair – which reached all the way to her waist – fell down around her face. Her eyes were narrow and swept upward on the outsides, giving her face a reptilian look, and her open mouth was turned up gently at the corners, almost – but not quite – smiling as the tip of her ever-so-slightly curled tongue touched the bottom-side of the man's cock just beneath the bulbous head, which she pressed to her upper teeth as her eyes looked up at the man's tormented face.

"Go ahead," Lorelle whispered, stroking one of the scaled wings with her fingertips, "touch it."

Robby lifted his hand slowly until it was less than an inch from the woman's flowing hair, then –

– a harsh buzzer sounded somewhere in the house and Robby's hand dropped as he spun around.

Lorelle touched his shoulder and said, "It's just the timer. Dinner's ready." She went to the kitchen.

Robby turned to follow her and see if he could help, but he couldn't take his eyes from the sculpture. It was quite clear what the man and woman were doing, but there seemed to be no joy in it. They seemed to be struggling rather than making love.

He glanced down at the dogs. They were no longer looking at the sculpture; they were watching him.

"You do like it, don't you?" Lorelle asked a few minutes later, carrying their dinner in on a short tray which she set on the floor before the fire. She'd changed from her jeans into a long black cotton skirt that whispered around her legs as she went to his side. "You don't think it's ... too much?"

"Too much?"

"You know, offensive? It's not exactly something most people would put in their living room, is it?"

"Well, I doubt you'd ever find one in our living room, but ... no, I don't think it's offensive."

"Is your family conservative? Religious, maybe?"

"Well, we go to a non-denominational church, but no, we're not what you'd call religious. In fact, neither is our church. It's very liberal. So's our pastor. A lot of love and forgiveness, very little fire and brimstone."

"You're frowning."

He realized he had been frowning as he stared at the sculpture and he tried to relax. "Sorry."

"Does it bother you?"

"No. No, I'm just wondering ... why does she have wings?"

"Have you ever heard of Lilith?"

He shook his head.

Lorelle stroked one of the wings proudly as she walked around the sculpture. "Lilith was Adam's first mate, according to Hebrew legend."

"Adam? As in Adam and Eve?"

She nodded. "After creating Adam from dust, God made Lilith from mud. But Lilith and Adam –" With a soft chuckle, Lorelle lightly caressed her creation as she circled it slowly, " – they didn't get along very well. They had a few ... differences of opinion. For one thing –" Lowering herself to one knee, Lorelle looked around the woman's face and up at Robby, " – Lilith considered herself Adam's equal." She put her hand on the man's smooth black chest and passed her fingertips along the ridge of the pectorals. "She wanted to do things –"

– down the flat, rippled abdomen –

" – that Adam didn't want to do."

– over the carefully detailed pubic hair –

"You might say –"

– running one fingernail up the length of the cock as she said with a lifted brow, "– she wanted to be on top."

Robby heard himself swallow dryly as he followed the path of her fingernail up and down the cock. He felt his own cock warm and stiffen.

"When Adam tried to force her into subordination," Lorelle continued, "Lilith fought him at first, then flew away, leaving him alone in Eden. Then Adam complained to God." She stood and came around the sculpture again, still moving slowly, speaking softly, until she was at Robby's side, wearing an amused smile. "God tried to persuade Lilith to come back, but she refused. So, God returned to Eden and created Eve." She leaned on one wing. "That was the inspiration for this sculpture. It's Lilith and Adam in their final struggle, just before she flew away. At least, this is how I imagined it."

Leaning so close that Robby could feel her breath, she whispered theatrically, "What will the neighbors think?"

Robby stared at the sculpture, unable to look at her, thankful for the darkness that he hoped hid his erection. Lorelle startled him by taking his hand.

"Go on, touch it," she said. "I like people to touch my work. That's why I enjoy making jewelry."

She put his hand on Lilith's smooth round hip. As soon as Lorelle let go of his hand, Robby immediately moved it up toward the wing, but –

– he caught the back of his hand on one of the thorn-like points and jerked it to his chest as the cut began to bleed.

"Oh, Robby!" Lorelle moved close and took his hand. "I'm sorry. Hurt bad?"

He shrugged. Actually, it did hurt, but that was okay; he'd needed the pain to divert his attention.

Lorelle knelt beside the tray before the fire and tugged him down with her. "Sorry, I don't have any Band-Aids," she said, dabbing the cut with a cotton napkin.

"That's okay."

She held his hand close to her eyes. "It doesn't look too bad. Probably hurts, though."

Once again, Lorelle caught Robby off guard – she lowered her head, placed her mouth over the cut and licked it with the tip of her tongue.

Robby sucked in a trembling breath and started to pull away, but her grip on his wrist tightened slightly and he froze, watching her until she lifted her head and whispered, "Does that feel better?"

He held his breath as several panicky thoughts shot through his mind:

I should go home, I should –

– stay here and see how far this goes, see what happens, what if –

– Dad comes over to see if we need help or Mom decides to do some dumb neighborly thing like bringing some cookies to the new neighbor, because they 're just across the street, what if –

– she really wants to do it?

Lorelle touched her lips to his hand again, but he pulled away, stood clumsily and said, in a cracked voice, "I should pruh-probably go, um, go home."

"But what about our dinner? It's getting cold." She remained on her knees in front of him, calm, her dark eyes showing a hint of disappointment.

"I-yum, I'm really not hungry." He tried to remember where he'd put his jacket.

"If you're not hungry –"

"And I should put something on this cuh-cut."

"Well, I can't let you just leave. Not after all the work you've done."

She raised an arm and Robby thought she wanted him to help her to her feet, so he offered a hand, but –

– she curled a finger over the top of his jeans and flipped her thumb over the button, unfastening it.

Robby stammered, "I-I-I –"

His zipper hissed as she pulled it down.

"I don't think you want to go, Robby."

She tugged on his jeans and undershorts until his erection sprang free and he closed his eyes a moment, concentrating on not falling, because his knees were weakening, trembling.

"Not really," she whispered, squeezing his erection and licking the head, never taking her eyes from his. "Do you?" She slipped her tongue into the moist slit at the tip of his cock and sucked hard, but only for a moment. "Do you?"

His only response was to kneel slowly in front of her. She never let go of him and, once Robby was on his knees, she began to stroke his cock. Her hand made moist smacking sounds as he became more and more wet.

"This is what you were doing last night," she whispered in his ear. "When I first saw you in the window. You were stroking yourself. Weren't you?"

He could only nod, pressing his face into her hair, inhaling deeply.

Lorelle dragged her nails gently over his scrotum, then cupped his testicles in her palm as she drew him into her mouth, sucking hard. She squeezed his balls a little harder.

Robby moaned as she pulled his jeans down his legs, tore off his shoes and clawed at his socks until his feet were bare, all the while jerking his cock with her other hand, pounding his groin with her fist. His hands clutched at her blindly until he felt her breasts beneath the sweatshirt, heavy and firm, felt the lump of her hard nipple pressed against the material, but –

– his hand suddenly weakened and fell to the floor as his heart began to beat impossibly hard and dangerously fast and his chest heaved with out-of-control gasps because he was seconds from coming. He didn't want to, not yet, but it was rumbling through his gut, unstoppable, and –

– he thrust his hips up off the floor and cried out as he came, his semen splashing over his belly, chest and legs as Lorelle continued to pump her fist up and down. He released a groan of disappointment and his hips shuddered when it was over, but –

– Lorelle did not stop. "It's okay," she hissed. "It's ooookay." In one swift movement, Lorelle sat up and pulled the sweatshirt over her head and pressed his hand to her bare breast, grinding it in a circular motion as she began to unbutton his shirt with her other hand. When the shirt was off, something tore suddenly and Robby opened his eyes. Lorelle's tattered skirt was heaped on the floor. They were both naked.

Swinging one leg over him, Lorelle straddled his chest and lifted his head with both hands. Robby's face was an inch from the triangular patch of dark hair; beads of moisture glistened among the tight curls.

"Look at it, Robby," she rasped. "Have you ever seen one before? Up close?"

He stared open-mouthed and licked his dry lips, panting.

"Do you like it?"

He lowered his hand from her breast and ran his fingers through the hair, touched the slick folds.

"Lick it, Robby. Eat it!"

Clutching his head between both hands, Lorelle pulled his face between her legs and squeezed her thighs together, laughing.

Robby inhaled deeply, slid his tongue over her fleshy lips and found the small hard nub hidden between them as Lorelle closed her fists on his hair and pulled until his scalp stung. As he licked her and sucked her folds into his mouth, he realized his erection had not gone away. Instead, it had grown so hard it felt as if the taut skin might split open.

Digging her nails into his scalp, Lorelle moved against his face and Robby's tongue slipped inside her as if sucked into a mouth, and he felt her opening move, felt it tighten around his tongue, which only excited him more. He stiffened his tongue and moved it in and out of her rapidly, slurping like an infant sucking the milk from its mother's tit, and Lorelle responded. A low growl rose from deep in her chest and became a breathless laugh and she moved on his tongue as if it were a penis. She reached behind her and closed her hand around his genitals, tugging on his erection and testicles at the same time until she pulled herself away from his face suddenly and slid down his body, painting a strip of clear glistening fluid down his chest and abdomen, which she rubbed in with her palm.

Lorelle devoured Robby's cock like a starving woman given a hot meal and Robby could not remain still. His arms and legs quaked and his hips rose to meet her. His head rolled back and forth as his hands clutched his hair and he groaned as if in agony. She reached beneath his ass as she sucked him, running a fingernail over the sensitive flesh between his buttocks and something inside Robby churned, roiled. Something deep in his gut whirled, like water being sucked down a drain and he felt as if he were being emptied.

His second orgasm came on like an army conducting a surprise attack.

As he emptied himself into Lorelle's mouth with spine-twisting bursts, Robby's skull began to shrink, squeezing his brain in an iron grip; he slapped one hand to his head and the other to his mouth to hold in the ragged scream that tried to tear its way up his throat.

They'll hear, he thought, feeling a jolt of shame as he envisioned, for an instant, his dad and mom bursting into the house to see what was wrong.

Lorelle squeezed Robby's testicles as she continued to suck on his ejaculating cock. He convulsed on the floor until he felt empty, then his movements slowed and he reached out to touch her, stroking her arms, her hair, her face. His body relaxed and he sighed as his movements slowed and he touched her more and more gently.

She crawled up his body, laughing.

"No," she whispered, "Don't stop now. We haven't gotten to the best part yet."

He opened his eyes, took a moment to search for his voice, then croaked, "What?"

"The best part," Lorelle said breathlessly, pressing her breasts against him. "Don't you want to be in me? Don't you want to fuck me? You've never done that before."

Robby gave her a weak frown.

"Oh, that's okay. I like that you haven't done it before. I want to be your first time."

"But I –" Robby stopped.

He was going to say, But I can't, but stopped. Lorelle was moving herself above him. He felt the scrub of her pubic hairs and felt her wet lips rubbing against his cock, which was still hard.

Lorelle lifted both of his hands to her breasts then leaned forward and squeezed them together over his face. He kissed them, took the rigid nipples into his mouth and rolled his tongue over them, his breath heaving through his nose as he licked and sucked and bit them until she pulled them away and –

– she pressed her mouth to his, stabbed her tongue into him and moaned. Robby tasted himself on her lips as she explored his mouth then sucked hard on his tongue. He wrapped his arms around her and held her tight, clutching her back as she reached down, gripped his cock, and slipped it inside her, writhing on it. Robby gasped, opening his eyes wide. Lorelle's long hair fell on him, tickling his chest and face, and through it, as if through a mist, he saw the sculpture just behind her. Lilith leaned toward them, pulling Adam's cock into her mouth – but she seemed to be watching Robby and Lorelle, smiling slightly, as if with approval.

Sodom and Gomorrah sat on the hearth, one on each side of the fire and quietly watched them.

Robby groaned as Lorelle's vagina closed like a fist, squeezing him to the verge of pain, then releasing just enough to slide up, then back down, then squeezing again, repeating the cycle over and over until –

– Robby felt the churning again, the sensation of being drained as he began to jerk beneath her, driving his cock upward as hard as he could, again and again until –

– his orgasm fell over him like a blanket of thinly sliced lead and –

– Robby lost consciousness....

When he awoke several minutes later, dazed and disoriented, Lorelle had already started all over again...

Chapter 5

An Afternoon Visit

KAREN had just changed out of her uniform when the doorbell rang. Normally she would be annoyed by the interruption so soon after getting home from work, but it was Friday and she was always in a better mood than usual on Fridays, knowing she didn't have to work for the next two days.

It was Lorelle Dupree. "I hope I'm not bothering you," she said.

"Not at all," Karen said. "Just got home from work. Come on in."

"Thank you. Where do you work?"

"Redding Medical Center. I'm a nurse. A very fortunate nurse because I've managed to get weekends off. That means Friday is actually my Friday." She chuckled.

Karen led her into the kitchen and Lorelle sat at the breakfast table. "I was just going to put on some coffee. Want some?"

"Sure."

Karen filled the coffee maker, remembering the discomfort she'd felt with Lorelle Dupree and wondering what it was about the woman that had unsettled her. It could have been any number of things – the fact that she was beautiful, she was a stranger, or because, in spite of what George said, it was odd (at least, Karen still thought so) that she'd invited Robby to come over and help her with the furniture and have a cozy little dinner for two. Or perhaps it was just that Lorelle Dupree was a new neighbor. Karen was naturally cautious around new, unfamiliar people. Perhaps she was even more so when she knew that person would be living across the street. Whatever it had been, she didn't feel it now. Instead, it was rather pleasant to have another woman to visit with for a while. Aside from Lynda, she had no female friends, and Lynda was as occupied with her family as Karen was with hers.

She pulled up a chair at the table as the coffee began to gurgle lazily. She looked much better than she had the night she arrived, much healthier, with some color in her face. Karen asked, "What about you? What kind of work do you do?"

"I'm an artist."

"Really? An artist? What are you doing in Redding?"

Lorelle laughed. "That's the reaction I've been getting from everyone. I didn't think Redding was that backward."

"It certainly seems like it sometimes."

They talked for a while about Redding and Karen made the standard hick town jokes, then did the standard backpedaling and said it wasn't all that bad after all – even though it really was.

She told Lorelle about the local points of interest – interesting to newcomers, anyway – like the dam and Shasta Caverns. As they talked and laughed, Karen became much more comfortable with Lorelle until her previous uneasiness was forgotten.

"So, what do you do, Lorelle, paint?"

"I paint, sculpt. But I make my living from my jewelry."

"You make jewelry? Oh, I'd love to see some of your work."

Lorelle held out her hands and Karen looked closely at the rings, impressed.

"They're beautiful," she said quietly. "You make these?"

"You like them?"

"They're gorgeous."

"Tell you what. Why don't you turn off the coffee and come over to my place. I was just unpacking all my pieces and I bet there's something over there you'd like."

"Oh, you don't have to –"

"No, really. That's why I came over here. I like to know my neighbors, and I was going to invite you over for a cup of hot spiced wine so we could get acquainted."

"Mmm, that sounds good. But really, my husband'll be home in a couple of hours and I haven't started dinner."

"Order a pizza. Or better yet –" Lorelle stood and gave Karen a conspiratorial wink, " – let him cook it. You work, too, remember."

Laughing, Karen went to the coffee maker and switched it off. "We're gonna get along well, you and me," she said, grabbing her coat in the hall as they headed for the front door. "I like the way you think."

* * * *

Robby stared at his English lit test as he hunched over his desk, but did not see it. Neither did he hear the occasional weary sighs of the other students laboring over the questions, nor the rustle of papers and tapping of pencils that punctuated the silence. Instead, his mind re-examined the events of the night before, going over them again and again.

He vaguely remembered waking in Lorelle's arms, in front of the fire, feeling weak and helpless as a newborn infant. She smiled, stroked his face, and told him he should dress and go home. But before he left, she gave him a gift – a silver neck chain with a sterling wolf's head pendant that held two tiny ruby eyes. At the door, she gave him one more kiss – a long hungry kiss that sucked his tongue into her mouth so hard it hurt – then he staggered across the street, unaware of the time, but hoping it wasn't too late. In the house, he closed the door quietly when he heard the television in the living room, quickly ducked down the hall and went straight to bed.

Getting out of bed that morning had been a chore and his mother had insisted he stay home from school because she didn't think he looked well. But, not wanting to miss the test, Robby assured her that he was fine and managed to shower and dress in time to catch the bus.

But he did look ill: pale and exhausted, with gray rings beneath his heavy eyes. His chest, shoulders and neck were spotted with light bruises where Lorelle had chewed on him and the ruby eyes in the snarling wolf's head looked an even deeper red against his ashen skin than they had the night before.

As he stared blindly at the test, he wondered why it had happened, what she had seen in him when he was so obviously below her standards. She was – how old? Thirty? Thirty-five? Older? It was hard to tell. He was just a clumsy teenager who couldn't drink, drive or vote, and whose experience with women did not extend beyond sucking on one of Janine Flugel's nipples and slipping his fingers down her panties while she jerked him off through his undershorts behind the gymnasium, during the autumn dance, a couple of weeks ago. He didn't understand it, but the more he thought about it, the more it seemed that understanding it was not necessary.

"Robby? Robby?"

He blinked as he looked around, fingering the sterling wolf's head. He was surprised to see everyone leaving their desks, slapping their books together and complaining about the test. Miss Weiss was leaning over his desk, frowning.

"Are you all right, Robby?" she asked.

"Huh? Yeah. Fine. Is ... did the bell ring?"

"Yes, and you haven't finished, have you?"

"Well, um ... " He looked at the test. Not only had he not finished, he'd barely even started. The first question was half answered and the rest of the paper was blank except for the doodles in the margins. The doodles ...

Robby moved to slap his hand over one of the scribbled pictures, but knew he was too late when he saw Miss Weiss looking at his crude drawing of Lorelle's sculpture.

She turned to him slowly and he wasn't sure if she was going to smirk or frown.

"You don't look well, Robby," she said. She was leaning

close and he could see the light sprinkle of freckles on her chest, but that – even combined with the smell of her perfume – did not elicit the usual blushing response. He just didn't have the energy to find her attractive.

"I guess I ... haven't been ... feeling too well today. But I didn't want to miss the test."

"Well, it didn't do you much good to come to school, did it?" She took the paper and stepped back from his desk. "Go on home and get some rest."

"I've got two more classes," he said.

"They'll still be there next week. Go see the school nurse and I'll let you make up the test on Monday."

He quickly gathered his things. "Thanks, Miss Weiss."

"But next time you're sick, stay home. Okay?"

He didn't look back as he hurried out of the room.

Dylan was waiting for him in the hall.

"What the hell's the matter with you man? You look like you fell out of the back of a hearse."

"Flu, maybe," Robby said without slowing his pace as he went to his locker.

"So how'd you do on the test?"

He said nothing.

"You do okay? I'm not sure if I got that question about –"

"I don't want to talk about the test, okay?" He didn't want to talk at all.

"Maybe you've got the swine flu, 'cause you've been a real pig's ass all day, you know that? What're you, on your period?"

"Sorry, Dylan. I just don't feel well." Actually, he didn't feel sick, just exhausted, and he only wanted to go home and sleep. He'd slept as if in a coma the night before, but still felt as if he would never get enough sleep again.

* * * *

After about half an hour of conversation over wine in Lorelle's kitchen, Lorelle went to her bedroom to get her jewelry. Karen seated herself on the sofa and gasped softly when she saw the sculpture. She gawked at it for a few moments, then turned away when she heard Lorelle coming, acting as if she hadn't even noticed it. But each time Lorelle turned away to open a new box of jewelry, Karen stole a look at the sculpture and wondered if it was Lorelle's work. If Lorelle had done it, she hadn't given herself the credit she deserved when she'd said earlier, "Oh, my art is nothing more than a hobby, really. I just happen to make a living at it." Still, there was something about the sculpture that made Karen squirm. It was not the deliciously sinister look on the woman's face or the look of anguish on the man's, and neither was it the leathery wings sprouting from the woman's back. It was ...

... the penis. It looked so real, black as coal, but shiny as if it were wet, generously leaking the clear viscous fluids that penises seemed to produce in abundance. Each time Karen looked at the sculpture, it was the man's stiff penis to which her eyes were drawn.

She was admiring a pair of sterling crescent moon earrings when Lorelle turned away to open the fourth box. Karen looked at the sculpture again, at the fat penis clutched in the winged woman's fist.

"Does it bother you?"

Karen jerked around toward Lorelle. "Pardon?"

"My sculpture. Does it bother you?"

"Oh, no. It's ... beautiful. I was wondering if you'd done it. I think it's ... wonderful."

"Ah. Well, some people are offended by it. And you were looking at it with a sort of distasteful grimace."

"Was I? I'm sorry. It has nothing to do with ... I mean, I really do think it's beautiful. I just ... well ... " She laughed, embarrassed that she'd even considered telling Lorelle what was bothering her, and finished off her wine.

Watch it, she thought. You've had more than a few of those.

"I'll get you another." Lorelle took the cup and was gone before Karen could protest.

So she looked at the sculpture again.

Coming back into the living room with another cup of wine, Lorelle asked, "What were you about to say?"

"Oh, nothing."

"Come on. No fair teasing. You were about to say something about the sculpture."

Karen laughed again. "No, it's nothing. Really, I guess I'm just not used to drinking this much wine."

"Is it the woman? I know she doesn't exactly meet the current standards of beauty."

"No."

"Her wings?"

"No, really, I'm just –"

"The man?"

"No, no, it's just, um ... his penis," she whispered suddenly with a wince, surprising herself.

Lorelle lifted a brow, "His penis?"

"God, that sounds awful, doesn't it?"

"Not at all. What about his penis?"

"Well, it looks so real."

"Does that bother you?"

"Well, um, it's very well done and ... I just ... well, I know this sounds crazy and you'll probably think there's something wrong with me, but ... I think they're so ugly."

Lorelle slapped her thigh, threw back her head and laughed. "I don't think there's anything wrong with you, Karen. I know a lot of women who think they're ugly. And –" She turned to her sculpture, " – in a way, I have to agree. Aesthetically, there's not a great deal to recommend them, is there?"

Snickering into her palm, Karen shook her head.

"How does your husband feel about your opinion of the male organ?"

"He doesn't know," she laughed.

"You haven't told him?"

"Do you think I should? Seems like most men would be crushed. They all seem so –" she snickered again, " – emotionally attached to that part of their body, so sensitive about it."

"Yeah. If you speak anything less than words of praise about it in their presence, they get a sort of hurt look in their eyes, like ... like a child does when he shows you his latest finger-painting and you ask, 'What's it supposed to be?'"

"Yes, exactly!"

They roared with laughter, nodding and slapping the sofa cushions. When their laughter began to die, Lorelle said, "But they do sort of make up for their unsavory physical attributes, don't you think? Penises, I mean."

Karen squirmed; her smile fell away and she sipped her wine, staring into the cup. "Yeah, I ... I suppose so."

"You don't sound too sure."

"Well, I ... yeah. Yeah, they do."

Lorelle frowned and touched Karen's arm with affectionate concern. "Is something wrong? Are you having problems at home?"

"Oh, no, it's nothing like that. George is great. He's different than any other man I've ever been with, or I wouldn't have married him. I mean, we don't talk about it much, but he ... well, I guess we've never talked about it. But he seems to understand."

"Understand what?"

"That I ... that I don't really ... " She sighed and scrubbed her face with her hand. "I don't know. Sometimes I think there really is something wrong with me. That I'm crazy, or something. I'd see a therapist if I thought it'd do any good. But I'm one of those people who believes that psychotherapy was invented by someone who saw a chance to make some major bucks without getting a real job." She laughed, but there was no humor in her voice.

"What is it, Karen?" Lorelle leaned toward her, eyes narrowing with concern. "You don't have to talk about it if you don't want to. But if you do, I'm willing to listen."

She thought for several long moments. She'd never shared her thoughts on the subject with anyone, not even Lynda. After taking a deep breath, she spoke very slowly.

"I don't just think they're unattractive. You know ... penises. I think they're ... well ... repulsive. All of them.

I've never seen one that I wanted to touch. I mean really wanted to touch. Even with George ... I love him, I really do. He's been so good to me. He's understanding and accepting, he doesn't make a lot of demands ... hardly any, really. And the ones he does make are reasonable. I know that sex is something he enjoys and ... he's so different from the other men I've been with. He's a very good lover, very giving. And I love him, I really do, but ... even so, I'm ... I can't ... well, it's hard for me to ... do it. I thought I would feel differently with time, but still ... it's just like all the others. A stubby, wrinkly, one-eyed worm. And he wants to put it in ... side me. I let him, of course, because I love him and want him to be happy. I don't want to lose him. But ... I don't enjoy it. Even now, after all these years. I can't get excited about it. And I know that, although he doesn't say anything about it, that bothers him. I know he'd like me to be very ... sexual. Like his first wife. But I just can't. Because –" Karen looked at the onyx erection across the room. " – of that. It has nothing to do with him, with the kind of person he is. It's just that ... thing." Smiling at Lorelle, she said, "I guess that's what bothered me about your sculpture. It's very beautiful, but –" She laughed again. " – it's got a dick."

Lorelle laughed too, then took Karen's hand and squeezed it.

"There's nothing wrong with you, honey," she whispered. "You don't need a therapist. That's just the way you feel, that's all."

"Well, if I don't need a therapist, what do I need?"

"You need a nice piece of jewelry." She began emptying the contents of the box onto the table. "And if you can't find one here, I'll make you one."

They went on sipping their wine as they sifted through the many pieces of jewelry Lorelle produced from the boxes she'd stacked on the floor by the sofa; and each time Karen found one she was especially fond of, she set it aside, until she found something she could not resist and had to try on. It was a pair of pyramid-shaped onyx earrings with an eye-shaped sapphire set into all four sides of each one.

"You like those?" Lorelle asked, smiling.

"I love them!" She put them on and ran her fingers over them as they dangled from her earlobes.

"You know, I have a necklace somewhere around here that goes perfectly with those earrings. Let me get you some more wine and we'll go find it."

A moment later, she returned with a filled cup for Karen, then led her down the hall into the bedroom, where a few unpacked boxes were stacked against the walls. She fished through one of them until she found a smaller box, and removed from it a necklace of onyx cubes – each of which sparkled with a speck of sapphire – joined by beads of sterling silver. She seated Karen at the dresser facing the mirror and rested the cubes on her chest, fastening the necklace in the back.

Karen pulled back the collar of her plaid shirt, but it wouldn't stay, so she unfastened the top two buttons and let the necklace rest against her bare skin. Lorelle reached over Karen's shoulders and gently patted the necklace, then placed both palms flat on her chest. They were warm against Karen's skin, smooth.

"What do you think?" Lorelle asked, resting her chin on Karen's shoulder.

"I love it."

"You have good skin," she said, gently stroking Karen's chest. "Perfect for necklaces, because you don't have any freckles or blemishes to draw attention to."

Karen closed her eyes a moment and told herself it was probably the wine that was making her feel lightheaded – she'd had too much, that was all.

"Let's try another." Lorelle removed the necklace and took another from the box, this one of sterling, with bits of onyx and opal.

In spite of the possibility that she'd had too much, Karen took another drink of her wine – a good-sized swallow. Lorelle put the second necklace on her, fingernails brushing her flesh, fingers carefully arranging her blond hair on her shoulders.

Karen's hands itched to pull her shirt closed and button it because she felt her nipples hardening against the material, and wondered if Lorelle could see them from where she stood.

Lorelle removed the pyramid earrings from Karen's ears and fished through the box for another pair.

"Ah," she said, holding up one earring, "this would go with the – oh, no, that won't work. There's only one of these." She set it down and continued looking.

Karen stared at the tiny delicate piece of silver Lorelle had set on the dresser and tried to take her mind off the lingering sensation of tightness in her breasts. She picked it up by its little hoop between thumb and forefinger and held it dangling before her.

"Here they are." Lorelle stepped behind Karen, carefully hung a pair of teardrop opals from her lobes and smiled into the mirror. "They go together perfectly," she said, tracing the edge of the necklace with her fingertips all the way up to Karen's neck, where her hands stopped, fingers squirming ever so slightly against her skin.

Karen's breath caught in her throat like sawdust.

"Don't you think so, Karen?"

"Yes, it's ... they're very ... yes, I like them. They're very nice." She returned her attention to the tiny piece of silver. Its shape was confusing at first – graceful curves that locked together smoothly.

"Do you like that?" Lorelle asked when she saw her staring at the piece.

"Oh," Karen whispered when she finally realized what all those little curves were. "Yes, it's very ... unique."

Two naked female bodies dangled from the hoop, their legs wrapped around one another as they ground their vaginas together. Holding the piece closer to her eyes, Karen could make out the amazingly intricate detail: erect nipples, flowery vulva, fingers, toes and facial features.

"You said there's only one?" she asked.

"Mm-hm. I made that for myself when I got my nipple pierced."

"Your nipple?"

"It was a lot of work, that one. That much detail isn't easy on something so small."

"I can't imagine having my nipple pierced." Karen frowned at Lorelle's reflection in the mirror.

"Well, I love jewelry and I'm always looking for new places on my body to put it." Lorelle stepped in front of her, took the piece of silver and unfastened her dress. It fell open in front like a bathrobe and beneath it, she was naked.

Karen's face burned and she clenched her teeth, angry at herself. Why? She thought. I've been around naked women thousands of times, for God's sake, why am I feeling this way?

Lorelle cupped her left breast, upturned the nipple – which was quite erect – and slipped the hoop through a minute hole in the hard brownish-pink flesh.

Karen touched her own left breast gently, almost protectively, feeling her nipples shrivel even further into solid pebbles beneath her shirt. "Didn't it hurt?" she whispered.

"Oh, not much. If it's done properly, it's not as painful as you might think."

Karen's eyes widened as Lorelle's hand moved toward her, slipped beneath her shirt, lightly touched her breast, and –

– Lorelle said, "Not much more than a pinch," as she closed her thumb and forefinger together on Karen's nipple, squeezing hard for just an instant, and –

– Karen drew a loud gasp as the pinch sent thin white tendrils of heat through her breast, into her throat and down through her abdomen. Her eyes locked onto the two tiny silver women dangling from Lorelle's nipple, flashing as they caught the light from overhead.

"See?" Lorelle whispered. "It's not so bad."

Karen started to speak, to say she had to go now and probably wouldn't be back, thank you but no thank you, she had a husband and two kids and all that, but –

– Lorelle squeezed again, a little harder, and Karen's back stiffened as she murmured, "Oooh-ooh."

Another whisper as Lorelle knelt beside the chair, smiling: "You like that, don't you?"

"Pluh-please, I-I really...I ruh-really –"

The third time Lorelle squeezed, she did not let go; instead, she rolled the nipple between her thumb and finger

Karen grew weak for a moment, slumping in the chair, gripping the armrests, breathing, "Mmmm ... "

Lorelle pushed her shirt open and touched her other breast, squeezed it gently and fingered the nipple.

Karen thought, What am I doing here? She kicked at the floor. The chair scooted back and Karen pulled her shirt together, fumbling uselessly with the buttons and stammering, "Look, I-I can't – I'm not – I really don't – I really just can't –"

"Yes you can," Lorelle whispered, standing and closing in on her again, so close this time that Karen couldn't rise from the chair. "It's all right, you can. There's nothing wrong. Look, it's just this –"

She took Karen's trembling hand and placed it on her breast, just below her pierced nipple and its sparkling silver lovers –

"See? That's all. Just this –"

– passed it slowly over her slightly rounded belly –

" – Just smooth skin, that's all, nice smooth skin ... and this –"

– then slipped Karen's fingers between her slightly parted legs, into the dark patch of hair, pressing them hard onto her mound –

" – just nice, soft lips. Feel them? Soft warm lips. Just you and me, that's all.

No one else, nothing else. No fat wrinkly penises, no stiff dripping hard-ons, no balls hanging in their little bags ... just this."

"Oh God," Karen breathed. She felt the growing heat and moisture between her own legs, closed her eyes as Lorelle knelt between her knees and unbuttoned her shirt the rest of the way, then kissed her breasts, licked them, sucked on her nipples so ... perfectly. Her teeth nibbled with just the right amount of pressure – not too hard, not too soft – then she took Karen's hand and pulled her out of the chair. Lorelle's dress fell to the floor on their way across the room. Karen shed her shirt, sat on the bed and let Lorelle remove her jeans.

The moment Lorelle's tongue touched her clitoris, Karen began to writhe on the bed, clutching the dark blue spread in her fists, breathing in rapid machine-gun bursts, and when her orgasm exploded inside her – more powerful than any other before it, almost smothering in its force – Karen screamed, and –

* * * *

– Jen's books hit the concrete sidewalk with a resonant slap. She froze in place as the other students just off the bus stepped around her and walked on down Deerfield.

Tara and Dana Crane stopped on each side of her and Tara asked, "Whatsa matter, Jen?"

"Did you hear that?" Her mouth was suddenly very dry and she no longer noticed the icy breeze. They'd stepped off the bus just a moment before she heard the scream and it had been very faint beneath the rumble of the bus's engine, but it had sounded, for all the world, like her mother.

"Hear what?" Dana asked, wrinkling his nose against the cold.

"I thought I heard my mom scream."

Dana cackled. "You watched that Nightmare on Elm Street movie on TV last night, didn't you?"

"No, really, I thought I heard my mom scream."

"Well I didn't hear it."

Tara shook her head. "Neither did I. Maybe it was a cat."

Jen listened hard, screwing her face up and turning an ear toward her house, but heard nothing.

"Better get home, Jen," Dana said. "Maybe Freddy got her!" He clawed one hand, stretched his eyes open wide and crossed them in that ugly way he knew frightened her.

"Stop it," Tara snapped, but Jen had already swept up

her books and trotted away, turning and walking backward long enough to shout, "Sometimes you're a real shit, you know that, Dana?" and then hurried home.

Her mom's car was parked outside the garage and the door was unlocked, so Jen knew she was home. She walked in slowly, closed the door and called for her mom, but got no response.

The living room was empty; so was the kitchen. Her mom's car keys were on the counter where she always put them when she got home from work. As Monroe crept through the kitchen, looking suspiciously from right to left, Jen called out again, but heard only silence.

Troubled she went to her room and dropped her books on the bed.

Something moved. Somewhere.

She listened at her bedroom doorway.

It came from the next room. Robby's room.

He's never home this early, she thought.

Standing in the hall outside Robby's closed bedroom door, she muttered, "Mom?"

More faint sounds of movement.

"Mom?" she called, a little louder. Then, in a voice filled with the panic that had clogged her throat, she shouted, "Muh-therrr?"

An angry voice ... the squeak of bedsprings.

Jen pressed her back against the hallway wall and held her breath.

"What?" Robby barked as he opened the door.

She stared at him as she emptied her lungs, relieved, and snapped, "What're you doing home?"

"I was sick."

"You look sick."

He was pale and slump-shouldered and his ribs seemed to stick out a little more than usual.

"Where's Mom?" she asked.

"I don't know. She wasn't here when I got home."

"Well, I thought I heard her scream."

"What? You're high."

"I am not! I heard her! At least ... it sounded like her."

"Well, she's probably down at the Cranes'. Now shut up." He slammed the door and Jen heard his bedsprings squeak as he went back to bed.

Still not rid of her fear, she went to the telephone in the kitchen and called the Cranes, but her mom was not there. Neither was she at the LaBianco's house.

Jen flicked on the television in the living room and tried to preoccupy herself with it, but she couldn't. Maybe she hadn't heard her mom scream, but she couldn't shake the feeling that something was wrong, something was different about today.

She sat cross-legged on the floor in front of the television and chewed her fingernails until the front door opened. She heard her mom's familiar sigh and dashed out to meet her.

Jen caught up with her in the kitchen and started to ask where she'd been, but only stared at her as she poured a glass of orange juice.

Mom did not look well. Her pretty blond hair was a sad mess and her face looked long and weary, almost as pale as Robby's.

"Mommy?" Jen asked, surprising herself, because she usually didn't call her that. She thought "Mommy" sounded childish.

"What, honey?" She didn't look at Jen, just rinsed her glass in the sink and put the carton of orange juice back in the refrigerator.

"Where you been?"

"Huh? Oh, just ... I was visiting with Miss Dupree. Our new neighbor. She invited me over to look at her jewelry. She's an artist."

Frowning, Jen said, "I ... I thought I ... well, when I got off the bus, I thought I heard you scream. Dana laughed at me, but I, uh ... I thought I heard you scream."

Mom's head snapped around toward Jen and, just for a second, she looked as if she were about to become angry. Then she blinked, smiled falteringly, and said, "Oh, I'm fine, honey. Really. It was nothing. Maybe a cat."

"That's what Tara said."

"Well, that's probably what it was." She went to Jen and gave her a hug.

Jen felt her mom's hands tremble as they pressed to her back and her breath seemed to be coming faster than usual, rumbling in Jen's ear.

"I'm fine." Karen said. "Really."

"You ... look sick."

Her smile crumbled. "I do?"

"Uh-huh. Like Robby. He came home from school early."

"I knew he shouldn't have gone," she muttered distractedly, touching her face. "Probably the flu. It's going around. You'd better take some vitamin C, honey. Go watch TV, okay? I'm gonna ... take a hot bath."

Jen watched her mom walk slowly from the kitchen and disappear down the hall, shaking her head as if mumbling to herself. The bathroom door closed and locked and water began running in the bathtub. Back in the living room, Jen plopped in front of the television again, but she paid little attention to

Something's different, she thought, chewing another fingernail – chewing it all the way into the pink bloody quick. Something's wrong.

Chapter 6

A Stranger

GEORGE was exhausted when he drove the car into the garage that evening. The radio station had recently undergone a change of ownership and, although he was immensely relieved to still have his job, he had the unpleasant task of firing some of the talent at the request of his new boss. He'd informed three disc jockeys of their termination that afternoon, as well as the sales manager, and it hadn't been easy. They were the best group he'd ever worked with, not a single rotten apple in the whole barrel, and he hated to see them split up. He felt worn and achy and wanted nothing more than to sit down in front of the television with a beer – maybe a screwdriver, or even a straight scotch – and get a little numb.

He knew something was different the moment he walked into the laundry room and couldn't hear a sound in the house. Even the washer and dryer were silent, and they were usually thumping with a load each evening. Dirty laundry was one of Karen's pet peeves and she washed something almost every day after work. And even if something wasn't in the wash, someone was usually knocking around in the kitchen or talking on the telephone or watching the television with the volume at full blast.

Tonight there was only silence.

He slipped his coat off as he walked through the kitchen and hung it on the coat rack in the hall. He could hear the television in the living room, the volume unusually low, and he stepped in to find Jen stretched out on the floor, sound asleep in front of a Cosby rerun. Kneeling beside her, he woke her gently and she smiled up at him.

"Hi, Dad."

"Hey, kiddo. Where is everybody."

"Sick."

"What?"

"Mom and Robby. I think they've got the flu. They're both in bed asleep."

"Have you eaten?"

"I made a sandwich. How was your day?"

"Not so good. Things are kind of tense at work right now. How about you?"

"Oh –" She shrugged. " – same as usual."

"Do you have any homework?"

"I always have homework."

"Well, if you want any help, let me know." He started building a fire in the fireplace. "You sure you don't want anything more to eat, Jen?"

"Nope. I'm not hungry."

It was not like Karen to go to bed without feeding anyone. She must have felt pretty bad.

Once he had the fire burning, George went to the bedroom to check on Karen. She was curled up in bed. The closet light was on, but the door was only open a crack. Light fell on her puffy face and gave her skin a white pallor.

No, she did not look well at all.

George turned off the light and closed the door on his way out, then went to Robby's room.

"Hey, Dad," Robby croaked. He was just waking up, sitting on the edge of his bed with his face in his hands.

"How're you feeling?" George sat beside him and put his arm around the boy.

"Better. I think."

"You look better. You were pretty ugly this morning. Think it was the flu?"

"Prob'ly."

"Or did you just wear yourself out at Miss Dupree's last night?" He laughed and squeezed Robby's shoulder.

A look fell over Robby's face for an instant, then was gone – a look of slack-jawed horror so strong that, although brief, it made George flinch inwardly.

"Uh, we just, y'know, moved furniture, and stuff," Robby said. "She made dinner, but I wasn't very hungry. Guess it was the flu coming on."

"Yeah. Probably."   George watched him a moment, waiting for another sign of that fearful look –

– Guilt, he thought, that's what it looked like –

– but it never came. "Must be the flu," he said, "because your mom's got it, now. She's in bed."

Robby rubbed his stomach and said, "I'm hungry. Anything for dinner?"

"I was gonna go to Carl's, Jr. and get a burger. Mom didn't cook anything. Want me to get something for you?"

He shrugged. "A burger. Some fries."

"Sure you can take it? You still don't look so great."

"Yeah. I think so."

"Okay, a burger and fries it is. Be back in a while."

On his way out, George asked Jen if she wanted to go along, but she was more interested in the TV.

* * * *

A moment before his dad had come into the room, Robby had awakened from a long murky dream. He felt hungover, drained, and it didn't feel like the flu. After Dad left, he still felt foggy and parts of his body still ached. It was dark outside his windows and that only added to his feeling of disorientation. Once again, he found himself going over the previous night in his mind.

If being with Lorelle Dupree was going to screw him up this much every time, he decided he would rather go behind the gymnasium with Janine Flugel and engage in a little frustrating groping and fondling. At least his schoolwork wouldn't suffer and he wouldn't feel so wiped out. And so ... guilty.

So dirty, he thought.

He put on his underwear and robe and went to the living room to watch some television. Jen was watching Cosby.

"Turn it to channel two," he said, falling onto the sofa.

"Why?"

"The Simpsons is on."

"So what?"

"I wanna watch it, that's so what."

"I was gonna turn it to Entertainment Tonight."

"Entertainment Tonight sucks."

"Oh, c'mon Robby, you always watch The Simpsons. You've seen all the reruns twice. I never get to watch Entertainment Tonight."

"Go ahead," he growled, "rot your brain. See if I care."

Jen changed the channel, said "Thanks," and gave him a kiss on the cheek as she left the living room. She came back with a Pepsi and sat down in front of the TV again. "Mom's sick, you know."

"Yeah, I know."

"Just like you."

"Yeah, I know."

Still staring at the television, she said, "She went to see Miss Dupree today. For a visit."

"Look, if you're gonna watch that stupid show, just watch it, okay? Otherwise, turn it to two."

Robby pulled the afghan from the back of the sofa and curled up beneath it, feeling achy, and Jen said nothing more.

* * * *

Jen sat Indian-style in front of the television as Robby's breathing grew slower and more rhythmic. She had difficulty paying attention to Entertainment Tonight and although she watched the screen, her mind wandered. Next thing she knew, the show was over and a half hour had passed in what seemed like a heartbeat.

She heard Dad's car pull up in the driveway and went to the door to greet him, but she heard voices outside. Dad was talking to someone. A woman.

He came in a few moments later and handed her a Carl's, Jr. bag that smelled of Western Bacon Cheeseburgers and fries and said, "Here, honey, give this to Robby. I'll be right back."

"Where you going?"

"There's something wrong with Miss Dupree's car and it's starting to rain. I'm going to see if I can help her before she gets soaked. There's something in that bag for you, in case you decide you're hungry." He hurried out the door.

Jen went back to the living room and put the bag on the coffee table; Robby was sound asleep on the sofa and she decided a hamburger wasn't enough reason to wake him. She crept around the sofa to the front window and parted the curtains slightly to peer outside.

Dad was jogging across the street to Miss Dupree's driveway, where she was shining a flashlight under the hood of her car. The wind blew tiny specks of moisture against the windowpane as Jen watched them for what seemed a long time, until Miss Dupree finally got behind the wheel of her car and started it up. Dad slammed the hood down as she turned off the engine and got out to speak with him. He shook his head, then she touched his arm, beckoning him toward the house. He seemed to think about it a moment, then shrugged and followed her and the bobbing beam of her flashlight into the house. The porch light went off, leaving only the glow from the windows.

Jen let the curtain drop back into place and went to the bag on the coffee table. She figured the small cheeseburger was for her, so she got it out and opened it on the floor, took a bite and channel-surfed on TV. But the burger tasted like cardboard and she couldn't find anything interesting to watch.

She wondered why everyone in the family was suddenly becoming so friendly with this Miss Dupree when Jen hadn't even met her yet.

She wrapped the burger in its napkin, stuffed it back in the bag and went to the window again. No sign of Dad.

She thought of the scream she'd heard that afternoon

after getting off the bus, still certain it had been her mom's
voice –

– I was just visiting Miss Dupree. Our new neighbor –

– and of the sudden change in Mom's face when Jen told
her what she'd heard –

– It was nothing ... maybe a cat.

Moving away from the window, Jen watched Robby a
moment, to make sure he was deep in sleep, then hurried
silently down the hall to do the same with Mom. After
slipping on her coat, she sneaked out the front door, opening
the screen slowly so it wouldn't screech and closing the door
behind her with a faint click.

She watched Miss Dupree's front door closely as she
crossed the front lawn to the street. If her dad came out,
she would hurry back inside. She didn't want him to think
she was spying on him, or anything. She wasn't exactly sure
what she was doing herself. But he didn't come out. By the
time she got across the street to the edge of Miss Dupree's
lawn, there was still no sign of anyone coming out of the
house.

The cold rain hit her face like icy needles shooting from
the sky and Jen hugged herself against the cold, wondering
what she should do. If she got too close to the house, she
wouldn't be able to run back home if Dad came out. But
what would be wrong with that? She could say she'd decided
to come over with him and meet the new neighbor. That
wasn't so bad, was it?

She stepped onto the lawn and moved slowly toward the
house, watching the window and door, and through the
whisper of the rain, she heard laughter. It wasn't the kind of
laughter you hear when someone tells a joke or does a funny
trick; it was lower and more ... secret.

Jen took a few more steps across the lawn and nearly
dropped to the ground when she heard a man's voice.

"What are you doing?"

She spun around and saw a shadow standing beneath the
streetlight, leaning on a cane in his right hand.

"Do you live here?" he asked. His voice was low but clear.

"I-I ... no, I live ... across the street."

"Oh."

She waited for more, but he just watched her for a while, his face invisible beneath the hat he wore, left hand buried in the pocket of his long coat.

"Why are you sneaking around?" he asked finally.

"I'm not."

"Oh. It looked like you were. And usually, young ladies who look like they're sneaking around are doing something they shouldn't."

He sounded very friendly; in fact, he sounded as if he were smiling. But Jen had heard plenty about strangers – especially strange men – who seemed friendly.

"If you live across the street, why are you over here after dark in the rain?"

"My dad's in there. He was helping our new neighbor fix her car."

"New neighbor?" He took a step forward, leaning heavily on the cane.

"Uh-huh." Jen didn't move, but her whole body was tensed, ready to run.

"What's your new neighbor's name?" His voice changed. He sounded nervous now, and his question took on a tone of urgency.

"Miss ... Miss ... " Jen clenched her fists, wondering if it was a good idea to tell him. Maybe he knew Miss Dupree and she didn't want him to know she lived here.

"What's your name?" the man asked, taking another step toward her and pulling his hand from his pockets.

Jen moved back.

"I'm not going to hurt you," he whispered. "Really. I just need to know – it's important – I need to know about your new neighbor. What is her name?"

"I'm ... I'm gonna get my dad now."

He lurched forward quickly. "No, please believe me, I don't mean you any harm. I want to help you. But you have to tell me about your new neighbor. What's her name? What does she look like?"

Not wanting to take her eyes from him, Jen walked quickly backward over the grass until she lost her balance and tumbled back on her behind, landing with a grunt.

"Oh," the man breathed, holding out his left hand and hurrying toward her, sinking the cane into the wet lawn and asking, "Are you all right? Are you hurt?"

Miss Dupree's porch light came on, spilling light over the lawn, and –

– Jen's fists closed on the wet grass and her throat tightened with fear when the light illuminated the man closing in on her.

His face was melting as he rushed forward, dribbling down one side of his skull like hot wax. He staggered closer, his gloved hand outstretched and –

– horrified, Jen tried to scream but released only a hiss of breath as she reached up and clawed at the hand, her nails digging into the glove's material, and –

– the man balked in the sudden light, then pulled back, slipping his hand out of the glove and the glow of the porch light was reflected dully on the bony silver fingers along which ran thin cables that disappeared into the coat sleeve. He gawked for a moment at the glove dangling from Jen's hand and snatched it away, stuffing it into his coat pocket. He backed up as the lock on Miss Dupree's door clicked.

Jen rolled over and bounded to her feet, rushing toward the door as it opened and voices filtered out from inside. She stopped on the porch and turned.

The man was gone.

Her mind raced. If she told her dad about the man, he'd wonder why she was wandering around outside Miss Dupree's house and might even get angry. If she didn't, she could tell him she was just coming over to see him and meet Miss Dupree, and she wouldn't have to mention the man at all.

But her hands were trembling and her heart was thundering in her chest. Wouldn't Dad want to know if someone like that creepy, hideous man was roaming the neighborhood? Would he even believe her, though, if she described the man to him?

Probably not.

Jen decided to play it safe.

"I don't want you to forget it," Miss Dupree was saying as she opened the door.

"Jennifer! What are you doing here?" George stood in the doorway with Miss Dupree's hand on his shoulder.

Jen blinked up at her dad, afraid he was angry because that was the only time he called her Jennifer. "Everybody was asleep," she said, trying hard not to sound as scared as she felt. "I thought I'd come over with you and ... and meet Miss Dupree."

The woman dropped her hand from George's shoulder and stepped onto the porch, smiling. "Well, I'm glad you did, Jen," she said. "I've heard a lot about you and it's nice to finally meet." She held out her hand. Jen took it hesitantly and they shook.

An enormous dog peeked out the door and Jen gasped.

"He won't hurt you," Miss Dupree said. "This is my dog, Sodom. You can pet him."

Jen reached out a hand and the dog sniffed curiously, then licked it. She smiled as she stroked his head.

"We should get home, Jen," her dad said. "You shouldn't be out in this rain. I don't want you getting the bug that's going around."

"It was nice meeting you, Jen. You're welcome over here anytime. You can come walk the dogs for me. They'd love that."

Jen waved to her as Dad led her across the lawn and into the street.

"You know better than to be walking around in this kind of weather," he said with annoyance.

"Well ... "

"Well what?" Now he sounded angry.

"Everybody was asleep."

"What difference does that make?"

Although she didn't know what she was apologizing for –
his anger made no sense to her – Jen said, "I'm sorry."

"All right," he grumbled as they went into the house.

In the living room, Jen took off her coat and saw that
Robby was gone – he'd probably gone back to bed. She sat
down in front of the television again. She heard Dad pop
open a can of beer in the kitchen and wondered if he was
really angry, the kind of angry that stuck with him for a
while.

She was still trembling and couldn't quite catch her
breath. If Dad came back into the living room now, she
would probably seem more guilty than he already thought
she was, so she decided to go to her room. As she headed
down the hall, Jen heard him murmur to himself in the
kitchen:

"Son ... of a ... bitch."

* * * *

Robby did not wake easily. His eyes felt glued together
and his body was heavy as lead. He thought he was on the
sofa in the living room, but when he finally pried his eyes
open to see who was shaking him, he was staring at the
Bangles poster on his bedroom wall.

"Robby?" Jen whispered.

He rolled onto his back and squinted up at her. "What?"

"Sorry for waking you."

"Whassmatter?"

"Are you sure you're awake?"

He rubbed his eyes and struggled to sit up. "Yeah, I'm
awake. What's wrong?"

She sat on the bed and glanced cautiously at the closed
door. "There was a man outside."

"When? What time is it?" He found his clock. "It's only
eight o'clock."

"A little while ago. Out on the sidewalk."

"So, what was he doing?"

"He talked to me. Wanted to know who our new neighbor was."

"He talked to you? What were you doing outside?"

"Well, Dad went over to Miss Dupree's to help fix her car, so ... um, I followed him over a little later. And there was this man."

Robby buried his face in his hands and groaned. His head felt like it was filled with sand. "Why didn't you tell Dad?"

"Just listen, okay? He wore a long coat, like an overcoat y'know? And a hat, too, like the ones detectives wear in the old movies. And he walked with a cane and, and he was really ugly, like part of his face was melting, or something. Like the guy in that old wax museum movie we watched last weekend? Remember? You know, the scary one? Wax House, or –"

"House of Wax. Vincent Price."

"Yeah, that one. And he had a silver hand, like a robot's hand. He wore a glove over it, but the glove came off in my hand and it was silver. Y'know, all metal? Just like in The Terminator after his skin came off!"

"God, Jen, will you just go to bed, or something, and leave me alone. And quit watching television." He rolled away from her.

"But he was there. He talked to me. He wanted to know who our new neighbor was. He said it was important. I think ... well, I think maybe he was, you know, looking for her, or something."

"Whatta you want me to do about it?" he mumbled into his pillow.

Jen got off the bed. "I don't know," she sighed. "I just thought I should tell somebody, I guess. Mom's asleep and Dad's ... I think he's mad at me for something."

Robby couldn't ignore the sadness in her quavering voice and rolled over again, facing her. Her lips were trembling and her eyes sparkled with growing tears.

"He's probably just had a bad day, or something," Robby said quietly. "Maybe if you waited till tomorrow –"

"But he was out there tonight!"

Robby sat up. "You're serious, aren't you?"

"Yes, I'm serious! He talked to me!" She seemed to sense she had his attention now and stepped forward. "And his face, Robby, you should've seen his face. He was so ugly."

He knew she was serious, because Jen hated to cry and was on the verge of tears now.

"Well, there's not much I can do about it, Jen. Is there? I mean, what do you want me to do?"

She bowed her head. "Nothing, I guess. I just ... wanted to tell someone."

"I'm glad you did. But he was probably just out for a walk."

"He's not from around here, that's for sure. And his face ..."

"Did you get a good look at him? A really good look? I mean, it's dark out there, you know. And raining."

She nodded slowly and turned to go.

"You gonna be okay?" Robby asked.

"Yeah. Sorry I woke you."

"That's okay."

She closed the door silently.

Robby curled up in bed again, but couldn't relax. He tossed restlessly beneath the covers for a while, then raised up and pulled the shade aside to look out his window.

It was raining hard now and wind made the tree branches wave. There was no one on the street, not even a car. Robby saw nothing more than a cat scurrying across the street, its head ducked low against the rain.

But it was a while before he got back to sleep.

Chapter 7

Midnight Guest

THE dark bedroom seemed stuffy and gave George a vague feeling of claustrophobia. He got out of bed, careful not to disturb Karen, and cracked the window. Cold fresh air blew in and he hunkered down, put his face in the draft and inhaled deeply a few times before going back to bed. He lay naked beneath the covers, warmed by the electric blanket, and tried not to think of Lorelle Dupree.

He failed.

He was still stunned by her proposition. It had come so unexpectedly, in the middle of such an innocent conversation, that it had caught him completely off guard. It was not unpleasant – even very tempting – but still a big surprise.

She'd asked him in for a beer and, when he mentioned that Karen had the flu, she'd said, "Then you haven't eaten?"

"Not yet, but I just went out to get some –"

"Well, let me fix you something. I've got some stew on the stove and I can slip some biscuits into the microwave."

"No, no, thank you, that's nice, but my son and wife are asleep and my daughter's up watching TV and –"

"Then there's no reason for you to hurry back. Kids are very self-sufficient, you know."

He laughed. "No, really. Thanks for the beer, but –"

She moved forward suddenly, pressed herself against him and put her arms around him, her lips close to his, and whispered, "If you stay, we can fuck. They won't even miss you."

He almost dropped the half-finished beer he was holding, then stammered for a moment, unable to form words.

"Anything you want, George," she went on, pressing her breasts hard to his chest. "You want to fuck me in the ass? How about between the tits? Or ... how long has it been since you got a reeeaaally good blow job?" In a singsong voice she added with a grin, "I'll let you come in my moouuth."

His eyes widened and he looked around as if she might be talking to someone else, but when she kissed him, he knew she was serious. It was a long, wet, noisy kiss and when she pulled away, he gasped for breath. If he hadn't forced himself to push her back and walk around the kitchen, scrubbing his face with his palms, he knew he probably would have returned that kiss. But he thought of Karen and Robby and Jen, and he reminded himself that they were across the street. Yes, it would be fun, and yes, it would feel good – but he asked himself if it would be worth the inevitable price.

"I'm sorry," he said, unable to look at her, trying to sound firm but not unpleasant. "I'm very flattered. Really. But ... my wife ... my family ... I just can't. I'm sorry."

She went to him, smiling, and placed her hand to his face. "Okay, okay." Leading him to the door, she said, "I hope this won't affect our relationship as neighbors."

"Oh, no," he laughed, wishing his erection would go away. "No, not at all. You're welcome in our house anytime."

"Really?"

"Really. It's as good as forgotten."

"I don't want you to forget it," she said, opening the door, and –

– there was Jen.

George sighed into his pillow, turning on his side. His erection brushed Karen's thigh. She didn't respond. Her throaty breathing went on without breaking rhythm. He pressed his cock to her again, cautiously, and let the moist head slide over her flesh, watching for some reaction, in which case he would pull away. He remembered Lorelle's offer – You want to fuck me in the ass? – and thought about that, imagined it, as he moved against Karen's leg. He hadn't thought of doing that in years. It was the only thing he and Laura hadn't done, the only thing she wouldn't do, even though he was eager to try it, if only once. Karen did not even twitch as he moved, a little faster now, and –

– a hand came to rest on his shoulder and George spun around, kicking at the covers, ready to shout at whoever had sneaked into the room, but –

– it was Lorelle.

George froze, elbows locked behind him, knees up. "Whuh-whuh – "

She laid a finger over her smiling lips and knelt beside the bed in the soft glow of the small night light plugged into the socket beneath George's night stand. She sat back on the floor, legs spread, arms resting on her knees; she was naked. Silently, her lips formed two words:

"Fuck me."

George's heartbeat was the loudest sound in the room and he looked over his shoulder at Karen. The slow breaths wheezing in and out of her open mouth were all that kept her from appearing dead. He eased himself off the bed, embarrassed by his wet erection, and whispered, "What're you – how did you get in here?"

She leaned forward and began stroking his cock as she whispered in his ear, "You said I was welcome anytime." Then she bent down and sucked him hard into her mouth.

* * * *

Robby was dragged slowly from the quicksand of a bog-like sleep by a thunderous bellow. He fought to sit up in bed, lifting his leaden shoulders from the mattress and rocking himself upright as he wiped at his gluey eyes.

Barking. The sound he heard was a dog barking – two dogs – from across the street.

He muttered the names Sodom and Gomorrah, but they came from his pasty mouth sounding like spitwads hitting a brick wall.

With great effort, still unable to open his eyes more than

a sliver, Robby turned and looked out his window, nearly tearing down the shade with his clumsy, sleep-numbed hand. He blinked, rubbed his eyes with a knuckle and tried to pull everything into focus.

There was movement in the street, but this time it was not a cat.

A man wearing a hat and a long coat staggered from Lorelle's yard, leaning heavily on a cane and glancing over his shoulder. He turned left, heading toward Mistletoe, kicking up a spray of water as he moved quickly though a puddle. The dogs barked more frantically from inside Lorelle's house and the man slowed, turned, and waddled backwards for a moment as he looked at Robby's house. Then he disappeared into the shadows.

Robby blinked some more, wondering if he was dreaming, and lifted himself up on his knees. The shade dropped from his hand and his arm fell heavily to his side. He felt drunk, drugged, beaten, and when he tried to climb off the bed, he felt as if he were going over a cliff. He hit the floor with a thunk and groaned.

It was the man Jen had seen.

No, Robby thought. Just dreaming ... that's all.

But what if it had been the man Jen told him about. Someone besides Jen and himself should know there was a weird guy sneaking around the neighborhood.

Robby decided to wake his dad, except –

– he was falling asleep on his bedroom floor, sinking quickly back into the muddy depths of the sleep from which he had not entirely surfaced. Robby shook his head hard, sat up against the bed and tried to stand, failed once, tried again, then staggered toward the door, leaning first on the night stand, then his desk, then a chair.

The hallway was dark and silent. Robby leaned against the wall for a moment and his head drooped until his chin rested on his chest and his breathing became slow, shallow.

"No," he croaked to himself, jerking his head up. He swayed like a drunk and took a deep breath, focusing his bleary eyes on his parents' bedroom door. He trudged forward, staggering from one wall to another, until –

– his legs gave beneath him, unable to hold his weight, and he fell in a heap on the floor only a few feet from his parents' bedroom.

Through the black smoke of his fatigue, Robby felt the onset of panic. Something was wrong with him. He was sick. Suddenly, the man he'd seen – or thought he'd seen – was unimportant and he could think of nothing else but getting help. He took in a breath and tried to cry out for his parents, but his voice was nothing more than the gurgle of a clogged drain and his eyelids lowered completely, plunging him into darkness.

"Duh ... Duh ... Daaad." The word was only breathed, barely audible to Robby himself.

He pulled himself over the floor with the distant sound of the dogs barking across the street still in his ears and –

– something else.

Robby heard his dad ... grunting. Although it was a sound he'd never heard his dad make before, it was unmistakable.

They're fucking? he thought vaguely. Mom must not be too sick.

There was a moment of pause, a moment of embarrassment, then the panic set in again and Robby realized the interruption couldn't be helped. He dug his fingers into the carpet and crawled toward the bedroom.

* * * *

George lay on top of Lorelle, trying to hold in his cries as he slammed into her again and again, approaching his second orgasm as he looked down at her grinning face. His semen glistened around her mouth and in her hair and she reached up, swept her fingers through it, then licked them like candy.

She pulled away suddenly and George had to gulp back the shout of protest that rose in his throat.

Sitting up, she reached down between her legs and slipped

three fingers inside herself. When she removed them, they were dripping wet. Lorelle rolled over onto her knees, ass raised high, and reached back between her cheeks, sliding each wet finger into her asshole slowly, one at a time.

George's breath came faster as he watched her, then stopped completely when she wrapped her fingers around his cock, pulled it toward her and pushed herself back to meet him.

He entered her with an almost painful groan and clawed her back as he pounded into her ass harder and harder and harder until.

* * * *

Robby heard a low, throaty groan, then a loud thump from the bedroom as if something heavy had fallen to the floor. Sprawled on the floor, mouth hanging open, Robby listened and, when he heard nothing more, became even more afraid.

What's happening? he thought, and took another breath, this time managing a feeble, "What's ... wrong? What's –"

The very air changed. The darkness seemed to thicken and Robby felt as if his breath were being sucked out through his eye sockets.

The house chilled, became so cold that Robby expected to see his breath puff before him.

Something moved behind the closed door, then –

– silence.

No grunting or groaning. Even the dogs had stopped barking.

Except ...

Something gushed outside, like a sudden burst of wind.

Again ... and again ...

Like the slow flapping of great wings.

Then Robby blinked several times rapidly, feeling slightly confused, and looked around at the dark hallway. He stood easily, the deadly fatigue gone, and went to his parents' bedroom door, listened.

Nothing but his dad's snoring.

Massaging his eyes, Robby returned to his room. As he got back in bed, he tried to imagine his mom and dad making love. He'd tried before, unsuccessfully, but this time the image that came to mind was clear and vivid, as if he were in the room watching them. He relaxed in his bed, strangely warmed by the vision of his parents naked and entwined.

Outside his bedroom window, rain pattered and wind sighed and, once again, Robby sat up and looked out. There was a light on across the street at Lorelle's. A shadow moved behind the newly hung curtains, which suddenly parted, and –

– Robby ducked quickly, pulling the covers up to his chin. He didn't want to see her. He didn't even want to think about her.

And for some reason, he did not want her to see him.

He was still awake a few minutes later when a pulsing red and blue glow seeped in around the edges of his window shade. He pulled it aside to see Lorelle walking out to meet a police officer getting out of his car. Robby slid his window open a few inches and listened.

Above the hiss and crackle of the car's radio, Robby could hear their voices, but could only make out some of the words.

" ... prowler a while ago," Lorelle said.

" ... good look at him? Or did ... "

" ... walked with a cane and wore a fedora ... dark overcoat ... scarred face, horribly scarred ... arm with a metal hand ... "

Robby closed the window and let the shade drop back into place.

Could she have seen him? There hadn't been any sign of life over there other than the dogs barking. And even if she had, how could she have seen his metal hand if he wore a glove over it, as Jen had said?

Outside, the car door slammed and the policeman drove away.

Robby tried to go back to sleep, but he couldn't relax. Something wasn't right....

Chapter 8

Something in the Air

IT was not a typical weekend for the Pritchards. On Saturday morning, the sun rose behind lead-gray clouds and was nearing its peak before everyone in the house was awake.

Jen crawled out of bed, put on her robe, then shuffled around the house, her eyes closed half the time. After a while she realized she was the only one up. She made herself some toast, turned on the television and stared blearily at some dumb cartoon. As she began to feel more awake, her thoughts kept returning to the hideous man she'd met the night before, and the nightmares through which he'd stalked her in her sleep. She decided that, when he woke up, she would tell Dad about the man. She was afraid if she didn't, he would be chasing her through her sleep for many nights to come, laughing through his twisted grin as his shiny steel hand clutched at her hair.

But when Dad finally walked out into the living room wearing his bathrobe, his hair looking like a clump of barbed wire that had been pressed into his scalp, Jen had second thoughts. He was pale and moved slowly with his eyes half closed.

"Morning, Dad," she said tentatively.

He went to the recliner, where Monroe was sleeping in a curled-up ball. He swatted the cat hard with his knuckles. Monroe hissed as he dove from the chair and shot out of the room.

Jen was startled. He usually lifted Monroe out of the

chair. She knew he didn't like Monroe, but she'd never seen him hit the cat before.

"You feeling okay, Dad?"

He made a noise in his throat and moved his head, but that was all.

It'll wait, Jen thought, turning back to the television.

* * * *

Every inch of George's body ached. He couldn't remember drinking anything more than a beer last night, but he felt as if he were suffering the hangover of a lifetime. His hands trembled and his legs were weak and he felt as if someone had stabbed a straw into his gut and sucked out his insides.

When he first opened his eyes that morning, he'd thought of a dream he'd had, a vivid sexual dream, no doubt inspired by Lorelle Dupree's proposition the night before. It wasn't until he realized that he was lying on the floor beside his bed – that he'd slept on the floor – that his dream took on a new meaning. He sat up and saw the red circles of irritated flesh just below his thighs, as if his knees had been rubbing vigorously on the carpet. He touched his unusually tender cock and smelled on his fingers the distinct, musky odor of his dream.

How had it happened? How had she gotten into the house? Before going to bed, he'd gone through his nightly routine of checking all the doors to make sure they were locked. It made no sense.

As he sat in the recliner, wincing at the blaring noise from the television, George remembered he'd left the bedroom window cracked all night long. But in the dream –

– It wasn't a dream, he thought, it was real –

– he'd been awake when Lorelle came in. He would have heard that window open – even if he'd been asleep, the sound would have woken him.

As he ran his fingers through his hair, George noticed that the movement made his back sting. When the sensation did not go away, he got up, went to the bathroom, dropped his robe and turned his back to the mirror over the sink, looking over his shoulder.

Thin red scratches striped his back.

He quickly washed his face with cold water and decided he would make a pot of coffee. Then, no matter what it took, George was going to forget all about it.

After scrubbing his face with a towel, he looked into the mirror and muttered hoarsely, "Just a dream. Thassall."

In the hall, he heard Karen stirring in the bedroom and hurried away before she came out.

* * * *

Karen had awakened suddenly, sat up and clutched her head in her hands, sick with guilt. She went over it all in her mind and could not believe what she had done. And she'd done it just across the street! Lifting her head slowly, she stared for a moment at the jewelry box on her dresser. That was where she'd hidden the tiny silver women Lorelle had give her. She thought of the way their legs were locked together, of what she and Lorelle had done.

It was still light outside, so she probably had time to fix a quick dinner. That's what she would do. Maybe she'd get take-out Chinese food – a favorite in their house – and treat them all like royalty, shower them with affection, pay each of them a lot of attention – more than she usually did, she was afraid. She felt groggy, as if she'd been drugged, and knew she could probably sleep a few more hours if she laid back down. But she couldn't do that. George would be home soon and the kids were probably hungry.

As she got out of bed, she saw the time on the digital clock: 10:41 A.M.

Karen slapped a hand over her mouth and groaned, "Oh, God." Her stomach turned and her throat felt thick, as if full of phlegm. She never slept that long, not without at least waking once to go to the bathroom, or something. She had never been a heavy sleeper.

Slipping on her panties and dress, she peeked out into the

hall, saw no one, and went into the bathroom. The woman who stared at her from inside the mirror was frightening: greasy hair, pale, splotchy skin with dark bags beneath her eyes, and hands that looked veiny and aged.

Turning away from the mirror, Karen sat on the edge of the bathtub and closed a fist around a clump of her flat, spiky hair, thinking about it all again.

All the licking and sucking ... all the wet noises they'd made ...

The worst part was that no matter how hard Karen tried to be repulsed by the memory, it only excited her and made her want more.

An abrupt knock at the bathroom door made her jump.

"Mom?" Jen called.

Taking a deep breath, struggling to keep her voice steady, she answered, "What, honey?"

"Do we have any more cocoa? I can't find any."

"May-maybe not. I-I'll come look in a minute. Okay?"

"'Kay." After a moment: "You feel better?"

"Yeah. Yuh-yeah, I think so."

"That's good." Her footsteps hurried down the hall.

Better than what? Karen thought. Had Jen sensed something wrong yesterday? Had she looked this bad yesterday?

Looking in the mirror again, she was certain she'd never looked worse.

She stood and ran a brush through her hair a few times, then stood at the bathroom door for several long seconds, wondering how she could bear to show herself in her own home.

* * * *

Robby felt better when he woke that morning, although he had not slept well. His dreams of Lorelle had been haunted by the dark, limping figure he'd seen out his window the night before.

He put on jeans and a shirt and went into the hall, where

his mom was just coming out of the bathroom. She quickly looked away from him and rushed by before he could say good morning.

The house was unusually quiet. Even the television was playing at low volume. Jen was not in her usual place on the floor and instead of cartoons, a news show was on. The Carl's, Jr. bag was still on the coffee table and Dad was slumped in the recliner, scowling at the television.

"Morning, Dad."

"What?" He looked up at Robby with a long face, his eyes deep beneath eyebrows so mussed that they seemed made of tangled black wires.

"Just ... good morning."

Dad turned back to the television without responding.

In the kitchen Mom was doing something at the counter, while Jen thumbed through a magazine and listened to her iPod at the breakfast table.

"Guess Dad's not in a great mood, huh?" Robby asked quietly as he sat down with her.

Removing the headphones, Jen rolled her eyes and said, "He's weird this morning." Tossing a glance at Mom, she whispered, "So's she. You think they're fighting?"

Robby remembered the sounds he'd heard in their room the night before. They hadn't been fighting then.

Something thunked to the kitchen floor and Robby turned to see his mom staring at the coffee can she'd dropped to the floor. Grounds were spilled at her feet in a pool. She said nothing, just stared at it, pressing her lips together tightly as if she were about to cry. Then she walked out.

Robby went over and picked up the can and set it on the counter as she came back in with a broom.

"I'll get it," she said, her voice unsteady, quavering. "Just leave it alone, okay? Just leave it alone."

Robby backed up to the table and watched her sweep up the mess. She didn't look at him or even acknowledge his presence.

Jen looked up at him and shrugged, as if to say, I don't know what's going on.

He didn't either, but something had made the whole house thick with tension and Robby did not like it. He started out of the kitchen and as he passed Mom, she breathed, "Sorry."

The tension in the Pritchard house that morning did not go away. The day stretched on silently, with the exception of the television and an occasional door closing. Or slamming. Robby did some homework and Jen went down the street to see the Crane twins. Karen made a big pot of potato soup, baked some banana nut bread and wrote a few emails. George worked on the broken lawnmower in the garage, cleaned out the fireplace and watched an old movie. They did the things they usually did on Saturdays, but there was no conversation, no laughter, not even any angry shouting. And those few words that were exchanged were done so without eye contact.

Late in the afternoon, Dylan called and asked Robby if he wanted to go to the mall. Anxious to get out of the house, Robby grabbed his coat and went outside to meet Dylan. He assumed they were going to walk – the Mt. Shasta Mall wasn't far away – but instead, Mrs. Garry pulled up in her car and Dylan waved from the backseat.

A light rain was falling and Robby stuffed his hands into his coat pockets as he hurried to the other side of the car. As he got in, he spotted Lorelle walking down her drive flanked by Sodom and Gomorrah, each on a leash. He turned away quickly, as if he hadn't noticed her.

Dylan watched her as they drove away, turning around in the seat to look out the back window. With a low whistle, he whispered, "God, they're gorgeous." Then, chuckling: "The dogs're pretty nice, too."

Robby ignored him and looked out his window as they turned onto Mistletoe and something caught his eye. A tan Ford Escort was parked on the other side of the street. A man wearing a hat sat behind the wheel, elbow propped against the closed window, his face in his gloved hand. His eyes met with Robby's and he sat up suddenly, pulling his hand away, and –

– through the rain-speckled glass, Robby saw the man's

mangled face, his down turned eye, the rictus curl of the left side of his mouth as it grinned halfway up his face.

The man watched Robby as they rode by and Robby spun around, clutching the back of the seat.

The Escort started up and pulled away from the shoulder, making a U-turn in the street.

"My God," Robby breathed.

"What?" Dylan asked, glancing behind them. "Someone you know?"

Robby stammered a moment, then fell silent. What could he say? *That was the man with the melting face and the steel hand that my sister saw last night.* It wouldn't sound good.

But the man was definitely following them.

"Something wrong, Robby?" Mrs. Garry asked.

He tried to relax in the seat and think of a response, but he was too upset – too frightened – to string words into a sentence, so he just mustered a weak smile, said, "No," and resisted the urge to look back again.

Dylan was talking to him about something, but his voice sounded far away and his words were garbled. Robby stared at the back of Mrs. Garry's head as Dylan rattled on.

They turned right on Churn Creek Road. The windshield wipers sounded like a soggy heartbeat as they swept from right to left and back again and –– Robby looked over his shoulder.

The Escort was still behind them.

Robby's hands began to shake in his lap and he considered asking Mrs. Garry to take him back home –

– *I could say I forgot something I had to do, or that I'm expecting a long distance call, or* –

– but they were already on Hilltop Drive and Mrs. Garry turned on the blinker, ready to turn into the Sears parking lot just ahead.

"I've got some shopping to do," she said as she looked for a parking space. "You boys do whatever you want in the mall. Dylan, I'll give you a call when I'm ready to leave."

"Okay, Mom," Dylan said.

She pulled into a space, killed the engine, and they got out of the car.

Robby looked around for the Escort but didn't see it.

"What's the matter?" Dylan asked. "You look like you're lost."

"Oh. Nothing. Let's go."

Still looking over his shoulder every few seconds, Robby followed Dylan into the mall.

I'm tired, that's all, he thought. I haven't been sleeping well and it's made me jumpy. Paranoid. That's all.

Inside the mall, they went to Hot Topic first and looked around for a while. Dylan whispered jokes about the overweight goth girl operating the register as they browsed the merchandise. As the left the store, Robby looked to his left at the glass doors through which they'd entered.

The man stood on the sidewalk outside, leaning on his cane as he stared in through the glass.

"Holy shit," Robby whispered, spinning around so his back was toward the window.

"What?"

"C'mon, we've gotta go."

"What the hell's wrong with you?"

"That man is following me."

"What man?"

"That –"

He was gone.

"You're still sick, aren't you?" Dylan asked, frowning. "You got a fever?"

Robby didn't reply. He just stared at the glass doors as his heart thundered against his ribs.

"I'm gonna go look at the pictures of the half naked women in the Victoria's Secret window." Dylan left him standing alone.

Robby turned away from the entrance and stared absently into the display window in front of Hot Topic. He tried to tell himself it was ridiculous to be so frightened by a total stranger. Just because his face was disfigured did not mean he was some kind of mad slasher, and it certainly didn't mean he was the same man Lorelle had reported to the police last night.

Maybe I am sick, he thought, touching his forehead for signs of a high temperature.

"Please listen to me and don't run away."

Robby gasped as he spun around to face the man who had appeared suddenly behind him.

"I don't want to hurt you. Just warn you. You have to listen to me." The brim of his fedora was low and his head was tipped forward so Robby couldn't get a good look at his face.

"Who are you?"

"Doesn't matter. All you need to know is that you're in danger. Your whole family is in danger. In fact, your entire neigh –"

Feeling a sudden jolt of anger, Robby growled, "Look, man, I don't have to listen to you, okay? I don't know who you are, but if you don't stay out of my neighborhood and away from my sister, I'll have you thrown in –"

The man lifted his head and faced him directly.

Robby's words disappeared in a gulp.

The left side of the man's mouth had been cut all the way up to his cheekbone, which appeared to have caved in, as if it had been split then sewn back together. The scar that remained had dragged the outer corner of his left eye downward and puckered his cheek like a colorless raisin.

"Look at me," the man whispered. "Look at me. Do you want this to happen to you? To your family?"

Feeling queasy, Robby backed up until he bumped into the window.

"Now, listen to me. You have to listen. You're all in danger. You know something's wrong. Deep down, I think you know. Don't you?"

Robby looked to his right and saw Dylan a few stores down standing at the Victoria's Secret window. He willed Dylan to turn to him, to see the man with the cane, but Dylan didn't move.

"She's evil," the man said quietly, moving a step closer.

Robby looked at him again. The man's face made him wince. He couldn't look at him for long. He turned his head toward Dylan again and tried to call his name, but his throat was full of sand and he only made a senseless, whispery sound. His hands tingled, as if freezing cold, and he waggled his fingers spastically as the man moved a step closer, almost touching him now.

Robby turned toward Dylan again. He still stood at the window, oblivious.

He whispered, "You know she's evil, don't you?"

Robby forced himself to peel his body away from the window and turn left. He threw himself forward, away from the man, nearly tripping over his own feet on his way to the exit. But he could not keep himself from glancing back over his shoulder.

The man stood facing him but did not pursue him.

"You'll see," he said, just loud enough for Robby to hear him. "She never sleeps. There's no time. Too many souls to eat."

Robby broke into a run as he faced front, darting around the people in front of him, dodging those walking toward him. A few people stared for a moment as he passed, then went back to the business of shopping.

All Robby wanted was to go home.

The cold drizzle felt good on his face. He kept running into the parking lot, then slowed to a stop and turned around.

The strange man was nowhere in sight.

Robby went to Mrs. Garry's car and waited in the rain, keeping a watchful eye out for the man.

"Where'd you go?" Dylan asked as he and his mother came out of the mall and approached the car almost half an hour later.

Robby shrugged. "Outside. I just ... lost interest to the mall. That's all."

By the time he got home, Robby wanted to get drunk. He wondered if his parents were busy enough not to notice him breaking into their booze.

Dad was stretched out in the recliner in the living room,

dividing his attention between a magazine and an old movie on television.

"Hey, Dad."

He nodded without looking up.

"Where's Mom?"

"Across the street."

"Huh?"

"She went over to Lor – Miss Dupree's house."

Robby muttered, "Oh. Yeah." Then he hurried into the kitchen, opened the cupboard, and took several big, long gulps of vodka from the bottle.

Chapter 9

Saturday Night

KAREN went to bed at ten-thirty, but lay awake for over two hours thinking about what she'd done that afternoon. Once, she'd gotten up to take from her jewelry box the tiny piece of silver Lorelle had given her. She'd looked at it for several minutes, fondled it, then put it away and returned to bed.

Now that it was over, she hated herself for it, but at the time she'd felt like a junkie in need of a fix. The house had been so quiet, so tense, and all she'd wanted was to feel better.

As she'd tried hard to keep herself busy in the uneasy silence, Karen could not stop remembering how good Lorelle had made her feel Friday afternoon. She remembered the orgasms, one after another, first touching her like feathers, then hitting like trains. She'd never known she could be made to feel that way, that she could achieve such intense and physically rocking pleasure.

When she first started baking the banana nut bread, she told herself it was for the kids because they loved it so much, but deep down inside herself where she seldom looked, she knew it was for another reason. It was an excuse to go over to Lorelle's.

And she had. She'd allowed it to happen again.

Now she lay in bed hating herself for it. But she didn't hate herself as much as she had the first time. And this time, she found herself hating George just a little for never making her feel that way.

Karen wondered as she lay in bed gently touching herself
if she would hate herself even less the next time. She left her
hand between her legs but feigned sleep when George came
in, hoping he wouldn't speak to her.

* * * *

Seconds after George had settled beneath the covers,
Monroe jumped up onto the bed, purring and prodding the
covers between George and Karen for a comfortable place
to curl up.

George tolerated the cat the rest of the day in the rest of
the house, but he'd told Karen countless times that Monroe
was to be shut out of the bedroom when they turned in for
the night.

It had been a long, bad day, cold – inside the house as
well as out – and irritating. He knew part of the reason
was the guilt, shame and confusion he felt about what had
happened in their bedroom the night before. But he didn't
know what was wrong with Karen. He'd hoped she would
try to snap him out of it and cheer him up as she usually did
when he was feeling low. But she'd hardly even spoken to
him and that irritated him. Then she'd gone over to Lorelle's
for a couple of hours and that made him nervous. What if
Lorelle was the kiss and tell type?

Guess what your husband did to me last night ... on your
bedroom floor ... while you were asleep.

After a while he realized that was ridiculous. Lorelle
lived across the street from them, for Christ's sake. It wasn't
likely she was going to shit where she ate. But when Karen
returned, she'd been even colder and more distant, and that
only made him feel crankier.

The cat on the bed was the last straw.

Usually, George swept Monroe up and put him out in the
hall. Not this time.

He jerked his foot from under the covers, and kicked
the cat off the bed. Monroe yowled as he became airborne
and his claws tore at the carpet when he landed. Karen sat

bolt upright in bed as George chased Monroe around the room, finally cornering him under the bed. Mindless of the scratches he would no doubt sustain, George groped under the bed as Monroe hissed and spat, finally closing his fist on a clump of fur and dragging the squawling cat out, carrying him by his fur to the door and throwing him hard into the hall.

"Dammit, George!" Karen snapped, getting out of bed.

"I've told you, that cat does not belong in here at night."

"Well, you don't have to do that!"

"Maybe it'll teach him to stay out of here altogether."

"God." She put on her robe and went after Monroe as George got back into bed.

He knew he was not going to sleep, though. Awful as it sounded, knocking Monroe around a little had actually felt good and he was pumped with adrenaline. There was even a slight stirring between his legs.

Karen returned a moment later and grabbed her pillows.

"What're you doing?" George asked.

"I don't like the idea of sleeping with someone who abuses animals."

"Then don't bother leaving." He got out of bed. "I will." He slipped on a pair of pants, a T-shirt, got a blanket from the closet, and took his pillow with him.

In the living room, he tossed the pillow and blanket onto the sofa and turned on the television. Saturday Night Live was just getting over and it occurred to George that Jen and Robby usually stayed up for it, but they'd gone to bed a couple of hours ago.

Everyone seemed to be behaving oddly.

Not at all tired, George went to the kitchen to make himself a rum and Coke, but decided to hold the Coke. Back in the living room, he peered idly out the front window and was surprised to see Dylan Garry across the street, shuffling down the sidewalk toward his house. He was walking strangely, almost dragging his feet, hands in his coat pockets, head hung low. Was he ... limping? Swaying? Maybe he was drunk. Probably. George wondered if he'd get into trouble when he got home. As far as George was concerned, a teenager drinking was no big deal, not when he could be out snorting coke or crack or –

Beyond Dylan, there was a soft light in Lorelle's bedroom window where she stood holding the curtains open. The light shimmered through the flowing sleeves of the sheer robe she wore. She was watching Dylan as he swaggered down the sidewalk, then she disappeared a moment, returning with a lighted candle which she set on the window sill.

The candlelight illuminated the black and red teddy she wore and flickered on her face as she smiled across the street at George. She reached down and lifted something ... a telephone. She punched in a number.

She's calling here! George thought, hurrying to the telephone in the kitchen, ready to pick up, so the ring wouldn't wake anyone.

Barely half a ring sounded before he snapped the receiver to his ear.

"Hel-hello?"

"George," she purred. "You're still up."

"Yeah, I-yuh, I couldn't sleep."

"I can't sleep either. Why don't we not sleep together."

"Look, Lorelle, last night ... what happened ... I don't know how you got in here, but I'm not sure I appreciated it. I mean, I'm married."

"Seems to me a married man should be able to get from his wife what you got from me last night. But I don't think that's the case with you. Is it?"

He sighed, rubbed his eyes hard with his fingers. "I'm sorry, Lorelle. I just ... it was nice, but I just can't –"

"I have a vibrator, George. I'd like you to fuck me in the ass while I stick the vibrator in my cunt." She sounded as if she were telling him what color she'd like to repaint her house. "Won't that feel good, George?"

His mouth moved, but he didn't speak.

"You think about it, George. But I don't like to be kept waiting. I'll leave the candle in the window. When it burns out, you've missed your chance. It's a short candle, George."

She hung up.

George paced the kitchen, poured some more rum, and finished it off. It burned in his belly and spread over him like a hot flash as he rubbed his temples, thinking ... thinking ...

George turned and Monroe hissed at him from the kitchen doorway. When he stepped forward, growling an obscenity as he pulled his leg back to kick the cat, anticipating the pleasure of his foot's impact with the animal's small head, Monroe spun around and disappeared.

Taking one more quick drink, he went to the hall closet to find his jacket.

*   *   *   *

Too many souls to eat ... too many souls to eat ... too many souls –

– Robby was ripped from his sleep for the third time that night, his sheets soggy with perspiration. It was a few minutes after four in the morning.

He'd sneaked a Thermos of vodka into his room earlier that evening, hoping to drink himself numb, but it hadn't worked as well as he'd hoped.

The man was a lunatic, that was all. Had to be. He wasn't talking about Lorelle, he was just ... babbling. But that didn't make him – or his words – any less disturbing. The whole encounter had been so surreal, so much like something out of a bad horror movie, that Robby couldn't bring himself to tell anyone about it, although he knew he probably should. But who? Dad was in no mood to listen to him, and Mom had looked even worse that evening when she got back from Lorelle's. When Robby asked her if she felt all right, she'd dismissed it as the flu and said she'd take some aspirin and go to bed early.

Robby had gone to bed early, too, hoping to drink himself to sleep. But he kept waking suddenly, covered with sweat, from one nightmare after another. He'd opened the window earlier, hoping to cool himself off, but it hadn't worked because now the top sheet clung to him like a second skin and his chest heaved as he stared wide-eyed into the darkness of his bedroom. Groaning, he reached over and flicked on his lamp and –

– Lorelle leaned over him and whispered, "Hello, Robby."

"Jesus Chrrr – where did you – how did you get in –"

She placed her fingertips over his mouth and hissed, "Ssshhh," as she slid one knee onto the bed. She was naked and her breasts swayed above him as she ran her hand over his sweaty chest. Leaning forward, she licked his belly and chest, murmuring, "Mmmm, I love sssweat." She took his cock into her mouth and silenced all of Robby's questions.

It made no sense. She couldn't just walk into their locked house at four in the morning, not without someone hearing her ... unless –

– I'm dreaming, Robby thought, that's all ... dreaming ...

He forgot about the man with the cane and the strange things he'd said. In a few minutes, he even forgot that Lorelle shouldn't be there. He knew he wasn't dreaming because dreams just weren't this vivid, didn't feel this good. He lost himself in what she was doing.

Robby came three times. He even cried out once or twice, certain someone had heard him, but no one came to his door. The fourth time, he fell into a deep, dreamless sleep, and didn't wake until just before noon.

Chapter 10

The Flu

IT was the cold and flu season, as the television commercials continued to remind their sniffling viewers, so it was not odd that the flu was going around on Deerfield. But this year it seemed to be hitting everyone at once, and this particular flu was a more frustrating strain than usual. It was not accompanied by typical flu symptoms. It came, instead, as a simple but overwhelming feeling of fatigue. Jen was the only one in the house with any energy. Robby and George spent most of Sunday dozing in chairs, on the sofa, or in bed, while Karen, like most mothers with sick families, tried to go about her normal activities, but with little success. They moved around the house sluggishly, with long pale faces, looking exhausted and annoyed.

George came to life only once all day, when Monroe, curled up on the sofa, hissed at him, then tried to dart out of the room. He kicked the cat against the wall and growled a few curses, sending Monroe screeching into the kitchen, where Karen, angered by George's treatment of her pet, shattered her coffee mug in the sink, splashing coffee on the wall and counter.

Robby was not so far under the weather that he could not feel the tension in the house and, by mid-afternoon, decided to get out, no matter how bad he felt. He called Dylan to see if he wanted to go for a walk, or something. Anything.

"Sorry, Robby," Mrs. Garry said, "But Dylan's in bed." Her voice was tight, as if it were holding back anger. "I think he caught your flu. He doesn't have a fever and he's not really sick, but he's very pale and shaky and can't seem to get out of his tracks."

"Oh?" Robby said. "Yeah, we've got it here, too. Guess it's going around."

"I guess so. I'll tell him you called." She hung up without saying goodbye.

Not interested in going out alone, Robby stretched out on the sofa and fell asleep watching television.

Karen, too began to feel a bit claustrophobic, and trudged down the street through the rain to visit Lynda, but things were not much better in the Crane household. The twins were in the living room watching television, but they stared at the screen with cold, angry faces and didn't look up when Karen came in. The atmosphere in the house was thick with tension. Lynda was chain-smoking as she sorted through a stack of old magazines in the dining room.

"I kept all of these for one reason or another," she said, puffing smoke, "but now I can't remember why."

"Where's Al?"

"In bed. He's ... not feeling well." Bitterness shaded her voice when she spoke of Al. "Neither are the twins. I think they've all got a flu bug, or something. And I'm ... well, I'm just ... not in a good mood."

"What's wrong?"

She shook her head and, for a moment, seemed near tears. "Al and I've been fighting. I think."

"What? Why didn't you call me? What's going on? What do you mean, you think you're fighting?"

"I don't know. Things were fine until Friday night and ... then he just seemed to be somewhere else. He wouldn't talk to me, he was grumpy. I woke up late that night and he wasn't in bed. I found him sleeping in the spare room. When I got up yesterday morning, he was in the front yard talking to that woman who moved into the Huitt place. She was out walking her dogs. He seemed friendly enough, talking and laughing, so I figured whatever was bothering him was gone. Then he came inside and it was ... more of the same. He wouldn't speak to me.

"Well, you know we've never been that way, we always talk if something's wrong, so I sat him down and suggested we do something that day, just the two of us. I figured I'd leave the twins with you and we'd go out to the flea market like we used to, or have a lunch together and I'd talk to him, find out what was wrong. He wasn't feeling well – I mean, he looked bad, too – but he went along with it, sort of like he really didn't want to, but just to shut me up, you know? And about that time, the twins saw that woman walking back down the road, and they were fascinated by her dogs and Al took them out to introduce them. I went out and met her, too, and she seemed nice enough. When Al told her we were going out, she suggested we leave the kids with her, so they could play with the dogs, and Al said sure, fine, and the kids were crazy about the idea.

"We went out, had lunch, and he wouldn't talk to me. And when I tried to find out what was wrong, he snapped at me, told me it was none of my fucking business, if he wanted to tell me, he'd tell me, and we came back home. When we got here, the twins didn't look so good either. They've felt bad ever since. I guess the flu's going around, but ... it's like I'm alone in the house and I'm sick of it. He still won't talk to me and I don't know why." She winced, on the verge of crying again, then coughed and tried to perk up. "Oh, well. We've been married all these years, and this is the first time we've ever had one of those long silent fights for no apparent reason. They happen to everybody, I suppose. Guess it was just our turn."

Karen didn't tell her that she was going through something similar with George. Instead, she tried to reassure her by blaming it on the flu.

"It's a bad one this year," she said. "Makes you ... I don't know, just sort of pissy, you know? He'll get better and things'll be fine."

But, although she tried to hide them, Lynda's worries did not go away and she was not the company Karen had hoped for. So she made an excuse and left. She went across the street to see Betty LaBianco.

Ed LaBianco kept their yard in impeccable condition and Karen sometimes thought he cared more for his lawn and garden equipment than for Betty. But as she went up their front walk, she noticed he'd left his Snapper mower in the middle of the front lawn. In the rain. She frowned as she passed the machine, knowing that wasn't like Ed at all.

Ed answered the door, looking as if he'd just woke up. He was a small, cheerful, balding man with a beak-like nose and pleasant smile. But he wasn't smiling now. He looked like he'd been crying; his round face was red and puffy.

"Betty's in bed," he said wearily. "She's not feeling well. And neither am I, really."

"Oh, I'm sorry to hear that. Well, tell her I stopped by, okay?"

"Yeah, fine."

"Oh, and Ed, your lawn mower's –"

He shut the door.

Karen stood on the step a moment, surprised by his abruptness, then started back home.

She'd left the house hoping to make herself feel better, but had only darkened her mood. Thinking that perhaps everyone else in the neighborhood had the right idea, Karen decided to go home and go to bed.

One house seemed untouched by the flu.

Lorelle Dupree was the picture of health as she walked her dogs down the drive and out onto the street.

* * * *

On her way out of the house, Jen met her mom coming back in.

"Where are you going?" Mom asked.

"I'm gonna go see Tara and Dana."

"Uh-uh. They're sick."

"Is everybody sick around here?"

"Looks that way." She went inside.

Outside, Jen saw Miss Dupree taking her dogs for a walk,

across the street. She stopped, smiled at Jen and called, "Hi, there."

"Hello." Jen stayed on her side of the street. She didn't want to be rude, but she couldn't get rid of the nagging feeling that there was something different about Miss Dupree, something unpleasant.

As if sensing that Jen would not come to her, Miss Dupree led her dogs across the street. No, that wasn't right – the dogs led her across the street.

"Would you like to walk with us, Jen?" Miss Dupree said.

One of the dogs pressed its nose into Jen's hand and licked her palm while the other lifted its paw and patted her arm to get her attention. Jen laughed and petted them.

"Why don't you come with us. Just to the end of the road and back."

"Okay."

As they walked slowly and Jen patted the dog closest to her, Miss Dupree asked her about school, her hobbies and friends, what she did during her summer vacations.

As they reached the intersection of Deerfield and Mistletoe, the dogs slowed to a stop, ears perked with interest. Suddenly each one bounded forward, pulling the leashes taut, barking viciously toward the left corner of the intersection.

"Calm!" Miss Dupree snapped, and the dogs became still, emitting low, throaty growls. Miss Dupree looked in the direction in which the dogs were growling and Jen did the same.

A tan car was parked at the intersection's corner, pointing west on Mistletoe. Someone sat behind the wheel, but the glare from the steel grey sky shined on the windshield, hiding the driver. The engine started and the car pulled away. Miss Dupree watched it go, her face stern. The dogs whined and looked up at her, as if asking what to do next.

"It's okay now," she whispered to them, turning to walk back down Deerfield. After a silent pause she asked, "By the way, where's Robby? I haven't seen him today."

"He's not feeling well."

"Oh, I'm sorry."

Watching Miss Dupree's face closely, although for what she wasn't sure, Jen said, "He's been kinda sick ever since he helped you move your stuff."

"Really? That's too bad."

"So's Mom. Since Friday."

"Oh?"

"Dad doesn't feel too good either the last couple of days."

"Then you must be very lonely with no one to keep you company. Why didn't you come over?"

Jen shrugged.

"You must get lonesome, anyway, with only a brother at home with you. Do you two get along well?"

Another shrug. "Okay, I guess."

"Really? I know some girls who don't even like their brothers."

"Oh, I like him okay. He's smart." She smiled. "He always gets good grades. Better than me. School's hard for me sometimes, but it always seems so easy for Robby."

"Does he help you with your homework?"

"Dad usually does. I wish Robby would, sometimes, but ... you know, he doesn't have time to do that."

"He has a busy schedule, does he? Does he pay any attention to you at all?"

Jen frowned, thinking it over. "Sometimes. Well ... once in a while. We fight over the TV. That kinda thing."

"But in a nice way. Does he ever pay attention to you in a nice way?"

"Oh, yeah, sure, some ... times." But not that much, she thought.

They stopped in front of Jen's house and Miss Dupree smiled slowly. "Would you like him to?"

Jen felt suddenly suspicious. "What do you mean?"

"Well, I think I know how you feel. You admire your brother. Look up to him. You'd like him to ... well, treat you with a little more respect, pay more attention to you, am I right?"

Jen relaxed her frown slowly as she nodded, but she didn't lose the frown inside where she was beginning to feel uncomfortable. Miss Dupree looked like a perfectly nice person with pretty eyes and the straightest, whitest teeth Jen had ever seen. But in spite of that, Jen had a gnawing feeling of suspicion. She studied Miss Dupree's face, then –

"Yes," Jen finally answered.

"Well, if you'd like, I think we can get him to do that."

"How?"

Miss Dupree gave her a big smile and touched her cheek with a gentle stroke. "I'll think of something."

Chapter 11

A New Toy

"LOOK, Miss Weiss, I've gotta go to my next class," Robby said, standing before her desk.

"I really don't care, Robby. We have to talk."

Robby put a hand on her desk and hoped it didn't look obvious that he was leaning so he wouldn't sway. He felt so weak and shaky, he wasn't sure he'd be able to stand up much longer.

"Pull up a seat," she said. Reluctantly, he turned to one of the small school desks and dragged it closer to her desk, then plopped into the chair as if his knees had given out.

"Okay, Robby. What's wrong?"

"Nothing's wrong, I just –"

"Please, Robby," she interrupted. "You weren't ready for the test on Friday, you're not ready for the make-up today. That's not like you. I know it's not like you." She paused, then: "You came up in a conversation today. With another teacher. It seems you have quite a reputation, Robby. Nearly straight A's. You're an outstanding student. So. What's wrong?"

"There's nothing wrong. I just ... forgot."

"You forgot."

He nodded without looking at her.

"I don't believe you, Robby. I admit I don't know you well, but I know you're not the kind of student to forget a test."

His jaw worked back and forth as he stared at the floor.

"Is it because you're sick?" she asked. "You don't look

well at all, you know. But if you're ill, why don't you stay home?"

He said nothing, hoping she would steer clear of the subject of home.

"Is something wrong at home? Is that it? Because if –"

Robby's head jerked back and forth suddenly.

"Are you sure?"

He looked at her and spoke quietly and slowly through his teeth. "Nothing's wrong, okay?"

Miss Weiss leaned forward over her desk and softened her voice. "If there is something wrong, Robby, it's okay. I mean, everybody has –"

"Look, I'll take it tomorrow," he said, his voice wavering slightly. His eyes left her and darted around the room. "The test. I'll take it tomorrow. Okay?"

She watched him a moment before saying, "Listen to me, Robby. If there's anything I can do ... or even if I can't do anything, maybe I can turn you to someone who –"

"Tomorrow? Please? I'll do it tomorrow, I promise."

"Okay, okay. Tomorrow, I'll give you the same test you just took. I want all the questions answered, okay? All of them. I want you to try, which you didn't seem to do today, because almost three quarters of the questions haven't been touched. If you don't ... well, I think I'll have to talk with your parents."

Panic widened his eyes slightly and his neck stiffened as he turned to her to protest, but said nothing for a moment as his hands fluttered nervously with one another over his books on the small desktop.

"No," Robby whispered. "Don't do that."

"Why?"

His mouth felt dry suddenly. "I don't ... want you to ... well, they ... wouldn't understand. That's all." Then, after a long pause: "Please?"

"Will you be ready tomorrow?"

He nodded quickly.

"Okay."

Robby stood so suddenly that the desk scraped over the

floor and he staggered toward the door, clutching his books beneath one arm.

"Robby?"

He stopped but looked at his feet instead of turning toward her.

"Are you ... taking any drugs? Or –"

"No," he whispered.

"You're not well. And I don't think it's just the flu. Are you sure there's nothing you want to talk about?"

"No," he said on his way to the door. "Everything's fine."

He was out of the room before she could say anything else.

Robby trudged down the hall, out of the building, and tried not to drag his feet as he crossed the grass toward the next building, where his biology class was about to begin. He expected Dylan to be waiting for him in the hall, but remembered he'd stayed home sick that day. Robby had been tempted to stay home, too, but there was really nothing wrong with him, except for the weakness that made him nearly unable to get out of a chair or carry his books, and he hated to miss school unless he really had to.

Unfortunately, he'd completely forgotten about the test. Staying home had been a better idea than he'd thought.

He heard whispering footsteps in the damp grass behind him, but ignored them, until –

– a hand touched his arm and a familiar voice said, "Your sister is in danger."

When Robby turned to him, the stranger's mangled face seemed to wither, as if he were looking at someone more hideous than himself.

"My God," he whispered, squeezing Robby's arm.

"Get away from me," Robby said, pulling away. He knew he didn't sound very convincing, but he went on anyway. "I'll have you thrown off campus. You know, you can get into a lot of trouble for coming to the –"

"No, no, please, wait." The man simply stared at Robby for a moment, then whispered, "She's already started. She's not wasting any time."

"Who?" Robby snapped.

"You're sick. You look awful."

"So I've got the flu. It's none of your goddamned busin –"

"Is anyone else in your family sick?"

"Why? What're you –"

The man stabbed his cane into the wet grass, as his face twisted into an angry scowl, and muttered, "She's moving faster now. It won't be long, she's –" He looked at Robby again.

"You've got to listen to me. I saw your sister today. With her."

"With who?"

"You know who."

"I don't know what you're talking about and I wish you would leave me the fuck alone!" Robby spun on his heel and hurried away.

The man hobbled quickly to catch up with him. "Does she come to your house at night?" he asked, stepping in front of Robby and bringing him to a stumbling halt. "After all the doors are locked? Does she just appear? Like a ghost? She can put everyone else into a deep sleep, you know. Even someone lying right beside you. So they can't hear what she's doing to you. She did it to me. But after a while, she doesn't need to, because everyone is so weak, so ill, that they spend most of their time sleeping anyway."

Robby prepared to deliver another threat, but he said nothing. Gooseflesh crawled across his back and his hands trembled. He wanted to hurry away, but couldn't.

"You don't look well," the man continued. "The flu? Is that what you've got? Yeah, that's what we thought it was. But I know better now. Because I don't think the flu would make my wife take a chainsaw to my son. Or to me. That's how this happened, you know." He touched his fingers to his mangled cheek. "She did this with a chainsaw. Five years ago. And she didn't have the flu. But we did have something else. A new neighbor," he whispered. "A beautiful woman. A very friendly woman. She was especially friendly to us and to the family three houses down."

When the man took a step closer to him, Robby's testicles crept up inside him.

"Do you know what happened to the family three houses down?" The man waited a moment, then: "The man beat his nine-year-old daughter's skull in with the butt of a shotgun, then tied his naked wife to a chair, stuck the barrel into her vagina and fired. If nothing like that has happened in your neighborhood yet, it will soon. I figured within the next few months, but I know now that it'll be sooner. Probably much sooner. I can tell by looking at you. It's going to happen soon and maybe in your house. Because she's there. Across the street from you. And she's already started, hasn't she? She's ... seduced you, hasn't she? Probably your father. Maybe even your muh –"

"You're insane," Robby croaked. His throat felt made of half-dry cement, his scalp was crawling over his skull and his eyes were beginning to mist. "Stay away from me. Just ... stay away."

"It won't be long before you realize I'm telling you the truth," the man said, his voice trembling with urgency. "The people around you will begin to change. You'll change. Your thoughts will not be your own. You'll need me," the man snapped. "When that happens –" He pulled a slip of paper from his coat pocket and stuffed in into Robby's. " – call me at that number. I can help you. I'm the only one who knows how." He turned and hobbled away quickly.

Robby walked numbly into his biology class and clattered into his desk, interrupting Mr. Hinchley's lecture. Normally, he would have felt self-conscious, but he didn't even notice the stares or Mr. Hinchley's icy glare. Robby opened his notebook on the desk, moving stiffly, mechanically. Mr. Hinchley's voice was a distant buzz. The only things on Robby's mind were the words of the man with whom he'd just spoken.

She's already started, hasn't she? She's ... seduced you, hasn't she?

Started what? Started what!

Robby heard nothing in biology class or the social studies

class that followed. He spoke to no one on the bus going home, and as he walked down Deerfield to his house he saw and heard nothing. Inside, Jen said something to him – something about Mom being sick in bed – but he heard little more than a garbled hum, didn't even see her, really, just went straight to his room and flopped onto his bed without even taking off his coat.

Sleep. Robby wanted nothing more than to allow himself to slide down to the very bottom of a deep, murky bog of sleep. His descent began the moment he felt the mattress beneath him. Mud and moss sucked him slowly downward, oozing between his fingers and legs, creeping up around his face and hair ... taking him away from everything.

But he wouldn't let himself sleep. He dragged himself off the bed. He had to talk to her, tell her what the man had said, and ask if she knew him.

Robby left the house, again ignoring Jen, crossed the street and rang Lorelle's doorbell.

Her muffled voice came from somewhere inside: "Come in!"

Inside, the first thing he saw was the sculpture. He half expected Lilith's head to turn toward him and grin.

"Who is it?" Lorelle called from another room.

He heard her footsteps hurrying down the hall. She appeared in a long black robe that was thin as tissue; he could see her naked body beneath it, but immediately lifted his eyes to her face, determined not to let the robe – or the body beneath it – divert his attention.

"I need to talk to you, Lorelle."

"I'm so glad you came over. I was just thinking about you." She reached for his hand, but Robby stepped back.

"No. We have to talk."

"We don't have to talk here, do we?"

"Yes."

"Robbyyyy." She smirked and shook her head slightly, as if she were disappointed in him.

"There was a man here. Friday. He walked with a cane. You called the police. I watched from my bedroom."

"Yes, there was a prowler. Why?"

"Who was he?"

"I don't know. Just a prowler." She took his hand again. "You look tired, Robby."

"I saw him again on Saturday. And today. At school." His voice was low, breathy; he stepped back and leaned against the wall because the strength seemed to be draining from his legs. "He says ... he knows you."

"He's probably just some crazy old street person who eats out of the neighborhood garbage cans. That's all. Come here. You look so tired."

She led him slowly down the hall – slowly, because Robby's steps were uncertain and clumsy – and into the bedroom, where she seated him on the bed, took off his coat and eased him back onto the pillows.

Robby felt himself sinking into that bog again and fought it, trying to sit up, but Lorelle pushed him back down, gently. Her hand felt cool on his chest, and above him he saw her nipples brush against the thin material of her robe. She melted in a watery blur as she began to unbutton his shirt.

"No," he breathed, "nun-no more. Please."

"I know you don't mean that, Robby." Her voice seemed to come from a great distance. "Just relax."

With his shirt off, she started on his pants. With his eyes closed, Robby felt her cool hand on his cock. He closed his eyes a moment, then opened them to see her slipping her robe off. She leaned forward and squeezed his cock between her breasts.

Robby moaned, tried to sit up, couldn't and fell back down on the pillows. He tried to think clearly, tried to remember what the stranger had told him about her but –

– she sucked his cock hard, squeezing the head between her tongue and the roof of her mouth, and all thoughts were crowded from his mind as he began to experience the familiar feeling of being drained once again ... emptied ... wrung dry ...

Moments before he came, images began to appear

and disappear in Robby's mind, like flashbulbs going off unexpectedly –

– a long rusty nail piercing smooth babyflesh –

– vivid, disturbing images –

– a shiny razor blade slicing through a tongue –

– that strengthened the pounding beneath his cock –

– a shotgun barrel sliding into a vagina and firing with a violent kick –

– and made him cry out with simultaneous horror and ecstasy.

By the time the first orgasm made him convulse like an epileptic having a seizure, Robby had completely forgotten the stranger's warning, and even the stranger himself.

* * * *

Jen was curled up on the sofa with a textbook open beside her and the telephone receiver pressed tightly to her ear. She wore an excited smile and hugged her knees, rocking back and forth on the cushion with one fist clenched.

She was excited because Woody Gibson was on the phone and wanted her to go out with him that night. Her fist was clenched because she couldn't afford the time with so much homework to do.

"I thought you might wanna see a movie," Woody continued. "And we can get something to eat, too, if you want. Like, at Harry's Diner, maybe?"

"Jeez, Woody, I'd love to, I mean, I really would," she said, thinking, You have no idea how much I want to get out of this tomb. "But I've got ... well, I know this is gonna sound stupid, but ... I've gotta study. See, there's a history test tomorrow and if I don't study for it all evening I'm gonna –"

"History?" There was a smile in his voice. "With Mr. Lee?"

"Uh-huh."

"Well, I can help you with that."

"You can?"

"Sure. I was in –"

Jen pulled the receiver away from her ear when she heard a sound. At first, she thought her mom had gotten out of bed and was coming down the hall, but the hall was empty.

" – member that I'm a year ahead of you. I took all of Lee's tests and he's so predictable I could –"

She heard it again, lowered the receiver and frowned. It was a soft, dry scratching sound.

"Can you hang on a sec, Woody?" she asked, then set the receiver down and stood.

She'd been jumpy lately. Things were very strange in her house and she didn't understand why – everyone was acting differently, walking around with long, pale faces, saying nothing, quick to anger and slow to apologize, if they apologized at all. So she was sure the sound was nothing and she was simply overreacting.

The third time she heard it, she realized it was coming from the front door. She went to the door, locked it and asked, "Who is it?"

The only response was a soft whine.

She opened the door a crack and saw one of Miss Dupree's dogs on the porch. Jen quickly opened the door, weak with relief, and said, "Sodom! What are you doing here?"

The dog stood and pressed his head to Jen's thigh.

"Did you get locked out?" She wrapped her arms around his furry neck and gave Sodom a hug as he licked her cheek, then he turned and started down the walk. "Where you going?"

The dog stopped and turned to her, waited a moment, then walked back up the steps and licked her hand. Turning, he went all the way to the sidewalk, then looked at her again and uttered a brief, quiet bark.

He wants me to come with him! Jen thought with a laugh. She hurried inside and grabbed the receiver. "Woody? Can I call you right back? It'll just be a couple of minutes, I promise. 'Kay?"

"Sure."

She got her coat, then followed Sodom across the street to Miss Dupree's house.

The dog stopped on the porch and looked back to make sure she was there, then lifted a paw and scratched at the front door. It swung open.

"Oh, the door wasn't shut," Jen said, going in. "So that's how you got out." She closed the door and looked around for Miss Dupree. "Hello? Miss Dupree?" No one responded, and Jen stepped into the living room where Gomorrah met her with a toothy canine grin.

Her breath caught in her throat when she saw the black sculpture in the corner. A rush of heat filled her cheeks and she stared open-mouthed at it for a moment; then, feeling embarrassed and guilty, she turned away, cleared her throat and called, "Miss Dupree? It's Jen. From across the street?"

Still no answer.

But there was a sound.

It came from down the hall.

Reluctantly, Jen followed the rhythmic thumping sound down the hall, flanked by Sodom and Gomorrah. The sound was coming from a room at the end of the hall. The door was open a few inches and Jen lifted a hand to knock, took a breath to call out again, but –

– she heard a long throaty moan and froze. She slapped a hand over her mouth and breathed, "Ooohh, shit" into her palm.

Miss Dupree was in bed with someone.

Jen's face grew hot and she felt the same chest-tightening feeling of dirty, forbidden excitement that she'd felt the day she'd watched Robby masturbating.

Then there was silence, except for the whisper of slow movement.

Sodom and Gomorrah sat side by side in the hall behind her.

Hand trembling, Jen pushed the door open a little further, leaned forward and peered into the room.

The shades were drawn and no lights were on, but in the murky room, Jen could make out the figure of Miss Dupree sitting up on a bed. She was naked and leaning over someone who lay still beside her. Miss Dupree's long hair spilled over the body beside her and her hand was ... it was ...

Jen pressed her lips together to hold in her abrupt gasp.

The man lying on the bed was also naked and Miss Dupree's hand was wrapped around his –

– thing, Jen thought, his thing –

– penis and she was doing to it exactly what Jen had seen Robby doing to his six years ago. Her hand and the penis glistened wetly in the darkness.

Jen's own breathing changed as she watched the gentle way Miss Dupree moved her hand on the erect cock. Jen swallowed hard, told herself she should go. She was about to back away from the door when –

– Miss Dupree looked up and said, "Hello, Jen."

She did not silence her gasp this time. "Oh! I-I'm sorry, Muh-Miss Dupree, really, I'm vuh-very sorry. I was just – Sodom came over and – I brought him back and –"

"It's okay, Jen, don't apologize," Miss Dupree said with a quiet laugh as she got off the bed and put on a black robe that flowed around her body like liquid darkness.

Jen could not keep herself from turning to the bed again; she watched the man's erection slowly shrink and droop to the side until it was resting on his thigh.

Miss Dupree led her out of the bedroom and quietly closed the door, put her hands on Jen's shoulders and whispered, "Don't be embarrassed, Jen. Really."

But she was. Her face was burning and she wanted to shrivel up and die. "I didn't mean to sneak in," she said. "Sodom was at our door and I followed him over here and there was nobody around. I called for you, but –"

"It's okay, sweetie, don't worry about it."

"I'll go now."

"No-no-no." Miss Dupree toyed with Jen's hair, brushing it from her eyes and pushing it back over the ears as she spoke. "Remember when I said yesterday that we might be able to do something that would get Robby to pay more attention to you?"

Jen nodded.

"Well, I think we can. Right now."

"How?"

"First of all, you have to promise me you'll do exactly as I say. And you have to promise that it will be our secret. Just between us. You won't tell you parents or any of your friends. Anyone. Okay?"

She nodded again, but her brow was beginning to wrinkle with suspicion. "Why?"

"I think you'll know why in a little bit." Miss Dupree stood and took Jen's hand. "Ready?"

"I guess so."

Miss Dupree led her into the dark bedroom and to the side of the bed.

It was Robby. He lay on his back, arms and legs splayed, mouth hanging open as he slept. And he was naked.

Jen let go of Miss Dupree's hand and started to back away from the bed, but the woman put her hand on Jen's back and gently pushed her toward it again. Jen's eyes traveled down her brother's body, stopping in the middle, where his thing lay to one side, shining wetly. She was startled by Miss Dupree's hands as they reached around from behind and pulled Jen's coat off, but her eyes did not leave her brother's cock.

With her mouth pressed close to Jen's ear, Miss Dupree whispered, "Have you ever seen it before?"

She looked up at Miss Dupree, hesitated, then nodded.

"Have you ever touched it?"

Bluish-white bolts of electricity shot through Jen but, at the same time, thick black guilt oozed up in her throat. What if her parents found out? What would Robby do when he woke and found her there?

She couldn't believe she was even considering staying there.

Jen shook her head and mouthed no.

"Well," Miss Dupree whispered, "if you do as I say ... he'll pay more attention to you from now on. I promise. He'll look at you very differently after today." She took Jen's wrist and eased her hand toward Robby.

Jen resisted at first, wincing at the prospect of touching him and at the thought of what might result, but –

– she could not forget the memory of watching her brother squeezing thick white fluid from his penis and she could not ignore the excitement she felt at seeing her hand just inches away from it, fingers outstretched and trembling.

Giving in, Jen let her fingertips brush the end of Robby's penis. It was soft and damp, and when she pressed a bit harder, it gave beneath the pressure like a stiff, dry sponge.

"Go ahead," Miss Dupree whispered, moving her hand closer.

Reluctantly, Jen wrapped her fingers around it. It was fat and warm. Her lungs released a long quavering exhalation as Miss Dupree moved Jen's arm slightly so that her hand slid up and down Robby's penis. Then Miss Dupree let go of her wrist, knelt, and began to untie Jen's red high-tops, removing them first, then the socks, whispering, "Let's get your clothes off."

* * * *

Sleep was like a lead weight on Robby's chest, but he remained vaguely conscious of the sensations he was experiencing. A hand on his erection ... hot breath on his testicles ... a mouth on his nipple ... at the same time.

No, he thought, that can't be ... can't be ...

But it was. There were two mouths on him, two soft, breathy voices whispering to each other.

What had Lorelle done? Who had she brought into the room?

Robby thought of the man at school with a mangled face. What was it he had said about Lorelle?

"Souls," Robby managed to whisper, his head rolling from side to side. "Too many ... souls ... to eat ... too ... many ... souls ... "

He struggled to open his eyes as hands and tongues moved over his body, as a hot, wet vagina slid down his erection. He fought to raise his heavy eyelids.

Oh, my God, Robby thought, feeling vaguely nauseated. He was unable to speak as he stared up at Jen's sleepy, half smiling face.

She was straddling him, eyes closed, hands flat on his chest, moving slowly.

Robby lost consciousness.

Jen never returned Woody Gibson's call.

Chapter 12

More Dark Thoughts

KAREN woke briefly and heard movement outside her bedroom. Just footsteps, and doors opening and closing, no voices. That's the way it had become, almost overnight, it seemed.

She lay in bed passing in and out of a doze, wondering what time it was. She could not focus her eyes enough to read the digital clock on the night stand.

Although she had not felt well at work that day, that was not the reason she had left work early. She'd been tired, but not sick. The real reason was that she could not stop thinking about Lorelle Dupree. Karen spent the day imagining her at home, working on something – a piece of sculpture, or perhaps a necklace or ring – and those thoughts made her wet. She'd walked around at work that day with her panties soaked through.

Only a fraction of the guilt she'd been feeling still remained. Even though she tried to feel guilty, she could not.

This is something that makes me feel good, she thought. I spend the day at a difficult job, then go home to another difficult job, and there's so little that makes me feel good ... so why shouldn't I indulge myself as long as no one gets hurt?

But, another voice inside her countered, what if someone is hurt? The children? Or George?

Well ... I'll just have to make sure that doesn't happen.

But the other voice continued: Of course, it's not like

George has done a lot to make you feel good lately, has he? In fact, the only time he's affectionate is when he wants you to make him feel good ... when his ugly, stubby penis is feeling restless. Isn't that right?

Karen tried to go back to sleep, but the inner voice prodded her.

Well, isn't it?

George is a good man, she thought, curling up beneath the covers.

True, true. But even a good man follows the orders of his stiff one-eyed skin snake, doesn't he?

She sat up in bed, barely able to lift her eyelids, and heard something outside the bedroom.

A sob.

Another, deep and thick with anguish.

Jen? It might even have been Robby. But why?

Karen considered trying to get up, but fell back in bed and lay there, thinking of the two late morning hours she'd spent with Lorelle that day. She'd been so eager – so desperate – to be with Lorelle again that she'd broken all the speed limits to get home as quickly as possible. Once again, being with her had made Karen feel so good.

But she did not feel good after going home.

She was lulled back to sleep by the rhythmic sobs that went on and on beyond her bedroom door.

*   *   *   *

George was not feeling well either.

He'd been so exhausted all day that he'd been incapable of getting much done, and his few accomplishments at work were so uncharacteristically sloppy that his secretary had suggested he go home early and get into bed. By three o'clock he agreed with her.

But he did not agree simply because he was so fatigued. That, he knew, was simply because he'd gotten so little sleep lately.

Since he'd gotten out of bed that morning – a formidable

task beneath the weight of his exhaustion – he'd been able to think of only one thing: Lorelle's last words to him before he'd left her house and sneaked back to bed the night before...

Next time, you can tie me up. Or, if you'd like ... I'll tie you up.

He called her several times from his office, but never got an answer, so he tried to busy himself with his work. But nothing could eclipse his thoughts of Lorelle Dupree.

He knew it was ridiculous. It wasn't like he was sneaking to a motel with someone his family didn't know about and had never met – she lived across the street, for crying out loud. Worse yet, he'd even fucked her in his own bedroom while Karen was asleep in bed!

So who says you can't do it someplace safer? he asked himself at his desk over a fast-food lunch he couldn't eat. And, if necessary, we can sneak off to a motel. It's not exactly unjustified, either. For the last twelve years, I've been married to a woman who thinks a libido is an Italian desert. Maybe if Karen had made some effort to overcome her lack of interest in sex ... maybe if she'd tried to use a little imagination in the bedroom ... maybe then this wouldn't be happening. Maybe if she took a little more interest in me than she does that fucking cat of hers ... maybe ...

George left work at three and was home in fifteen minutes. Jen was the only one up. She sat in his recliner wearing her bathrobe. A most unusual expression rested on her pale face. She stared at the television, but did not seem to be seeing it. Her eyes were dark with concentration beneath a huddled brow, but a gentle smile curled her mouth slightly at the corners. She sat with her knees spread far apart. There was something strangely adult about the way she looked, sitting in his chair with contrasting expressions struggling together on her face.

"Where is everybody?" George asked.

"In bed. They're sick."

"You don't look so good yourself."

"Just tired."

"You should go to bed."

She did not look at him, just shook her head.

"You've got school tomorrow, Jen. If you're not feeling well, you should go to bed."

"I'm ... just ... tired," she said with slow deliberation, as if speaking to a retarded child.

"Well, that's what people do when they're tired, dammit, they go to bed!" he snapped.

She didn't move.

"Did you hear me?"

"I heard you," she muttered.

"Goddammit, go to bed!"

He waited until she finally got out of the chair and went down the hall, walking by him as if he weren't there.

George went to the bathroom, urinated, then washed his hands, freezing for a moment as he looked at his reflection in the mirror.

Have I missed that much sleep? he wondered.

Wrinkles webbed from the outer corners of his eyes and his face seemed to sag on his skull like an ill-fitting garment. He ran a brush through his hair and brushed his teeth before going to the kitchen and pouring himself a drink. Coffee was what he really needed, but he knew a couple of drinks would make it easier for him to do what he wanted to do.

Twenty minutes later, he went to the phone and punched out a number.

"Hello?"

"Hi," he said.

"George! You're home early."

"Yeah, I was ... well, I felt kind of ... actually, I was thinking maybe I could ... that maybe I'd, you know ... "

Lorelle laughed. "Tell me, George. Has anyone ever dripped hot wax on your bare skin?"

"Nuh ... no ... "

"Come on over. I'll tie you up and we'll see how you like it."

Chapter 13

There Goes the Neighborhood

ROBBY awoke with a taste of dirty socks in his mouth and a vivid memory in his mind. For a few minutes, he tried to convince himself the memory was of a dream brought on by what had happened yesterday afternoon, but his gut told him it wasn't.

Sometime during the night, he had awakened to find a ghost kneeling beside his bed, groping under the blankets and between his legs.

"Let me do it again," Jen had whispered, as her fingers fumbled for his cock, her face the color of dirty teeth in the sodium glow of the streetlight outside. "I wanna do it again, Robby, okay? Please?"

"Go back to bed, Jen," Robby slurred, pulling away from her. "Just ... go."

"Oh, c'mon, Robby. I promise not to watch Entertainment Tonight anymore, okay? I promise. I know how much you hate that show. And ... I know how much you love what I want to do to you."

Robby had cried himself to sleep that afternoon, his bed shaking beneath the uncontrollable sobs that he could not fight. He'd not only been upset by what he'd done, but also by how much he'd enjoyed it ... how much he'd enjoyed Jen's hands stroking his cock ... how much he'd enjoyed nuzzling the fine hair between her legs with his nose ...

The sobs almost returned as she kneeled beside his bed in the night, reaching for him.

"Go away!" he'd hissed again and again, pulling the covers up tight around his chin.

As Jen left his room, pouting and naked, she'd said something in a sad whisper.

What was it?

He sat up in bed, trying to remember, trying to wake up. It had seemed important at the time.

Robby crawled out of bed, dressed and got his books. He didn't want to take time to shower or eat breakfast. He had to get out of the house and avoid seeing anyone, if possible. Especially Jen.

Angry voices came from his parents' bedroom. Robby considered pausing outside their door to see what they were fighting about, but didn't want to take the chance of getting caught. In the bathroom, he splashed cold water on his face, brushed his teeth and combed his hair, trying to ignore his hollow, gaunt reflection in the mirror.

Jen was curled in the recliner wearing her bathrobe when he passed the living room. She turned and looked at him, her face empty for a moment, then warming suddenly, as if it had taken her a moment to recognize him. Robby stopped in the living room doorway. He wanted to speak to her, to say something that might begin to make up for what he'd done, but his voice was trapped in his constricting throat because –

– Jen's hand was beneath her robe, between her spread legs, moving as she stroked herself and smiled at him with her brows raised high above her heavy-lidded eyes, and –

– Robby suddenly remembered her words as she left his room the night before, spoken in a breathy whisper full of disappointment. She said you'd pay more attention to me.

He hurried out of the house and into the cold drizzle, lifting his face to the gray sky as he crossed the grass. He breathed deeply as the chilly moisture sprinkled his face.

Robby's foot kicked something and he stopped, looked down. Four newspapers were scattered at the edge of the lawn where they always landed when the paperboy threw them each day. They were wrapped in plastic because of the weather, but two of the wrappers had torn and the papers inside were soaked.

Four days of newspapers. It was always delivered early, before Robby went to school, so one of them was probably today's, Tuesday's. Dad usually brought it in and read it over breakfast.

He hadn't since Saturday.

He hasn't been feeling good, Robby thought as he stepped across the sidewalk and onto the street. *He just hasn't thought about it, that's all.*

Across the street, there were lights on behind the curtains of Lorelle's windows. She seemed to be a very early riser despite the late hours she kept.

She never sleeps.

The mailbox was full of mail. The aluminum door hung open a couple of inches and the corners of wet envelopes, sales papers and advertisement flyers stuck out of the box.

Robby stopped and stared at the box, pulled it all the way open and looked in at the sopping stack of mail, all of it ruined. He usually brought in the mail, and if he didn't, it usually occurred to someone eventually.

It had occurred to no one.

Frowning, Robby walked on. Jessie sat in the middle of the road, head hung low, her tail curled beneath her rump.

"Hey, Jess," Robby called, but his voice was hoarse and flat.

The dog's head lowered even more and her tail twitched cautiously over the pavement. Her fur was wet and slicked to her body.

Robby walked over to the dog and patted her head. "What're you doing out here, Jess, huh? How come you're not inside?"

Dylan usually let Jessie into the garage at night, especially if it was raining. But Dylan had been sick, too. Maybe he'd forgotten.

But why wouldn't his parents do it? Robby wondered.

Jessie hunkered down close to the pavement with a whine,

looking up at Robby fearfully, as if he were about to strike her.

Robby bent down to pet her, murmuring, "What's the matter, Jessie? Huh? What's –"

She pressed her chin to the ground and whined again, clenching her eyes shut.

Robby heard someone shouting behind him, a voice muffled by distance and walls. He stood slowly and turned back toward the Garry's house, the last house on the left, as glass shattered. Another voice joined in, both shouting at once. The front door opened, then slammed. Mrs. Garry stalked across the grass to the car parked in the drive, got in and slammed the door. After starting the engine, she revved it and popped the clutch. The car shot backward into the street and turned until the headlights faced Robby.

"C'mon, Jess," Robby said, slapping his thigh as he backed toward the sidewalk.

Mrs. Garry shifted gears and the car kicked forward.

"Jessie, come on."

The dog remained in the middle of the street, hunched down like a frightened child.

Robby whistled, made kissing sounds with his lips, and kept slapping his leg as he called, "C'mere, Jess, c'mon, Jessie-girl, come here."

The car's speed increased and Mrs. Garry's eyes stared straight ahead as if they saw nothing in her path.

Robby dropped his books, bolted forward and clutched Jessie's fur, dragging her over the pavement. The dog wailed horribly, pulling her head away from him, as if dodging a blow. Her black claws scraped over the road as Robby heaved her toward the sidewalk, his weakened arms trembling with the effort, his head pounding. The dog suddenly gave a sharp bark and clambered to her feet, jumping onto the sidewalk as Mrs. Garry roared by in her car, eyes front, mouth moving rapidly, angrily, flashing teeth as she shouted silently at no one.

Robby watched her run the stop sign at the intersection and take a squealing left turn. He bent to give Jessie a reassuring pat, but the dog scrambled away with a yelp, trotting down the street. Robby stood on the sidewalk, numbed by what had just happened.

Winona Garry was one of the most easy-going even-tempered persons he'd ever known. Robby couldn't believe she'd nearly run over him and her own dog.

He stared at the Garry house for a moment. It looked dead. Empty. Apparently Dylan was still sick. He was usually out by now, heading for the bus stop with Robby.

Still sick, Robby thought. Like everybody else.

Moving slowly, trembling from his exertion, Robby picked up his books from the wet pavement, tried to dry them off with his jacket sleeve, then started toward the bus stop again, so disturbed that he was mumbling to himself, trying to sort out what had just happened. He noticed that the Crane's mailbox, like his own, was stuffed with days of mail. Robby stopped to peek into the box at the soggy stack.

There were three plastic wrapped newspapers in the driveway. One of them was beneath the left rear tire of Al's Mazda.

Not a whole lot of interest in the mail or the paper these days, Robby thought.

The LaBianco's weren't interested in theirs, either. And coming from inside their small house, Robby could hear Mr. LaBianco's normally quiet voice raising to an angry roar.

Sheri MacNeil's porch light was still on and all her curtains were closed. She was usually at her kitchen window by now, waving at passing children as she made breakfast and watched Good Morning America on the small television on her kitchen table.

But when he stopped again and looked around, Robby realized there were no children passing her house. There were a few standing at the intersection, waiting for the bus, but not half as many as usual. And they were so quiet.

He walked on slowly, facing front, but looking out the corners of his eyes at the strange sights that only a longtime resident of the neighborhood would notice – more mailboxes stuffed with neglected mail, more ignored newspapers scattered on lawns and driveways, a small jagged hole in the front window of the Petrie house, no loud rock music coming from Donald Gundy's bedroom window as he got ready for school.

Robby walked to the intersection and stood behind the Crane twins and two other children. The twins were talking softly between themselves; the other two were silent.

"I thought you were sick," Robby said.

"We are," Dana said, facing the street and sounding cranky.

"Sorta." Tara's voice was gentler, almost a whisper. "But we're better."

"Shouldn't you stay home until you're well?"

Tara said, "Mom wants us out of the house for the day. She's ... in a bad mood."

"So's Dad," Dana snapped.

Robby hesitated, not wanting to sound nosy, then asked, "How come?"

"I think they're sick, too," Tara said. "But mostly, I think they're fighting."

He wanted to ask why, but the bus rumbled off of Victor Avenue and slowed to a stop at the curb and the children climbed aboard.

Robby stood alone on the corner hugging his books –

– The flu? Is that what you've got? –

– feeling a chill that had nothing to do with the weather –

– Yeah, that's what we thought it was. But I know better now –

– and listening to the sound of his own bus in the distance –

– Because I don't think the flu would make my wife take a chainsaw to her son. Or to me –

– as it neared the corner. It would stop, the doors would hiss open, and the driver would wait for Robby to get on, then it would take him to school, where he would be expected to forget the deeply disturbing feeling of wrongness that he felt now, and concentrate, for six hours, on teachers and books. He spun around and hopped over the small shrubs that ran along the front of the Holcombs' yard, then ducked behind the fence that faced Mistletoe until the bus came. It slowed at the abandoned corner, then picked up speed and rolled on down the lane.

Robby left the Holcombs' yard and started down Mistletoe. Although he wasn't going to school that day, he couldn't go back home, either. There was something else he had to do.

* * * *

When the telephone rang Ronald Prosky was lying in bed in his room at the Motel 6 on Hilltop Drive, thinking about sleep.

That was about the best he could do these days – think about sleep. For nearly a year after the loss of his wife and son, there had been no nightmares. In spite of his grief, he had other things to think about, like the surgical reconstruction of his face (for all the good it had done) and adjusting to his prosthetic arm. Then, after his life settled down a bit, Marie and Gordon had come back to haunt his sleep. Each time he drifted off, he saw them naked in bed together ... and then he saw them bloody and dead. He heard his son's screams and smelled the gasoline vapors from the buzzing chainsaw, felt his own warm blood on his face and tasted it in his mouth and he saw his right arm lying on the bedroom floor. And worst of all, he saw her, again and again.

Now he couldn't even fall asleep long enough to have a nightmare. He was afraid to sleep, not because he would relive his family's death, but because he knew she was near.

She was working differently now. The people who lived on Deerfield had changed in a matter of days. It usually took months before the changes in her victims became visible, then a couple of months after that before they became violent. In less than a week, the Pritchard boy had taken on the gaunt, pale look that usually overcame one of her victims after three months or so of seductive teasing and careful priming.

She was working much faster now, as if driven by something to finish here in Redding and move onto the next neighborhood ... or apartment building ... or mobile home complex ... anyplace where families lived in reasonable contentment and safety.

It could begin at any moment, the torture and killing, and there was nothing Prosky could do to stop her. Unless –

The phone rang.

Prosky sat up on the bed, hoping it was the Pritchard boy; that he'd decided, for whatever reason, to help Prosky.

"Hello."

"Um ... hi. It's me. The guy you talked to yesterday? At school? My name's Robby."

Prosky shot to his feet and a broad smile of relief twisted the scarred flesh of his cheek. "Yes, Robby?"

"I ... I'm scared." His voice broke and dropped to a whisper. "I'm really scared and I think I need help."

Chapter 14

The Stranger's Story

THE man picked Robby up at the Shell station on the corner of Mistletoe and Hilltop. He said his name was Ronald Prosky and although Robby tried to conceal his nervousness – actually, it was more like fear – and to avoid looking at Ron's face, he knew it was obvious because Prosky tried immediately to put Robby at ease.

They went to the International House of Pancakes just a couple of blocks away and got a booth in the back, where they each had a cup of coffee.

"Please don't be nervous, Robby," Prosky said quietly. "I know that my appearance is off – putting and I'm a stranger to you, but if we can just talk a while, I think you'll feel better. "

Robby fidgeted, wondering if he'd made a mistake – maybe this guy was just a streetwalking lunatic who ate out of trash bins and lived in his clothes.

"Okay," Robby said hesitantly, "so what do you want to talk about?"

"Your new neighbor."

"What about her? I mean, yesterday, you seemed to think you knew everything about her, so what do you want me to tell you?"

"What has she done?"

"She hasn't done anything."

Prosky stared into his coffee for a moment, then took a deep breath. "Okay. Maybe it'll be easier if I tell you what I know about her. Then you can talk." He took a deep breath, then let it out slowly. "Five years ago, I was a reasonably successful investigative journalist. I had a wife and a sixteen-year-old son. We lived in a suburb of Chicago, a nice friendly neighborhood. A lot like your neighborhood, Robby. Then Lily moved in. At least, that's the name she was using then." He took a long sip of coffee before continuing. "She was a beautiful woman. Very nice. Friendly. Generous. It was the kind of neighborhood that welcomed new neighbors, so everyone started to get to know her. I really got to know her.

"My wife and I had been married for nearly nineteen years by then. It wasn't a bad marriage, but ... well ... " He looked away from Robby and winced, as if someone had stuck him with a needle. "I guess I'd gotten ... bored. And I didn't even know it at the time. At least, not until Lily let me know that I was –" he cleared his throat abruptly, " – welcome in, uh, her bed any time. She was ... god, she was gorgeous. Women like that do not proposition men like me every day. So I took her up on it. She assured me it would be discreet and just between us.

"So, I was having an affair. And what an affair it was. I mean, she was the kind of lover men only dream of having. But as the months passed, something happened. I began to change. I noticed I wasn't as coordinated as usual, I wasn't as strong. I was always tired, couldn't get enough sleep. And when I did sleep, I had these dreams. Incredibly vivid. I dreamed that Lily came to my room and we made love on the bedroom floor or on the bed beside Marie while she slept, and she never woke, no matter how noisy we got. I didn't think much of it, until it got worse – the fatigue and the dreams – and then I woke one night and she was there. On top of me. In my bed. It wasn't a dream, she was really there, and I didn't know how she got in. I didn't know how she got out, either, because I lost consciousness at the end. I always did with her. I asked later, but of course she wouldn't tell me."

The inside of Robby's mouth had turned to soggy felt and he gulped his ice water down quickly, then sucked on some crushed ice. The glass clattered against the tabletop when he set it down because his hand was trembling. He wasn't sure he wanted to hear any more.

"Then I noticed something," Prosky continued. "It had been happening gradually, right in front of me, I just hadn't noticed. I wasn't the only one not feeling well. My son and wife were tired all the time, pale and sickly. They didn't talk much. None of us did. And if we did, it was bad, you know, we ... we fought, said hurtful things to each other. That just wasn't like us. Things had changed, and they were changing still.

"I tried not to see Lily much anymore, but she would come to me. One night, I decided to stay up, find out how she got in, so I drank a bucket or so of coffee and took some little white pills. It was still tough staying awake. I felt so ... drained all the time. I sat in the living room, in the dark, waiting. When I heard a noise outside, I looked out the window and saw my son climbing down a tree outside his second-story bedroom window. He walked over to Lily's house. I realized that I wasn't the only one being neighborly.

"The next day, I had a private talk with him, told him I knew, and that it had to stop. Some father, huh? It's okay for me to fuck her, son, as long as your mom doesn't find out, but you can't. Anyway, when I told him to stop, I saw such ... hatred in his eyes. Hatred like I'd never seen in anyone, and he was my own son. And he said – no, no, he spat – 'Why? Are you fucking her too?' I told him to stop, he said he'd stop when he was ready. So, the next day I hired someone to cut down the tree in front of his window and had a new lock put on his bedroom door, one that could be locked from the outside. See what I mean when I say I changed? I was jealous of my own son, so I locked him up. Like a prisoner. Marie wanted to know what was going on, so I told her. She went to his room. They talked. That's what she said, anyway. They talked –" He chuckled icily. " – for nearly three hours.

"All of this began to affect my work. My editor – whose position I was supposed to take over later that year, because he was leaving – noticed a drop in my quality, said I was irritable and preoccupied, and suspected I was drinking or doing drugs. I told him I'd take care of it, problems at home, all that shit. But I couldn't, I just couldn't. Not long after that, he informed me I wouldn't be promoted. The position was going to someone else. Someone ... more responsible. More reliable.

"That very day, I went home and found my son and wife in bed together. Fucking. Everything exploded. We hated one another. I don't know how we stayed in the same house. It was like ... drinking. I had developed a bad drinking problem in college, see, so I know what it's like. You're not yourself, you don't even know yourself. The bottle does something to you, makes you do and say and think things you wouldn't even consider under normal circumstances. That's the way I was then, I hated them for what they'd done. And they kept doing it. I hated them so much I didn't stop to think why they'd done it or what was happening to us. Instead, I decided to go on seeing Lily, to see her even more. Fuck 'em, I figured.

"About that time, the man down the street killed his family and himself. A couple of weeks later, a woman at the other end of the street ran over her own son with her car. Not accidentally. And somewhere in the back of my mind I realized that everyone in the neighborhood – or nearly everyone – looked sick, weak, like they had the flu, which is what everybody said they had. Except the flu goes away. This didn't. It got worse. After a while, some of them even stopped bathing. They wore dirty clothes. I remember seeing Mrs. Denny – about fifty, normally a real cow – walking naked out to her mailbox, scratching her crotch and hacking, and I realized she'd lost about sixty, maybe seventy pounds. She looked like a corpse.

"And again, I realized – almost subconsciously – that something was wrong. It was like a little voice inside me that couldn't get above a whisper, trying to tell me that I had to do something because things were going really bad. But I didn't listen to it, because there was another voice, a louder one, talking over it, telling me that my wife was a cunt and my son was a spoiled little shit and the only person I had to think about was myself and what made me happy, and what made me happy was fucking Lily. So I kept it up while everything crumbled down around me."

Prosky stopped, tugged at his collar as if he were choking, and stared silently out the window for a moment. "I haven't talked about this in a while," he whispered. "It's ... hard."

Robby didn't know what to say. He couldn't feel pity for the man because he was too busy fearing for himself ... for his family.

"My wife and son fought," he continued with a broken voice. "Like lovers. More passionately than she ever fought with me. And other times, I could hear them somewhere in the house. Moaning obscenities to one another. I got fired. I didn't know what to do. My wife didn't work and I was afraid of how she would react if I told her. So I got drunk. First time in years. I went on a real skull-grinder, spent my last dime at the nearest bar and walked home – staggered, really – talking to myself like some wino, even singing, for Christ's sake. But after I turned onto my street, I saw something that sobered me up. Fast.

"At first, it looked like smoke and I thought something was burning, because it was the middle of summer and I knew no one was using their fireplace. But it wasn't smoke. Smoke drifts. This was moving. It was white as a summer cloud and ... liquidy. And ... maybe it was because it was floating by a streetlight, I'm not sure, but ... it seemed to glow. Just a little. It moved through a tree in front of Lily's house and over the street, formless, but moving with purpose. And it went straight to my house. I stood there with my mouth hanging open and watched it hover outside my bedroom window. The curtains were drawn, but the window was half open. Then, like milk being sucked through a straw, it flowed into the window and was gone.

"Whatever it was, it was in my house! I practically forgot I was drunk, ran down the street, let myself in and went upstairs. Halfway up the stairs something hit me, I don't know, something like ... a drug. Yes, it was like I'd been drugged. My feet weighed a ton and I could hardly keep my eyes open. It wasn't the booze, I was pretty sure at the time – and I'm certain it wasn't, now. It was an effort, but I made it down the hall, fighting to remain conscious. I fell into the room and ... and I ... I saw ... " He shook his head. "She was there. Naked. Pulling the bedcovers back as Marie sat up reaching for her. When Lily turned to me, my knees gave out and I fell as she slapped her hand to Marie's forehead. Marie dropped back like a rock, unconscious, and I was losing it, too, just on the edge, but fighting, scared shitless. Then there was this ... this rush, like all the air in the room was being sucked to the center of it, and she was gone. Replaced by this-this-this writhing cloud that blew back out the window. Then I passed out.

"I woke up a few hours later, I think. Went to bed. Marie never mentioned it the next day, but she didn't talk to me anyway. I tried to tell myself it was the booze, or a dream, but I couldn't deny it anymore. Something horrible was happening. Something horrible was wrong with Lily. But what? I didn't know what to do, where to start. Then I remembered something.

"She had this sculpture. Black onyx. It was –"

"Lilith," Robby interrupted, surprising himself.

Prosky nodded slowly. "That's the one. I'm not sure what made me think of it at the time. I guess what I'd seen the night before shook me up. I started thinking more clearly – I started thinking, period – and I remembered the first time I went to her house. I'd never heard of Lilith, didn't know who she was, and when I admired the sculpture she told me the story of Lilith. What I remembered was the way she told me the story; so passionately, lovingly, and all the while sort of watching me out of the corner of her eye, as if she were waiting for some reaction, some specific response."

"She did the same thing with me," Robby said.

"And what did you think?"

"Well ... " Robby shrugged. "I guess I wondered why she was making such a big deal out of the story. You know, being so dramatic about it. I wondered if maybe it, you know, meant something."

"Exactly. That's what I thought. And after seeing her in the bedroom with Marie that night, going up in smoke in front of me like that, I started thinking about it again. And her name ... Lily. It was a hunch. So the next day, I went online and looked up this Lilith woman. I learned a lot. I didn't believe any of it at first. Didn't want to believe it. But I knew, deep down inside, I knew it was true.

"One of the things I learned was how to keep Lily out of my house. I followed the instructions in one of the books. Then I waited. I didn't sleep, I didn't eat. I tried not to drink, but didn't try hard enough, I guess. She didn't come back.

"But during the next week, I noticed a change in the house. Things got worse. I'd have these flashes of violent and uncontrollable anger. But I tried to keep my mind off my anger by burying myself research. I read everything I could find about Lilith, learned about her, tried to figure her out. And I slowly realized exactly what she'd been doing." He leaned back in the booth, rubbed the back of his neck a moment, then leaned forward again. "Are you religious, Robby?"

"Funny. She asked me the same thing."

"Really? Well, I guess religious is the wrong word. Maybe spiritual is more accurate. Do you believe in a god?"

"I guess so. We go to church once in a while, and I –"

"No, I mean, do you really believe in a higher power? A force of goodness?"

"Well ... "

"You're undecided. So was I. In fact, I didn't believe in anything. I went to AA before I got married, and they teach alcoholics to depend on a higher power, but I never really believed it. I used it, but I never believed it. But when I began to realize what Lily was and what she was doing to us, that changed. I mean, you won't see me in church, and I sure as hell don't send checks to the fucking 700 Club. But I definitely changed."

Robby was growing more and more tense and impatient and didn't want to wait any longer. "What is she?"

"I'm sorry, I got sidetracked. I'll get to that in a minute. Things got worse at home for all of us. I'd get these violent urges and I'd have to break something. I broke most of the breakable things in my office, I think, and a few dishes in the kitchen, for no reason at all. I realized we were all going through a sort of withdrawal. From Lily. I don't think Marie or Gordon knew what I'd done to keep her away. It was in plain sight and pretty hard to miss, but they weren't paying much attention to anything then. But I'm sure they suspected something, because Lily didn't show up at night anymore. And that's what was doing it. She'd gotten into our blood. She'd made us crave what she did to us. I guess ... that's what pushed Marie over the edge.

"She and Gordon got into a fight. She chased him out to the garage and took ... took my, urn ... she used the ... chainsaw. On him. Then me. My face ... my arm. I ... shot her. Killed her." He closed his eyes a moment and shuddered.

"As they were carrying me out to the ambulance, I saw her. Lily. Across the street and down two houses. Standing on the sidewalk. I went crazy, started screaming something about demons and evil. They thought I was nuts, of course, in shock, or something. In the ambulance, I realized I'd better cool it or they'd put me in the psych ward. But I've never been able to get that image out of my head: Lily standing on the sidewalk, smiling, with those two fucking dogs."

"Sodom and Gomorrah?" Robby asked.

"No. They weren't the dogs she has now. These were two Dobermans. Cain and Abel."

"More biblical names."

"Yeah. Cute, huh? She has an interesting sense of humor. I tried to kill one of the Dobermans. I'm not sure which. About a year later." He laughed in a way that frightened Robby for a moment. "Well, what I did should have killed it, anyway. Her, too. A normal person – a human – would have died." He removed his left glove, revealing the hand that had so frightened Jen. Light reflected dully on the thin metal tendons and knobby knuckles as Prosky turned the palm up, doubled his fist with soft metallic clicks and hisses, then snapped his fist back abruptly.

Robby flinched as a deadly, shining twelve-inch blade shot from the heel of Prosky's metal hand.

"I slashed her dog with it," Prosky whispered through clenched teeth. "Then I put it into her stomach, twisted it, cut up, then down. I expected her guts to fall out onto my shoes. I was looking forward to it. But she just smiled. She laughed while I watched her wounds close. They were gone in seconds." He pressed the tip of the blade to the table's edge and pushed it back into his hand until it locked with a click; then he put the glove back on and leaned close to Robby. "I've been just a few steps behind her all this time, but now I've finally found her again. And I'm scared, Robby. In less than a week she's done to your neighborhood what it took her six months to do to mine. She's moving faster than ever now. I was hoping to find someone like you to help me stop her, but now I don't know. It might be too late. Things might have gone too far already."

Robby's eyes stung with misty tears, not because he was crying, but because he was terrified. The back of his neck seemed to crawl up into his scalp and he had to take a steadying breath before he could speak.

"What is she?" he breathed.

"I know it sounds insane. I thought so, too. But you know, don't you, that there's something very wrong with her."

Robby nodded.

"She's not human. Your new neighbor is a daughter of Lilith. Conceived ages ago on the shores of the Red Sea in an orgy of demons. She's a sexual vampire. A succubus. She's sucking the life – the soul – right out of you."

After telling his story, Prosky explained that his wife's brother, Anthony Scolari – a very wealthy and prominent businessman in Chicago with a lot of connections, some of a rather dubious nature – had come to the hospital as soon as he heard what had happened and immediately made arrangements for Prosky to be treated by a cosmetic surgeon Scolari knew. Insisting that everyone leave Prosky's room in intensive care, Scolari said, "This may not be the time for it, Ronnie, but I've got to ask. What happened? I know my sister, and I know she wouldn't just do this. So what really happened, huh?"

"You ... won't believe me."

"Let me decide what I will and won't believe, okay?"

Groggy from the drugs that had been pumped into him, Prosky said, "If you want ... I'll explain it in detail later. For now, I'll tell you this. One person is responsible for what happened. But you have to swear ... to keep it between us. I can't ... I'll never be able to ... prove it. Don't ... tell the police."

"I never intended to tell the police."

"Our neighbor ... Lily Kress."

"You're sure?"

"Dead sure."

"All right, then. We'll talk about it more when you're better. Don't worry about anything. I'm making sure you're in good hands."

Lily was not mentioned again for nearly four months. Prosky was still in the hospital, learning to walk again and adjusting to his new arm, which had been arranged and paid for by his brother-in-law. Prosky had never seen a prosthesis quite like it and asked why he'd been given such an unusual arm. He was told that the arm met the specifications given by Scolari.

A week before Prosky was to leave the hospital, his brother-in-law paid him a visit. They exchanged small talk for a while, then Scolari said, "Would you like to tell me what happened?"

"Not really."

"How about if I insist?"

"Look, Anthony, I don't really know what happened myself."

Scolari sat on the bedside and spoke quietly. "Look, Ronnie, let's be straight, okay? I think you know that I do a lot more than buy and sell stocks and run a little corporation. I think you know I've got some friends who do things that aren't quite within the law. We've never talked about it, but it's always been there, right? I'm sure Marie told you plenty. So this isn't going to come as a big surprise. I had a friend put a tail on your neighbor lady. Frankly, I was planning to have her killed. Okay? I mean, I was pretty shook up, you know? She moved. To Indiana. My man followed her. A week after she settled into her new place, we lost contact with him. He was found beside a creek, several miles from her neighborhood. He was also found in a garbage dump about a mile from there. And we never found all of him. So ... are you sure you don't want to tell me what happened?"

Prosky was shocked, but he still did not tell his brother-in-law the whole story.

"You say this woman's responsible for what happened but you can't prove it, so you can't go to the police, and yet you mean to tell me you're turning down an offer of help from an outside source? You think this is all her fault, and yet you can honestly say you don't want her to pay for it?"

"You want to know the truth, Anthony? I'd like to kill her myself."

Scolari smiled. He lifted the prosthetic arm and carefully removed a pin from the wrist. "Do this," he said, nodding at the arm as he held out an arm, made a fist and snapped it back.

Prosky did as he was told and the blade appeared.

Scolari was still smiling. He cleaned his manicured fingernails with the steel pin as he spoke. "It's your decision. You can forget it if you want. You can even have another arm if you want. But I've got somebody else watching her now. I know where she is. It's up to you."

Prosky had been following her ever since.

Robby told him everything. He was hesitant at first, then spoke with more ease, relieved to finally face the fact that something was not right, and even more relieved that he did not have to face it alone. When he spoke of Jen, he lost his control and began to cry, unable to continue.

"It's okay, Robby," Prosky said. "At least you're seeing it now, before it's too late for you. I'm not going to lie, it might be too late for them. But maybe not. You might be able to help them."

"Huh-how?"

"Remember I told you I never used to believe in a higher power? That all of this changed that?"

Robby nodded.

"Well, like I said, I'm not gonna send money to any of these tall-haired, diamond-ring-wearing televangelists with a private jet and a few limos. But I do believe in ... something. Some force of goodness. And a force of evil. I know that's a touchy topic of conversation, but we don't have time right now to debate our differences of opinion about the ... the creator, or ... whatever. So, I'll just say this. I think there's a piece of both of those forces in all of us. Good and evil. Call it whatever you want, I think we've got it in all of us. And it's up to us which side tips the scale. Sometimes we can influence that scale for others, too. Like right now. Your family. You love them, don't you?" "Course I do," Robby croaked. He wanted to say, This is bullshit! Horror movie bullshit! But he couldn't, because he knew he would not believe his own words.

"Well, Robby, you need that love right now. It can help you tip the scales in the right direction for your family. Lorelle is trying to suck that love out of you and replace it with something ... bad. She creates hatred where there was once love. You're seeing it in your family right now. But she can only do that if she's allowed to do it." He took a drink of his coffee.

Robby gulped down the lump in his throat. "Well? What do I do? What do we do? To stop her, I mean."

Prosky put his mug down on the table with a thunk and contentedly smacked his lips. His smile was terribly distorted, but it was still a smile. "I thought you'd never ask."

Chapter 15

If I Had a Hammer

EVERYONE was home. Karen and Jen did not leave that morning. Karen called in sick and when she realized that Jen was not getting ready for school, she asked why.

"I don't feel good," Jen said.

Karen had hoped to be alone, but Jen didn't look well. "Okay," Karen said. "Whatever you think."

It was the only time they spoke that morning. They watched television silently, and Karen went back and forth to the coffeepot, trying hard to stay awake. She felt unbearably weary.

George came back from the radio station three hours after leaving the house. Neither Karen nor Jen asked why he was back so early and he did not offer an explanation. He really didn't want to go home because he knew Karen had not gone to work, but he couldn't function. There were ball bearings tied to his eyelids, his shoes were full of metal shavings and his brain was covered with a thick layer of dust. Trying to work was useless, so he gave up and went home.

Karen and Jen were in the living room and they both looked awful. He stuck his head in for a moment, then turned and headed down the hall, pausing a moment to think, they're sick, too. Maybe they need something. Then: Fuck 'em. He went to the bedroom and began changing his clothes. He stopped, naked except for his socks, to frown at himself in the mirror over Karen's dresser.

"Fuck 'em?" he muttered, puzzled by his own callous

attitude. He thought, They're sick. Karen takes care of you when you're sick. What's the –

Monroe hissed, shot out from under the bed and clawed at George's feet, coming so close that George felt the cat's saliva splatter his ankle. Anger spewed up from George's middle like lava from a volcano as he kicked Monroe against the closet door, then reached down and took a handful of the cat's flabby flesh. Monroe yowled as George carried him out of the bedroom and down the hall to the front door.

Karen was already out of the recliner and standing in the living room doorway, fists clenched, eyes narrowed. "No, George, no!" she shouted.

"Everybody else on the street lets their cats outside! What makes this cat any different?"

"He's never been an outdoor cat. He can't take care of himself, he'll get hurt!"

"My ass," George growled, opening the front door. "He'll kill anything that moves! He's a cat, not a goddamned retarded blind child!" He flung Monroe out the door; the cat spun head over tail through the air before rolling over the grass with a pathetic screech.

Karen ran after him in her bathrobe, crying, "You son of a bitch! You goddamned monster!"

She swept Monroe up in her arms, but George didn't stay to watch any more. He turned away, knowing she'd bring the cat back inside. Then he froze. He suddenly realized he was naked.

Jen was staring at him. He didn't make a habit of parading naked in front of his daughter. He felt a rush of embarrassment and thought that she was probably embarrassed, too. But she wasn't.

Jen's gaze was aimed straight at his crotch. Her left index finger was locked between her lips and her checks were sucked in deep beneath her cheekbones. Her right hand was under her robe, between her legs. Her eyes were narrowed in the same way they would be if she were smiling. He realized she'd been watching him for a while, ever since he'd come out into the living room. It looked almost as if she were –

George hurried down the hall, trying not to think about it.

Back in his bedroom, he put on jeans and a blue chambray shirt, ignoring the slight tingle that passed through his cock when he thought of the way Jen was sucking on her finger..

* * * *

Robby knew everyone was home before he went into the house. Both cars were in the driveway and after seeing her still in her robe on his way out that morning, he knew Jen hadn't caught the bus to school. Inside, he hurried straight to his room, giving no one time to speak to him. He dropped his books on his desk, removed his coat and sat on his bed.

He felt as if someone had been pounding his brain with a meat tenderizer. He'd been told too much too fast and was still trying to process all of it. On top of that, he was still heavy with fatigue.

But it ain't the flu, he thought morbidly.

Before dropping Robby off at the corner, Prosky had given him several pages printed off the internet. He'd folded them into a small square and put them in his back pocket.

"Read these today," Prosky said, "then meet me here tonight at nine. Bring a sack of burnt woodchips from your fireplace and a dry towel."

Robby took the papers from his pocket and laid back on his bed to read them. On the first page Prosky had written, From – DEVILS AND ANGELS by Thelonius Pascali, 1962. A quarter of the way down the page was the heading, LILITH AND HER DAUGHTERS.

At first, Robby thought it was the same story Lorelle had told him the night he first saw her sculpture. But as he read on, he realized she had been careful to leave out a few important details.

According to Mr. Pascali, after Lilith fled the Garden of Eden and Adam told god of her rebellion, god sent three angels named Sanvi, Sansanvi and Semangelaf to retrieve her. By the time they found her on the desolate shore of the Red Sea, she was engaged in sex with countless demons and giving birth to a brood of baby girls – as many as a hundred a day, many of which she ate alive between couplings to appease her hunger, which was almost as voracious as her sexual appetite. When she saw the three angels, Lilith was enraged and told them to go away. They told her they'd been instructed by god to return her to Eden. With the blood of her daughters on her lips, she laughingly told them there was nothing in Eden that interested her. She was perfectly happy with her demon lovers.

The angels were appalled by what they saw and watched in horror as Lilith's daughters – winged, reptilian creatures – crawled through the dirt, maturing at an incredibly rapid rate, some of them writhing with the insatiable demons before flying away. Once again, the angels asked Lilith to return with them, saying they dreaded relaying to god what they had seen and could not leave her behind in such decadence knowing that she was feeding on her own infants.

Lilith still refused, but she sneeringly promised that if the angels were to write their names near a newborn, she would spare the child.

As a result of that promise, parents took precautions for centuries to protect their babies from Lilith. Until a girl was twenty days old and a boy eight years, parents would draw a circle in charcoal on the wall above the child's bed containing the words "Adam and Eve, barring Lilith" and on the door they would write "Sanvi, Sansanvi, Semangelaf."

"But what of Lilith's legions of daughters, the succubi?" Pascali wrote. "Infants were of no interest to them. Instead, they engaged in another of their mother's favorite activities: seduction. Stealing into bedrooms by night and placing all other members of the household into a deep sleep, the succubus seduced men – sometimes women and even children – in their sleep, sucking from them not blood but their energy, vitality, and any goodness they might process;

the ability to give, to feel compassion, or even to love those closest to them.

"The succubus, in human form, was irresistibly beautiful and had the ability to prey on each victim's most secret weaknesses. She returned night after night, using her beauty and charms to convince her victim that there was nothing wrong with their lurid relationship, all the while stripping the unsuspecting man or woman of all humanity and reducing him or her to little more than a wild animal, until she reached her ultimate goal: to consign the victim's soul to eternal damnation.

"Working in league with Satan's minions, the immortal succubi are said, in legend, to roam the earth to this day. If that were true, then it is indeed safe – but sad – to say that in today's society of low moral standards and self-centered lifestyles, a succubus in human form could quite likely lead a normal life, carrying out her evil deeds nightly without ever raising suspicion."

Robby slapped the pages onto the bed and sighed. It all sounded like some kind of pornographic fairytale. In fact, it was probably too ridiculous to work as a fairytale.

But it fit. It fit so well, it made Robby's blood run cold.

He had the rest of the pages, but they were just more of the same, all of which confirmed that Lorelle had left out an important part of the story, a part that she apparently felt was too revealing – although Robby knew that, had she told him the whole thing, it wouldn't have crossed his mind in a million years that she was a demon.

Robby sat up on his bed and stared at his shoes for a long time, knowing it was going to be a long wait till nine o'clock. The house was silent and Robby craved the sound of another voice. He needed to talk to someone, particularly about the crazy thoughts he was having. He knew Dylan had stayed home from school and hoped he was not too sick to talk. Robby had to get out of the house and didn't want to be alone.

With his coat on, he started down the hall. A door opened behind him.

"Robby?" Jen whispered.

His back stiffened.

"Robby? Where you going?"

He walked faster and rounded the corner.

The living room curtains were closed and the room was dark. His mom sat before the television looking thin and weary, the glow of the television turning her face a soft electric blue.

Outside, Robby hurried down the street, never looking at Lorelle's house, hoping she wouldn't see him and call him over.

Mr. and Mrs. Garry's cars were both in the driveway. It wasn't unusual for Mr. Garry to be home – he was a carpenter and his work schedule was sporadic – but Mrs. Garry was a telephone operator, worked five days a week and seldom took a day off. As he neared the house, Robby heard Ozzy Osborne playing so loud that the bass was rattling the front window. That was even more odd than Mrs. Garry staying home from work. Dylan's parents insisted that he listen to his rock music on headphones so they couldn't hear it.

Robby knocked hard, but knew they would never hear him above the music, so he opened the door a crack and called, "Hello?"

Somewhere beneath the thunder of the music, Robby could hear the television playing.

"Hello? Dylan? Mrs. Garry?"

No response. He went inside and closed the door, wincing at the music's volume. Rounding the corner of the entry way, he saw Mr. Garry's slippered feet from behind, propped up on the ottoman in front of his plush, overstuffed chair.

"Mr. Garry?" Robby said. "Is Dylan around?"

The feet didn't move.

He got a whiff of what smelled like shit and wondered if he'd stepped in something on his way over.

Stepping forward, he tried again: "Um, Mr. Garry? I was just wondering if –"

Robby stopped when he noticed that someone had spilled something on the carpet and splashed the television screen.

Judge Judy was on and dark fluid speckled Judy Sheindlin's face.

"Mi-Mi-Mister...Garry?" Robby's voice was lost beneath the music.

Keeping a distance from the chair, he walked around it, saw Mr. Garry's bare calves, saw his bathrobe lying open in front, his right hand lying palm up on the armrest. What looked like chocolate pudding clung to the front of the terrycloth robe, except ... it wasn't exactly the color of chocolate.

Mr. Garry's mouth was open.

So were his eyes.

So was his forehead.

In fact, most of the top of his skull was gone and the pudding-like substance had dribbled over the edge of the opening, into his eyes and down his cheeks like thick dirty tears and onto his robe.

Robby staggered backward, hit the end table by the sofa and fell on his ass, gagging. He rolled over and tried to scramble to his feet, but his stomach convulsed and bile burned his throat.

"Dylan!" he gurgled, wiping his mouth and gasping as he climbed the sofa to his feet. "Duh-duh-Dylaaaan!"

He ran down the hall toward Dylan's room, the source of the music that was pounding through the walls. He tripped over a shoe and fell face-down to the floor. Except he didn't land on the floor. He landed on something soft and wet.

Mixed with the odor of feces that he'd smelled in the living room was the rosy smell of Mrs. Garry's perfume.

Robby propped himself up on his arms and realized that the shoe he'd glimpsed before tripping over it had not been empty. Mrs. Garry was wearing it and she lay beneath him, face up, arms spread at her sides. Her left eye was closed as if she were asleep, but the right half of her face was no more than bits of shattered bone and bloody shreds of flesh. Robby babbled as he tried to get off of her, slipping twice before –

– her left eye opened, blinked, and she hissed a wet parody of his name: "Aaww-eeee? Aaww-eeee?"

With a childlike whimper, Robby crawled clumsily down the hall, trying to stand, until he saw the hammer on the floor. He'd seen it before. It belonged to Mr. Garry. The clawed end looked as if it had been caked in mud, but he knew it was not mud that filled the gap in the forked claw. He stared at it, motionless for a moment, then carefully stood, staying close to the wall as he passed the hammer.

"Dylan?" he called, only a few steps from Dylan's closed bedroom. His voice was hoarse and broken. "Dylan? Please? Are you there?"

Dylan did not reply, but as Robby went farther down the hall he heard something ... a voice ... it sounded like Dylan's voice ... high and shrill ... singing along with the loud music.

He looked back at Mrs. Garry. Her fingers twitched like the legs of a dying spider, tensed, then became limp. Robby took the remaining steps to Dylan's room and put his hand on the doorknob. He clenched his eyes shut before opening the door.

The music hit him like a wall and he opened his eyes to see –

– nothing more than the mess that was Dylan's bedroom.

"Dylan?" he called, knowing there would be no response.

He backed out, closed the door and heard the voice again, singing along like a small child. It was coming from the bathroom.

Robby called his friend's name again as he ran to the bathroom and thunked the half-open door with his palm.

Dylan was slumped, naked and pale as snow, in the bathtub, his head leaning against the tub's edge, eyes closed, lips moving slightly as he tried to sing, arms lolling in a foot of dark-red water. His bloodstained clothes were crumpled on the floor.

Robby dropped to his knees beside the tub and rasped, "Dylan! Dylan, what's ha-happened?"

Dylan's eyes opened slowly and he tried to lift his head, but failed.

"They ... won't let ... me go ... " he breathed.

"Go where?"

"Her house."

"Whose house?" Robby asked, but he already knew.

"Luuuhh...Lorelle's." Dylan smiled weakly. "Jealous?"

So he killed them, Robby thought, and took a bath to wash off the blood. Jesus Christ, it's already started...

Dylan lifted first one hand, then the other, out of the bloody water slowly and made playful little splashes, like a small boy playing in his bath, and Robby saw the long vertical slashes in his wrists. They were small chasms from which black-red blood flowed to darken the water.

"Jesus Christ, Dylan!" Robby screamed, looking around the tub until he spotted the razor blade on the edge beside Dylan's head. "Jesus, why did you do this?"

"Dint ... wanna ... go ... to jail."

Robby stood and dashed around the bathroom, searching for some sort of bandage and murmuring, "Oh god, oh god, oh god ... " He found nothing and returned to the bathtub. "Listen to me, Dylan, okay? Stay awake! I'm gonna call an ambulance. Okay? Dylan?"

Dylan's eyes were closed and his head was turned away from Robby. He was not singing anymore.

Chapter 16

Succubus Interruptus

KAREN woke slowly, thinking the sensation of teeth and lips on her nipple was only part of a dream. But as she rose closer to the surface of her sleep, she heard breathing ... felt hot breath on her skin ... the weight of a naked body on top of her own.

She reached down and felt soft, warm flesh, silk-smooth hair, and opened her eyes to see Lorelle, whose mouth curled into a slow smile filled with promise.

Karen jerked upright and turned to George who lay beside her, still as the onyx statue in Lorelle's house, his breathing so shallow it was almost invisible.

Sensing her panic, Lorelle reached up and touched her fingertips to Karen's cheek, brushing them over her lips, then crawled down her body and nestled her face between Karen's legs. Her tongue snaked through curls of hair, teased the lips of Karen's pussy, delicately separated the folds and traveled slowly up and down the crevice between them.

Karen turned once more to her husband. When he didn't move or make a sound, she allowed the tension to flow from her, feeling her body relax more and more with each sweep of Lorelle's tongue. She moaned softly, and before long, she was squirming, then writhing with pleasure that continued to build. Karen slapped a hand over her mouth to contain the cries she felt rising from her chest.

Karen reached up and closed a fist on a handful of Lorelle's thick hair as the first orgasm came, then another, and a third, each one battering her more than the last, until –

– Karen couldn't breathe and she was certain her heart had stopped beating and then –

– there was nothing. Not even dreams.

* * * *

"I saw it on the news," Prosky said, as Robby got into the car with a brown paper bag and a towel. "I'm sorry. Very sorry. Are you all right?" But even as he asked the question, Prosky knew the answer. The dark patches of skin beneath the boy's eyes and his deeply sunken cheeks made him look malnourished. He moved with the sluggishness of someone deeply depressed and spoke in a low, hoarse voice that Prosky had to strain to hear.

"No," Robby said. "I'm not all right."

"Believe me, Robby, I know how you feel, and I'm sure you're not in the mood for this right now. But we have to do it."

He nodded indifferently, staring out of the window. Then he chuckled.

"What are you laughing at, Robby?"

"The news. That bitch on the news tonight. She said Dylan was listening to Ozzy Osborne when he did it. And ... he was. But she interviewed some clown – some psychologist or something, I don't know – who said it was the music ... the secret Satanic messages in the music ... that made Dylan snap. Isn't that funny?"

"Yes," Prosky whispered, his gut wrenching for the boy, "unfortunately, it is."

Neither said anything for a while, just stared down Deerfield.

"They all went to bed about half an hour ago." Robby sighed finally. "I almost did, too. I'm exhausted."

"No. You can't do that, and you know it. Let's go. We don't want to wait too long."

"Better be careful. There might still be some reporters hanging around. They've been circling like vultures all day."

"Right. And remember, Robby, the dogs ... whatever they are, they aren't dogs. If they see or hear us, so does she."

Leaving the key in the ignition in case they needed to get away quickly, Prosky opened his door and got out. A moment later, Robby did the same.

Looking down Deerfield, Prosky felt a chill. It looked like a dark alley. Mist hovered around the two streetlights. The rain had stopped, but the air was still damp. A soft bone-chilling wind blew some soggy leaves onto the wet street and into the messy gutter. A cat shot through a clump of shrubbery and crossed the street, dragging its left hind leg limply as it disappeared into a darkened front yard. On the whole street, only one house was lighted; the porch light shined and a dull glow came from behind the closed curtains of one window, while a candle flickered in another.

Lorelle's house.

"She's awake," Prosky whispered, taking the bag from Robby and checking the contents: fist-sized chunks of fire-blackened wood. He handed the bag back to Robby and said, "We'll have to be careful. Stay away from the streetlights, okay?"

As they started down the street, the rubber tip of Prosky's cane kissing the wet sidewalk with soft smacks, he watched Robby shuffle slowly beside him, hands in his jacket pockets, and Prosky began to worry. The boy's mind was – quite understandably – on other things, and he didn't appear capable of being careful. Prosky stopped, faced him and whispered urgently, firmly, "Listen to me, Robby, I know what you're feeling right now, but what happened to your friend and his family only proves that things are getting worse fast. So we have to do this, and we can't afford to be caught or interrupted. We've got to be very careful and very quiet. You can't shuffle your feet like that and you've got to pay attention to what you're doing. Otherwise, more people will die."

Robby seemed to think that over as he turned his eyes toward Lorelle's house.

"You can grieve later," Prosky said. "Right now, you've

got to forget about it, cold as that sounds, and concentrate only on what we're doing here."

Robby changed slowly. His sagging shoulders lifted and his back straightened. He took his hands from his pockets and turned to Prosky, taking a deep breath. Unfallen tears were pooled in his eyes.

"Yeah, you're right," he whispered. "Let's go."

* * * *

George woke from a sweaty dream about Lorelle to find her kneeling beside his bed, silently sucking his cock. Her right hand was tucked beneath his ass and her middle finger was pressed hard against his rectum.

Her eyes met his, glistening in the soft light bleeding through the curtains and she lifted her head and laughed.

"Hello," she said.

Until she spoke, George thought he might still be dreaming, but her voice broke through the bedroom's silence like a rock through a windowpane and he sat up suddenly, still heavy from sleep, hissing, "Ssshhh!"

She only laughed again.

"You've got to stop this," he breathed. "I don't know how you keep getting in here, but it's got to stop. Things are bad enough around here without my wife waking up to find –"

"She's not going to wake up. She's dead to the world."

George turned to Karen and watched her sleep. She was perfectly still; George could not even hear or see her breathing.

Lorelle wrapped her fingers around his cock again and led him off the bed with a gentle tug until he was on his knees. She hunkered down before him and continued sucking.

George's discomfort left him quickly and, as before, he forgot there was a third person in the room.

She licked his belly and whispered, "Fuck me like a dog, George. Hard." She turned around and squeezed him hard in her fist as she eased him into her,

slamming her ass backward against him. Grabbing his

wrists, she wrapped his arms around her and pressed his hands over her breasts.

"Ahhh," George moaned, moving faster inside her as he smiled in the dark. But his smile faltered a moment later and he winced as images of pain began to flash on the backs of his eyelids –

– teeth being knocked from a bloodied mouth with a rock –

– changing with each thrust of his hips –

– erect nipples being snipped off with garden shears –

– and he began to move faster –

– sleeping eyes being pierced with fish hooks –

– and faster, until his smile slowly returned.

* * * *

Standing on Robby's porch, Prosky took the towel Robby had brought and carefully wiped the dampness from the front door, whispering, "Let's hope it doesn't rain now."

"Dad's gonna be pissed when he sees this," Robby said. He reached into the bag for a piece of the wood, handed it to Prosky and asked, "What do I tell him when he sees it?"

"Tell him the truth."

"Are you serious?"

Lifting the wood, Prosky began to write on the door. "Yes. Tell him. All of it. Tell him everything."

"He'll think I'm crazy. And with the mood he's been in lately –"

"Just tell him." He finished the first name, Sanvi. "He might not believe you at first, but when he sees her reaction to it, he'll think twice." The second name, Sansanvi. "If you can convince him, maybe he'll spread the word." The third name, Semangelaf. "It might be the best thing that could happen." Then Prosky drew a circle around the three names and –

* * * *

– George was seconds away from an explosive orgasm, digging his fingers into Lorelle's round ass, when she craned her head back and released a scream that made his scrotum shrivel like a raisin and filled the room with the smell of rotting meat and shit and –

– the bare skin of her back split open, revealing glistening blackness, and something shot upward, hit George in the face and knocked him back and –

– he hit the side of the bed and lost consciousness before he slid to the floor.

* * * *

Prosky dropped the piece of burnt wood leaving the circle unfinished as the scream tore the night in half. It did not seem to come from just a single person – it was a sound that might have come from the gas chambers in Nazi concentration camps, the combined screams of dying cultists in the jungles of Guyana; the cries of the unsuspecting outside Chernobyl as the air they breathed turned to fire and flesh and muscle began to peel away from bones.

There was a sweeping shift in the air and –

– Robby dropped the bag, spilling woodchips down the porch steps and onto the walkway and –

– the dogs began barking inside Lorelle's house across the street and –

– glass shattered and wood splintered with a piercing crack as a window to their left burst outward and something black arced up into the air, its sickening scream growing even louder as it headed straight for the streetlight that stood between the Pritchard's house and Lorelle's and –

– the streetlight exploded and sparks rained onto the street, sizzling on the wet pavement as darkness swallowed that section of the block.

"What is it, what is it?" Robby cried, pressing himself back against his front door.

Looking up into the darkness, Prosky said, "She was in

the house." A gust of cold wind stung his face as he stepped down from the porch, searching the black sky.

Dry flapping sounds moved over them, the sound of great wings slicing the air as the scream faded, then rapidly grew louder again as –

– a black shape swept downward led by two burning red eyes, heading straight for the porch, dropping so low that Prosky could feel a rush of air that swept his hat off his head. He dropped his cane and fell to his knees, covering his head with his arm and crying out like a child, actually afraid he was going to wet himself. The creature left behind a smell that conjured images of piles of rotting, vulture-eaten corpses stretching to the horizon of a hot barren desert.

Prosky got up and finished drawing the circle on the door. "Go in the house!" he shouted at Robby as the creature retreated. "She can't get to you in there!"

"No!"

"Go inside!"

"I'm not going back in there!"

"Robby, I'm the one she wants! Now go!" He stuffed the chunk of wood in his coat pocket and groped for his cane. Robby remained at his side. "Dammit, Robby, will you –"

"I'm coming with you."

They didn't have time to argue. The rush of putrid air was coming again as Robby moved ahead of Prosky, whose hobbling jog held him back until –

– two strong hands clutched Prosky's shoulders, digging steel-hard claws through his coat and shirt, piercing his skin like knife blades. He cried out as he was lifted from the sidewalk and swept above the street like a leaf on the wind.

Robby's cried out after him, shouting Prosky's name, his voice fading.

Prosky kicked his legs helplessly as he rose higher, heading straight for Lorelle's house. The stench of decay filled his nostrils like mud and made him gag. Still clutching the charred wood in one gloved fist, he swung his other arm up until he felt the cane connect with something hard and crusty. The creature released a wet snarl that reminded

Prosky of the sound of muscle being peeled away from bone
and he struck again, harder. The snarl became a scream
and the third time, when he stabbed the cane upward and
felt its tip sink into soft tissue, the creature's grip loosened.

Prosky struggled and fought, swinging the cane again
and again until, with a frustrated screech, the claws released
him. The ground rushed up at him like a giant fist.

He slammed onto Lorelle's front lawn and rolled. His
breath gushed from his lungs and he knew at least one rib
had broken, but the sweep of powerful wings overhead
made the pain easy to ignore.

He opened his eyes and saw Robby's sneakers an inch in
front of his face.

"C'mon!" he rasped, clutching Prosky's arm. "Let's get
outta here!"

Movement hurt, but he did his best to ignore the pain.
Still gripping his cane, Prosky crawled on his knees and
elbows first, then stumbled to his feet and started down the
street toward his car with Robby.

The sound of wings was gone. So was the awful smell.

Even the dogs had stopped barking.

All they could hear was the sibilant whisper of the wind,
their rushing footsteps and gasping breaths.

Then glass shattered.

A frenzy of vicious barking echoed through the night.

They could hear the dogs behind them, their claws clicking
against the pavement and splashing through puddles, their
slobbering pants for breath between each fit of barking.

Prosky tried to run faster and ignore the piercing pain in
his ribs, but he fell behind Robby.

Then she came again with a scream like a rake dragging
over a chalkboard.

Robby moved further ahead, glancing back over his
shoulder, eyes more white than brown.

The car parked at the end of Deerfield grew closer as the
pain in Prosky's chest grew more debilitating, preventing
him from drawing enough breath as he ran.

The stench fell over him again, making breathing even more difficult.

He desperately willed someone to hear, to come outside, knowing she would not want to be seen by others, not here where she lived and preyed on those around her. But Prosky knew that no one would come. They were all sleeping ... very deeply.

* * * *

Robby reached the car, opened the driver's side door and got in, sliding over to the passenger's side. He looked out at Prosky and began screaming, "Hurry hurry my god hurry!"

Prosky dove into the car and started to pull the door closed as he tossed his cane into the back seat, but –

– one of the dogs was on him. It closed its jaws on his left leg, trying to drag him back out of the car.

The second dog was fast approaching and Prosky knew that if it got there, he wouldn't stand a chance. He snapped his left fist back, releasing the blade, and slashed.

The dog reared its head back with a pathetic wail when the blade caught its snout, digging a deep gash over its nose and lips. But it dove forward again immediately and –

– its eyes flashed a deep glowing red as the gash peeled back, opening like a blooming flower on black raisin-like flesh that sagged grotesquely over a flat simian face and a mouthful of jagged yellow fangs glistening with clear fluids. As its right front leg lifted, bony clawed fingers sprouted from the paw, swiping at Prosky's abdomen.

The creature no longer bore any resemblance to a Malamute, or any other kind of dog. As it lunged forward, Prosky drove the blade into its throat and pushed with all his strength. The creature tumbled backward out of the car and Prosky jerked his arm back, pulled the door closed and locked it. He started the ignition as the creature threw itself against the car, rocking it like a boat on choppy waters, and clattered onto the hood.

Prosky babbled obscenities as he jerked the car into gear, then cried out in shock because –

– the other one was on top of the car now, pounding on the roof so hard that it was crumpling inward like cardboard.

Robby was slouched way down in the seat making small, horrified sounds in his throat.

Prosky's foot jammed the gas pedal to the floor. The tires spun on the wet pavement for a moment, then the car roared away from the curb and sped down Mistletoe.

The creature on top of the car rumbled over the roof, down the back window, and Prosky glanced into his rearview mirror in time to see it fall off the trunk, gracefully landing in a sinister crouch in the road as the thing that had been Lorelle rounded the corner, flying no more than six feet from the ground.

"Son of a bitch, it's her!" Robby cried, looking over his shoulder. "Drive, hurry, go, go, drive!"

The creature hunkering below her hunched its shoulders and sprouted two frail-looking wings, broke into a run and lifted itself into the air.

Robby babbled, "Oh Jesus shit fuck goddamn!"

The creature clinging to the hood of the car like a stone gargoyle perched on the corner of an ancient skyscraper opened its mouth in a wet grin as its wings broke free and spread wide, blocking Prosky's view of the road. It lifted its hands – three fingers and one stubby thumb each – and scraped it black claws over the windshield, leaving deep trenches in the glass, then flattened its palms against the glass and pushed.

The windshield sparkled with silver webs a second before it fell in pieces onto the dashboard, sprinkling their laps.

Black arms rippling with stringy muscles reached into the car as if to embrace Prosky and –

– he crushed the brake pedal with his left foot.

The red eyes widened as the creature snapped backward and fell to the pavement.

Robby slammed into the dashboard, then crumpled in a heap on the floor.

Prosky hit the accelerator again and all four tires rumbled over the body on the road. The creature's scream was so loud, Prosky could feel it vibrate through the body of the car.

It sickened him.

He glanced in the mirror. She was only a few yards behind him, and the smaller creature only a few feet behind her, while the other twitched in a heap on the road.

Prosky sped up, nearing the intersection of Mistletoe and Churn Creek Road, icy air slapping his face through the broken windshield. The light was red. He ignored it.

A pickup truck coming from the right of the intersection screamed to a stop, missing Prosky's car by mere inches as Prosky swerved and continued toward Hilltop.

"Where's a fucking cop when you need one?" he shouted at the steering wheel.

He barely slowed as he turned right on Hilltop, relieved to see the Motel 6 sign less than a block away. Prosky looked in the rearview mirror and saw –

– nothing.

They weren't there.

But he knew they were not gone.

"I think we're safe for a little while," he said.

In a flat, numb voice, Robby repeated, "For a ... luh-little while." There was blood on his face and a lump had swollen on his forehead where he'd slammed into the dashboard.

Prosky's tires squealed as he drove into the motel parking lot, not bothering to slow down for the speed bump as he drove around to his room at the back of the building and slammed to a stop in front of his door. He killed the engine, pulled the keys from the ignition and staggered around the car without his cane, leaving the door wide open. The deadly blade still protruded from his left hand.

Robby got out and followed him, moving haltingly as he glanced cautiously in every direction. Fishing the key from his coat pocket, Prosky unlocked the door and kicked it open. He pressed the tip of the blade against the doorjamb until it slid back into his hand with a click. He stepped inside, leaning against the door as he took the charred wood from his coat pocket and wrote quickly as Robby watched.

First, the circle.

Outside, the sound of traffic from Interstate 5, which ran behind the motel, was interrupted by the flapping of great wings as –

– Prosky hurriedly wrote the first name, Senvi, then –

– the first sound was joined by a second as two pairs of wings grew nearer, and –

– Robby whispered, "They're coming," as –

– Prosky wrote the second name, Sansanvi, and –

– a third sound joined in and all three drew closer as –

– Prosky wrote the third name, Semangelaf, and threw the door shut, turned both locks and dropped the wood to the floor.

It hit the carpet with a quiet thump.

He moved away from the door slowly, leaning against the wall for support, groaning painfully with each stabbing breath.

Robby stared at the door and backed away from it, until his legs hit the bed and he flopped down onto the edge, staring with his mouth open. "D-do you, uh...you think –"

Scraping outside.

Claws scraping over pavement.

Low slobbering growls.

Prosky stiffened against the wall.

Thick oppressive silence, until –

– the scream.

It was the same scream they'd heard coming from the Pritchard house when Prosky wrote the three angels' names on the front door.

It stopped and, for about three seconds, there was silence, until –

– chips of wood exploded like shrapnel from the door as two black, three-fingered hands burst through effortlessly, curled their fingers, dug their curved claws into the wood like hooks and pulled.

The door was torn outward, ripping through the doorjamb and away from its hinges as if it were made of paper.

Prosky started to move away from the wall but the slicing pain in his ribs and his weak leg cut him down and he hit the floor hard, grunting, "The headboard –"

The hands threw the broken door backward. It crashed into the side of the car, shattering the window on the passenger's side.

" – Robby, on the headboard –"

Robby crawled over the bed and pressed his back to the wall, curling into a ball.

" – the piece of wood on the headboard, Robby." Prosky crawled toward the bed, shallow breaths wheezing in and out of his lungs.

The empty doorway was filled with silent darkness that seemed to move like spilled black paint.

"Put up the ... the puh-piece of wood on ... th-the head-board, Rob-Robby!" Prosky hissed.

The darkness swirled into a shape.

Robby looked at the headboard, saw a square piece of wood lying flat, leaned forward and tipped it up. Written in black on the piece of wood:

ADAM AND EVE BARRING LILITH

The shape solidified and moved slowly forward, like darkness peeling away from darkness.

"Lean it ... against the wuh-wall, Rob – "

She burst into the room, her black scaled body glistening in the light, and stood over Prosky with her wings spread. The wings darkened the room, filled it with shadows. When she spoke, her voice was like a gorge being vomited from deep inside her:

"They're not like me, Prosky," she said through a slobbering grin. "They're only demons. They don't give a fuck about three angels." She bent down, swept him up and turned him to face her, holding him in the air for a moment

by his shoulders. Then she hefted him effortlessly until he
was lying across both of her large hands and –

– she snapped him like a twig.

The crack of bone was like a gunshot in the small room.

Robby felt sick and had stopped trying to control the
convulsive shakes that were raging through his body. He
tipped the piece of wood up and leaned it against the wall
and curled up on the bed like a frightened child. He felt like
a frightened child.

The Lorelle creature stepped over Prosky's body and
came toward the bed, burning eyes locked on Robby.

He felt his insides shriveling. Why didn't she stop? Why
wasn't it working?

Then she saw the piece of wood and stopped. Her black
lips pulled back over her fangs and she exhaled a long,
wet hiss as her wings folded over her back. She turned to
him again and stared for a long time as she began to walk
backward. Her lips curled into a hideous mutation of a grin.
When she reached the doorway, she spoke.

"Come over later, Robby," she said in her thick, distorted
voice. Then, with a chuckle: "I'll suck your cock."

She was gone.

Robby stayed on the bed for a while, his whole body
shaking so violently that the headboard rattled noisily
against the wall.

People would be coming soon. They would want answers
to their questions and they would expect Robby to provide
them. He couldn't do that. Not yet. He needed help. He
needed someone.

Robby got off the bed and went to Prosky's twisted body.
There was no need to check for signs of life. He was bent
backward at an impossible angle, mouth and eyes frozen open.

Robby's chest ached. It wasn't a physical pain – it was
his fear and sudden feeling of isolation, of abandonment.
Prosky had been his only ally, the only one who could help
him save his family from her. Prosky's death felt to Robby
like ... his own.

What could he possibly do now? Surely anyone he talked

to about a woman who was really a succubus and who
had flying Malamutes would laugh at him at best, or try
to have him put away at worst. He didn't know what he
was going to do, but he had to do something. He needed
transportation.

Kneeling beside Prosky, he shuddered as he reached down
with an unsteady hand and pulled back a flap of the man's
coat until he found a pocket. He hesitated, then winced as
he slipped his hand into the pocket.

He removed the car keys and got away from the body as
quickly as possible.

Standing just inside the doorway, he peered out to see
if either Lorelle or her pets were waiting for him, but saw
nothing. With one glance back at Prosky, Robby headed for
the car.

Claws clicked against pavement.

Robby swallowed his scream and broke into a run.

The door on the driver's side was wide open and Robby
dove in, pulled it closed behind him and locked it.

Hell of a lotta good that'll do, he thought, looking at the
glassless windshield and passenger-side window.

The keys jangled as he fumbled to find the right one, and
his breaths were coming hard and fast as –

– claws screeched on the door and –

– Robby chose a key and slipped it into the ignition
successfully as a small whimpering sound grew in his throat,
and –

– a head popped up in the window beside him and –

– Robby screamed and threw himself down on the seat,
arms over his head protectively.

Nothing happened.

He heard rapid-fire panting and lowered his arms
cautiously. He looked up to see the dirty face of a scraggly-
haired mutt grinning in at him, its pink tongue bobbing as
it panted happily.

Robby heard himself giggle coldly as he started the car.
The curious dog dropped away from the window and Robby
drove away.

Steering was difficult because his hands and arms were shaking so much. The car jerked forward and slowed a few times at first as his foot jittered on the accelerator.

What if he got pulled over? With all the broken glass, the chances were good.

License and registration, please.

Um, here's my license, officer, but ... I don't know where the registration is. This isn 't my car.

Whose car is it?

Belongs to a friend of mine.

And where is your friend now?

He's lying dead on the floor of his room at the Motel 6. He was killed by a succubus, officer.

"Wouldn't sound good," Robby muttered with a chuckle. "Wouldn't sound good at all." His chuckling became laughter as he stammered, "Nuh-no, uh-uh, nosiree!" And as he drove across town his laughter dissolved into deep, quaking sobs and his vision was blurred by tears. He began to feel dizzy, light headed, as if he were slipping down in the seat, further and further, until –

– he reached his destination. The right front tire of his car bumped over the curb and stopped on a strip of grass that ran along the sidewalk. He turned off the ignition, got out and staggered across the lawn in front of a small modest house. There were no lights on inside or out.

Robby fell heavily against the wall beside the door and pressed a thumb to the doorbell. He pressed it again and again, knocked several times, then pressed down on the button so the bell rang over and over.

"Yes!" a voice called inside. "Coming! I'm coming!"

Footsteps thumped over the wood floor inside.

The porch light came on. Locks clicked and the door opened.

Robby pushed himself away from the wall and swayed before the open door.

"Robby? Robby Pritchard?"

"Pastor ... Quiller ... man ... "

Robby fell into the pastor's arms and lost consciousness.

Chapter 17

A Domestic Squabble

MOMENTS after a senseless and infuriating dream about Karen, George awoke clenching his teeth in anger as hot knives twisted in his eye sockets, and in his mind he heard himself scream, Awww, hell, I might as well just break her fucking neck and get it over with before she wakes up!

He sat up, blinked his sticky eyes, and tried to massage the throbbing from his temples, thinking, My God, what's wrong with me, what am I thinking, what's happening to me?

Then: A dream...just a dream...

Pain rippled through his stiff body as he tried to pull himself from his stubbornly oppressive sleep. He was cold, chilled to the bone, and he realized, finally, that he was on the floor beside the bed.

Slowly, he rose and sat on the edge of the bed, still feeling irritated, close to anger. Looking across the room, he muttered, "What ... in ... the hell," when he saw that the window was gone. Not broken ... gone.

George groaned and scrubbed his face, searching for some memory that would explain the gaping hole in his bedroom wall, but could remember nothing. Except ... Lorelle ... soft flesh and graceful shoulders ... taut back muscles moving urgently ... rhythmically ... sighs and moans and then –

– George's hands jerked away from his face and he gasped at the memory.

An explosion of movement, something black shooting up

toward him through two bloodless slits that had split open in Lorelle's back like misplaced vaginas and then –

– nothing. Not even dreams.

He walked naked to the torn-out window, puzzled by the absence of broken glass on the floor until he saw the window scattered in pieces on the grass outside.

It had been broken out, not in.

"Excuse me, sir," a sharply-dressed blonde woman called out, hurrying across the lawn from the sidewalk. She held a microphone attached to a cord that disappeared into the bulky black leather bag at her side. "Could I ask you a few questions?"

There were others behind her, another woman and three men, as well as two cameramen. They jogged across the lawn, microphones clutched, rattling cameras perched on their shoulders.

George stepped back, overwhelmed by a rush of paranoia that rivaled the worst of his pot-smoking days.

The questions came all at once:

"Do you know Ronald Prosky?"

"What happened to your window, Mr. Pritchard?"

"Can you explain the symbol on your front door?"

"Is there any truth to the rumors that Dylan Garry killed his parents in a satanic ritual?"

Prosky? Symbol? Satanic ritual? What were they talking about? George felt dizzy, disoriented, as if he'd awakened in the wrong house – the wrong life.

"Mr. Pritchard?" the blonde woman called. "Sir? Would you care to comment on any connection there might be between –"

"Please," George said hoarsely, moving toward the hole in the wall, "please, I answered questions yesterday. I'd rather not –"

"Do you know if your son had any interest in Satanism, Mr. Pritchard?"

A bubble of anger began to grow in George's stomach and he clenched his fists at his sides.

"Does your son listen to heavy metal? Ozzy Osbourne or Metal –"

"Is there any connection between the disappearance of Ronald Prosky and –"

"Is the symbol on your front door a Satanic –"

"Were you shocked to hear of the murder of –"

"Get off my lawn," George said, just loud enough to rise above their voices.

The blond woman stepped forward. "Mr. Pritchard, if you could just –"

"Get off my fucking lawn, lady," he shouted as he went to the large hole that had replaced his bedroom window. His knuckles turned white as he clutched its splintered edge, leaned out and, through clenched teeth, shouted even louder, "Get off my fucking lawn, do you understand? All of you! Get off my lawn!"

Their rapid-fire questions came to a staggering halt and they stared at him, mouths open, caught in mid-sentence.

The inside of George's skull felt ... red. A bright, flaming red. He spotted others – two men, one wearing a suit and holding a microphone and the other with a television camera – scrambling out of a van with KCPM-24 painted on the side and he roared at them, "All of you! Stay away from my fucking house!"

The two men stopped, then backed away.

George wanted to slam the window shut and the fact that he couldn't made him even angrier. Instead, he turned and stalked across the bedroom for his robe but stopped, glanced down and found his penis jutting rigidly before him. He reached down to touch it and stopped when he saw the splinters of wood protruding from his palms and fingers, their tips embedded just beneath his skin.

Reporters, for God's sake, he thought, staring at his hands as he gritted his teeth together. I wake up and my fucking window's gone – just gone – and then I've gotta deal with reporters closing in like fucking scavengers and I get two handfuls of splinters and I'm sick on top of that, probably the damned flu everybody else in the house has given me, and she's sound asleep! Like a fucking baby! George stared at his wife, her head buried in her pillow, then looked at his hands again.

He bit his lip and fought back the urge to close his fist and drive the splinters in deep, just to feel the pain and have something real to scream about, because a scream was rolling inside him – a bright flaming red scream – building up, pressing at his throat from below, and he was opening his mouth to let it out when –

– Karen sat up in bed and croaked, "Whahappened? What's ... why's it so cold in ... the window ... Monroe ... did Monroe get out?"

"I hope so," he growled in a voice like two wet rocks being rubbed together hard. "And I hope his fur's lining somebody's fucking tires." He stormed out of the room, not bothering to don his robe. His erection was still pounding uncomfortably, almost painfully. In the bathroom, George found the tweezers and began to pick the splinters out one at a time, holding his hand close to his face, cursing and wincing with each biting tug, then tossing them into the toilet.

And his penis remained rock-hard.

He finished his left hand and started on the right, fingers trembling, lips moving rapidly and quietly as he breathed obscenities –

" ... fucking splinters ... like picking hairs from a goddamned caterpillar ... shit-eating reporters with their fucking vans and fucking microphones ... goddamned window, what the fuck happened to the goddamned window ... "

– and grew steadily angrier, moving faster, as if he were pressed for time. He was, in a way; George knew that if he did not finish the tedious plucking soon, he was going to put his hand through the medicine cabinet mirror, just slam his fist through the glass, that ought to take care of the fucking splinters, that ought to cut the little fuckers out, by god, then he wouldn't have to –

"Want me to do that for you?"

The voice was so soft, it almost failed to penetrate

George's intense concentration, and it was only when he realized he was no longer alone in the room that he knew he'd actually heard it, but he still wasn't sure what the voice had said, so he looked up, frowning.

Jen stood in the doorway smirking, wearing a tight blue crop-top and panties, her eyes half-closed, blonde hair a medusa-like tangle around her face.

"What?" George barked. "Oh, uh, yeah, I've just, um ... got some ... splinters, is all."

"Want me to do that for you?" she said again. She wasn't staring at his hand.

Suddenly, George became aware of his nakedness again, crushingly aware of it, and he dropped the tweezers into the sink to reach for a towel, but Jen stepped in front of him and took his hand.

"I promise I won't hurt you." Her eyes darted between his face and his cock, lingering below his waist a bit longer each time.

George said, "Just go on, okay? I'll do it, just go –"

She reached out casually and wrapped her fingers around his erection, "It's a lot bigger and harder than Robby's."

George blanched and slapped her hand away, stepped back abruptly and blurted, "Robby's? You've – you mean you've – Robby's been – what have you –" His fingers curled into hooks and his jaw worked, clacking this teeth together, "Oh, yeah," he hissed, thinking, There's a sickness in this house all right, but it ain't the fuckin' fluuu! "Get out!" he roared. "Go on, get out, I'll deal with you later. And Robby, too. Where's Robby? Where the hell is Robby?"

She stumbled backward, her eyes opening to their full size and a little beyond. "He's ... in his ruh-room."

"Well you tell him to stay there because I'm gonna be coming for him in just a few minutes, you understand? Now get your ass out of here!"

Jen backed out of the bathroom and pulled the door closed.

"Son of a bitch!" George rasped, pacing the bathroom.

"I've got a seventeen-year-old son who's – my god, what's happening? What the fuck is –"

He stopped.   Stood in front of the mirror, his chest heaving.   Stared at himself for a moment.

He was pale, thinner than usual, and the creases in his forehead seemed to be deeper than ever before.

And his cock was pounding ...

... tingling ...

... echoing the touch of Jen's cool hand ...

"Sshhhit," he groaned, sitting on the toilet, his right hand stinging.

The tingling. It wouldn't go away.

He touched his cock, rubbed it as if he could wipe the feeling away, but he only leaned his head back, closed his eyes and sighed, rubbing it again.   And again.   And again, squeezing out its thick fluid and slicking it over the shaft as he thought about Jen's hand ... her smooth, cool hand ...

"God," he whispered, and it sounded a little like a sob, a dry, sickened, miserable sob.   "My ... god."

When he came, George moaned behind closed lips and collapsed against the side of the sink, pressing his cheek to the cold surface of the counter and drawing long, deep breaths.

* * * *

Robby sat on his bed in his robe, hunched forward with his elbows on his knees, hands clenched together.   The local news station, KQMS, was playing on the radio and Robby rocked back and forth, tapping a knuckle to his pursed lips as he waited anxiously for the story.   He'd heard a teaser earlier, but nothing more.

It would come soon enough, he was sure.

Pastor Quillerman had told him to leave Prosky's car parked at the curb outside –"It won't be the first abandoned car on this street," he'd said – then he'd driven Robby home and told him to get some sleep.   But that had been impossible, so he'd just gone to bed and stared at the ceiling until dawn. He had not even wanted to come home.

"You should be there, Robby," the pastor had said. "You should all be together now, you need one another."

Robby had been surprised by Pastor Quillerman's reaction to his story, by his immediate acceptance of it as truth.

After collapsing in Quillerman's doorway, Robby awoke several minutes later on the sofa with Quillerman kneeling beside him, waiting with a cup of hot tea and an encouraging smile.

"I think you're going to be okay, Robby," the pastor said. "But you look like you've been through one very unpleasant experience. Want to talk about it?"

Robby sat bolt upright, swung his legs off the side of the sofa and leaned toward Quillerman.

"Pastor, you've gotta help me, you've gotta help my family, all of them, my whole neighborhood, th-they're ... something's wrong with them."

Quillerman frowned, handed Robby a tea and sat on the sofa beside him. "Exactly what is wrong with them?"

Robby didn't know how to tell him. "I don't know, they're all so ... angry. Everyone is fighting or yelling all the time or not talking at all and ... and ... " Robby closed his eyes a moment, embarrassed. "There's a lot of, um, sex going on in my neighborhood these days."

"Do you know what's causing all this?"

Robby nodded. "The new neighbor."

Quillerman released a long, heavy sigh as he looked down at his maimed hand. "Tell me, Robby. Everything."

So Robby had done exactly that, although he choked on the word "succubus," certain the pastor would think he was on drugs. But Quillerman nodded slowly and listened. When Robby was finished, Quillerman was silent for a long time. Then he looked Robby in the eye and said, "You were right to come to me. You should have come sooner. You're sure your friend is dead?"

Robby nodded.

"Pity. Sounds like he's been on quite a crusade."

"You mean ... well, you ... you believe me?"

He stared at Robby thoughtfully a while, then held up his injured hand and said, "This –" and pointed to his glass eye, " – this –" and to the scar on his forehead, " – and this –" to his leg, " – and this ... I got them all when I was just a little boy. I was ... running from my parents, both of whom wanted to kill me." His voice trembled when he said it. Robby had never heard that voice falter before. "We had a new neighbor then, too, Robby. Right next door. So, yes. I believe you. I know exactly what you're talking about, I assure you. And I think I know what to do about it."

He'd listened to a brief outline of Quillerman's plan, then had followed the pastor's instructions to go home.

"In the morning, talk to them," Pastor Quillerman had said. "Tell them everything, whether they believe you or not. If you have to, tell them again and again. They may call you crazy, but deep inside, they'll know you're right. I'll get over there as soon as I possibly can."

Robby heard the Cuisinart whir to life in the kitchen.

On the radio, a local chiropractor was listing the many benefits of making an appointment with him today.

The bedroom door burst open suddenly and Robby nearly fell off the bed as his dad rushed in and slammed the door behind him.

"What've you been doing with your sister, Robby?" he asked with quiet menace.

"What?"

"Your sister!" George moved in on him quickly and Robby flinched. "What've you been doing with her? Making out with her? Fucking her, maybe? Couldn't you go out and find yourself a real girlfriend?"

Robby stood and backed away from his dad, his face sagging with fear.

"Dad, you don't – I haven't – let me explain what's –"

"You'd fucking well better explain!" George shouted, rushing toward him until their noses were almost touching.

The doorbell rang.

"Well? I'm waiting, Robby. I'm serious, boy, I want to know what's –"

It rang again.

The Cuisinart did not stop.

"Son of a bitch," George hissed. He spun around, opened the door and leaned into the hall. "Karen! Get that!"

No response.

The doorbell rang again.

He murmured, "Me. Everything falls on me around here." He turned to Robby and aimed a rigid forefinger at him. "I'll be right back. We are not dropping this." He pulled the door closed hard as he left.

Robby could hear him stomping down the hall. He waited a few moments, then quietly followed. He peered cautiously around the corner at the end of the hall and watched his dad go to the door.

George opened the front door to find the mail carrier smiling at him. He was a short, bearded man with thick glasses and a toothpick dangling from his lips. Behind him stood the reporters and cameramen he'd seen outside his bedroom. They rushed in as if attacking, stabbing their microphones toward George and vomiting questions all at once.

"I told you people to stay away from my house!" George barked, waving his arms toward the street. "Now get the hell out of here! I answered enough questions yesterday and I don't –"

The blonde woman stepped forward and asked quickly, "Could you explain the writing on your front door, Mr. Pritchard?"

"What writing on my –" He stopped and stared at the black circle with three odd names written inside. "I don't know what –"

"Did you know Ronald Prosky?" another reporter asked.

"Who?"

Robby's breath caught at the mention of the name.

As if on cue, the other reporters moved forward.

"Is it a religious symbol, Mr. Pritchard?"

"What happened to your window, Mr. Pritchard?"

"Do you think the murders were cult related?"

The mail carrier said, "Um, Mr. Prosky? You haven't been getting your mail for a few days. It's gotten pretty wet."

George stared at the stack of soggy mail in the man's hand while the reporters kept asking questions. He raised his arms and shouted, "Hold it, okay? Just hold it a second and let me get my mail."

The reporters were quiet, but did not move.

George frowned at the soaked mail as he took it. "Why'd you keep delivering our mail if it was getting wet?" he snapped.

The carrier shrugged and spread his arms. "Hey, if you're gonna be gone, or something, it's your responsibility to put a hold on it. Otherwise, you gotta walk to the box and get it, okay?"

George pointed to the circle on the door and asked, "Did you do this?"

"'Course not, jeez. Look, I gotta go." Annoyed, he turned and headed for his red, white and blue Jeep idling at the curb.

A moment after he left, the reporters began firing questions again. George interrupted them with a shout.

"Okay! Look, I don't know what this thing is –" He stabbed a thumb over his shoulder at the door. " – and I don't know who put it there, probably some neighbor kid, okay? I don't know who Ronald Whoever is, never heard of him, and I don't want to answer any more questions. I'm sure there are other people in the neighborhood who knew the Garrys a lot better than we did, so why don't you go bother them!"

He slammed the door. "Who drew on the door?" he growled, turning around. "Who the hell drew on the front –"

"I did." Robby stepped from the hall looking ill.

"You did? Well, what the hell is it?"

Robby looked over his shoulder, all around him, then

gestured for George to follow him back to his bedroom. There, Robby told him everything.

* * * *

Karen was making a stew.

She'd been up for nearly an hour and she still did not feel awake. She wasn't sure if what she'd seen when she first woke – the empty hole where the bedroom window used to be, covered by fluttering curtains – had been real or the lingering echo of a dream she'd been having, and she hadn't gone back into the bedroom to check. She didn't care. She didn't care that her family hadn't had breakfast yet, or that she was missing another day of work and Jen and Robby were missing school. She could not even make herself care much that an entire family that used to live down the street was now dead. All she cared about at the moment was making a stew that would last for a while so she wouldn't have to worry about cooking. And ... Lorelle.

Since she woke, Karen had been unable to think a thought that did not involve Lorelle ... the touch of her hand ... her tongue ... the hot moist brush of her breath on Karen's skin ...

What they had done in bed beside George last night was as vivid in her mind as if it had happened minutes ago.

She stabbed a long carrot into the top of the Cuisinart and watched as the spinning blades sliced it into thin orange coins, feeling an undercurrent of satisfaction as the carrot danced a blade-spinning jig and its pieces clattered against the transparent plastic.

The window over the sink looked out on the long rectangular back yard where trees swayed in an icy wind and steel-gray clouds swept across the sky.

Beneath the whir of the Cuisinart the telephone rang, but it was white noise to Karen, unimportant. On the third ring, George shouted, "Answer the goddamned phone, Karen!"

She switched off the Cuisinart and stared blinking at the telephone as if she'd never seen it before. The six steps

across the kitchen felt like a long journey with bricks tied
to her ankles and, when she lifted it, the receiver felt heavy
as lead.

"Hello?"

"Karen." The voice was warm honey oozing into Karen's
ear and she leaned heavily against the wall and closed her
eyes.

"Hello, Lorelle."

"I hope I'm not calling at a bad time."

"No."

"I just noticed your car was home. Are you sick?"

"I'm feeling a little, you know, under the weather." She
tried to keep her voice from trembling, but hearing Lorelle
brought to life memories of last night when Lorelle woke
her with a gentle kiss. The sensations and smells and tastes
rushed back vividly as if she were experiencing them all
again.

"Do you feel too bad to come over for a while?" Lorelle
asked. "Just a little while. For a visit." There was a smile
in her voice.

Karen suddenly felt self-conscious, clumsy. "Well, I'm
ma-making some stew, but I could, you know, finish that
later, or just finish it up ruh-really quick and cuh-come over,
unless you want me to –"

"That would be fine. I'll be waiting." She replaced the
receiver softly at her end.

Karen licked her dry lips and hung up the telephone,
walked slowly back to the counter and quickly began
feeding more vegetables into the spinning blades of the
Cuisinart. She dumped the chopped vegetables into a pot,
quickly chopped the meat she'd thawed in the microwave,
slicing her thumb open in the process, then put it all on
the stove.

It was three-forty.

Leaving her mess untouched and her bleeding thumb
unbandaged, Karen got her coat from the hall closet and,
trembling with anticipation, put it on over her baggy sweats
and slipped on a pair of tennis shoes. As she passed the

living room doorway, she saw Jen on the sofa, her knees curled up to her chest, hands tucked beneath her nightshirt, arms moving slightly. Karen started to tell Jen she was going across the street for a little while, but didn't bother. The girl's eyes were closed anyway and she was oblivious even to the television.

Karen opened the front door and saw it. She frowned for a long moment, not sure what she was looking at, then realized it didn't matter what it was. Someone had defaced their front door, but it wasn't important. She would clean it off when she got back. She wanted nothing to hold her up now. She stepped out onto the porch and started to pull the door shut when it was jerked from her hand.

"Where are you going?" Robby asked urgently. He stood in the doorway, eyes wide, leaning toward her as if he were about to tell her something horrible.

"Juh-just ... I-I was just ... " Think fast, Karen told herself. "I was just going across the street to get some seasonings from Lorelle. I'm making a stew."

George appeared behind him looking agitated, a little angry. "What now, Robby?" he grumbled.

"Don't go, Mom."

"Why?"

"Just don't go. You can get 'em at the store, can't you? You'll need more later anyway, won't you? Probably. I'll go with you."

Karen sighed, annoyed, and said, "I don't want to go to the store, Robby. That's why I'm getting some from her."

"Don't."

"What's wrong with you?"

George gripped Robby's shoulder and spun him around. "That's what I want to know. What's wrong with you, what are you on? Drugs? Have you been doing drugs?"

"No, Dad, really, I told you what's —"

"Okay, that's enough," George said in that tone he used when he was deciding how to discipline one of the kids. "Clean this shit off the door. Now. Then you and I are going to have a talk and this time you're going to listen."

"No, Dad, please don't –"

"You clean it off right now or there'll be hell to pay and you'll wish you'd –"

"No."

"What?" George's voice was soft, level. "What did you say?"

Robby looked and sounded near tears, his lips trembling as he whispered, "I won't clean it off."

Karen watched as George's face was overcome by a look of anger so powerful that it seemed to alter his features. He began shouting at Robby, using obscenities uncharacteristic of him, and Karen stepped toward them and snapped, "What is going on here?"

"Shut up!" George barked. "Just shut up and go get your fucking seasonings, okay, just go!" Then he turned to Robby again and continued shouting.

Karen imagined how they must look to the neighbors – the three of them shouting on their front porch on a damp cloudy day, George and Robby in their bathrobes, she in her sweats, all three of them looking deathly pale and exhausted; and for the first time that day she forgot about Lorelle and wanted to cry, wanted to scream.

"Stop it," she said tremulously, quietly at first, then louder. "Stop it." And louder still. "Please stop it!"

George stopped, glared at her, and started to speak, but someone from down the street spoke first.

"Take it inside, for crying out loud!" a voice called from across the street. "Somebody's trying to sleep!"

George looked down the street at the Weyland house. Paul Weyland's face was leaning close to the screen over the bedroom window.

"It's my fucking porch, Weyland," George roared, "and I'll yell on it if I want to! Keep your goddamned dog off my lawn and maybe I'll be quiet! How would you like it if I came over and shit in your yard"

The window slammed shut.

Karen began to feel nauseated and tears stung her eyes.

"George, please," she whispered, "Leave him alone and let's just go inside, okay? Let's go inside."

"What? You're not going over to Lorelle's?" George snapped. His mouth curled into a malignant grin. "According to Robby, here, you're going over there to fuck her. You want me to leave him alone? Fine. I will. I'll just let him go on thinking that you and I are fucking the neighbor. Okay? That's okay with you?"

A clump of ice formed in Karen's gut, then shattered, its pieces tumbling through her veins.

They stood there for a small eternity, their eyes darting back and forth between one another. Then George's eyes held on her and he grinned.

"Welllll," he said, dragging the word out into a long whispery drawl, his head bobbing up and down slowly. "Maybe Robby's not on drugs after all. Are you? Fucking her?"

Karen tried to gather her thoughts but they only tumbled around noisily in her mind, words heaping one on top of another in an orgy of confusion.

This happened? How? Did? How happened this how did it my god how happened this Jesus Christ how did this happen my god Jesus Christ HOW DID THIS HAPPEN?

Her tears spilled and her throat felt thick, as if something were oozing up from her stomach. She knew that nothing she could say would make any difference. She saw in George's eyes an anger that had reached such a height even words meant to comfort him would only serve to feed his fury. She had seen that look before – only a couple of times, because George seldom got angry – but never like this, never so fiery and dangerous.

Karen turned and walked back into the house, her vision a kaleidoscope of tear-blurred colors, picking up her pace when she heard George's heavy footsteps following her.

"So is it true?" he snapped, and she could hear a cold smile in his voice.

Karen could not respond. She headed for the bathroom.

"Answer me."

As she opened the bathroom door, he clutched her elbow and spun her around. She stiffened and stared at the floor.

"What the hell's going on here?" he hissed through clenched teeth. "Robby's spouting some crap about demons and Jen's acting like-like-like I don't know what and now you're giving me this-this – what is this anyway, are you – is there something ... going on ... be ... tween ... "

She lifted her eyes to his and saw in his face – slack-jawed and drunk-looking – that he knew.

"Son of a bitch," he breathed, then laughed coldly, hatefully. "So ... how did Robby know, do you think? Huh? Maybe –"Another laugh, louder this time. " – maybe he's fucking her, too." His laughter grew louder still and more rapid-fire, like a machine gun. A strip of sweat glowed on his upper lip and a bead of it rolled slowly down his cheek. "Wouldn't that be a hoot? Huh? Wouldn't it?" He leaned back against the wall and shook his head vigorously and his laughter faded to quiet hiccups, then he sucked in a deep breath and released another booming round of laughs trying to speak at the same time. "I-I-I ha-haven't ... slept well ... need some sluh-sleep I g-guess."

Karen backed into the bathroom a step, frightened. George's sickly pale face was turning a rosy red and his cheeks seemed to swell as he kept laughing ... laughing and laughing ... until he leaned forward and put his face in his hands and was silent. His shoulders jerked slightly, but the loud belly laughs were gone. His fingers curled, their tips pressing into his face.

Frowning, Karen wiped her teary eyes with a knuckle and stepped toward him. She pressed a fist into her abdomen where she was feeling a heavy churning sickness – a combination of dread and guilt and pity – and reached her other hand out, slowly placing it on his shoulder.

"Don't," George mumbled into his palms, then straightened and lowered his hands. His face was deep red and puffy and the laughter was gone. "Don't ... duh-don't –" His fist moved like a striking snake, slicing the air between them and hitting the wall with a thunderous whump, rattling a collage frame on the wall and sending it crashing to the floor. " – touch me!"

George moved toward her suddenly, his bottom lip curling down past his lower gum and his shoulders hunched like a melodrama villain. Karen fell backwards into the bathroom with a sharp cry and slammed the door, fumbling with the lock until it clicked.

George pounded on the door with both fists and screamed, "You open this fucking door and open it right now, you hear me? Do you hear me, you fucking dyke?"

He stopped for just a moment to listen for a response, then began to slam himself against the door as –

* * * *

Robby rushed back into the house.

He'd been standing on the porch, enjoying the cold and the quiet, staring at the three angels' names. Then he'd heard his dad shouting, followed by the pounding, and he'd hurried inside.

The noise had stopped by the time Robby reached the hall, which was empty. From the other end, he heard his dad's voice:

"Kitty-kitty ... heeere kitty-kitty-kitty ... c'mon, puss-puss-puss, kitty-kitty."

From the bathroom: "George don't you dare hurt that cat!"

"Come out and stop me." He came out of the master bedroom and went into the guest room. "Heeere kitty-kitty-kitty ... "

"Mom?" Robby said quietly outside the bathroom.

"Robby? Robby, please, do me a favor. Take your sister and ... and just go out for a while, okay? Will you do that for me?"

"No, Mom."

"Puss-puss-puss? Kitty-kitty-kitty?"

"Go to a movie, okay? There's money in the ceramic elephant in the kitchen. You can take the car."

"No, mom, I'm not leaving while he's like this."

"Oh, h-he-he's just up-upset." Her voice sounded thick with tears. "He'll be fine after while."

"C'mon, Monroe ... where are ya, fella ... kitty-kitty-kitty ... "

"He's not just upset and he won't be fine." Robby hissed. "Nobody's gonna be fine. Mom, this is happening to everyone on Deerfield, I think. I think this is probably what happened to the Garry's."

"Robby," she gasped at him for suggesting such a thing. "Your father is just a little –"

"It's her, Mother, and you know it."

"I ... Robby, you're ... I don't know what you're talking about."

"Come out and talk to me. Please."

"No."

"Because you're afraid of him. See? It's her, Mother, she's sucking the life out of all of us, sucking out everything that's good and –"

A piercing snarl sounded from the guest room.

"Gotcha!" George shouted with a laugh.

"Leave him alone!" Karen shouted from the bathroom.

George stepped out of the guest room carrying Monroe by the nape of the neck. The tip of his tongue poked from the corner of his broad grin.

"Dad?" Robby said.

He pushed Robby aside as he walked by briskly.

"Damn you, George!" The lock rattled, the door opened and she stepped into the hall. "Leave that cat alone!"

His laugh faded as he rounded the corner toward the kitchen.

She followed him.

Jen's door opened and she peeked out cautiously. "What's –"

"Just stay in there for a while, okay?" Robby said, then followed his parents. He was halfway to the kitchen when he heard the Cuisinart come on.

Karen screamed.

Robby stumbled to a halt in the kitchen as George

backhanded Karen in the face, slamming her against the refrigerator. She slid to the floor as George removed the plastic top of the Cuisinart and held the squirming cat over the opening.

"Dad, stop it!" Robby shouted as he dove forward, wrapped his arms around George's waist and tried to pull him away from the counter.

George swung his elbow back hard and caught Robby's chin. Robby hit the floor hard and slid backward over the tile. His teeth had closed on the inside of his lip and he could already taste blood.

George pushed the cat's behind into the transparent plastic casing. Monroe was too fat, though, and stopped within an inch of the spinning blades.

Karen screamed incoherently, reaching out to George imploringly.

"You don't need it anymore!" George roared. "You've found another pussy!"

Robby got to his feet as Jen came in still wearing her crop-top and panties. She screamed shrilly, relentlessly.

Robby went for his dad's shoulders, screaming in his ear, "Dad, will you stop and look at what you're doing, think about what you're –"

George shook Robby off, turned and backhanded him with a fist. His knuckles hit Robby just below his left eye and returned him to the kitchen floor.

Turning his back on the others, George used both hands to push on the cat. The animal fought and clawed and spat and released a long, piercing yowl.

Karen and Jen continued to scream.

None of them heard the front door open, but they all heard the booming voice.

"George Pritchard!"

The screaming stopped.

All four heads turned to see Pastor Quillerman standing in the kitchen doorway.

None of them moved.

Pastor Quillerman crossed the kitchen and jerked the Cuisinart's plug out of the wall, glaring at George.

"I think," he said, his voice a low rumble, "that we should talk."

Chapter 18

Into Temptation

FOR a while that morning, bars of sunlight had managed to pierce the blanket of clouds overhead. It had even looked, briefly, like the clouds were going to break up and give way to blue sky. But it wasn't long before the sunlight was swallowed up and the sky was once again a low ceiling of grimy steel.

The street was thick with reporters from all the local television stations and some from Sacramento and San Francisco, even a couple of networks – CNN and MSNBC.

Although it was the reason they had all come to the neighborhood, there was very little activity at the Garry house. A police officer had arrived earlier that morning with a man and woman – presumably relatives, because they looked grief-stricken, but they wouldn't speak to any of the reporters – and had taken them through the house. Then they'd gone, leaving the house dark and empty once again.

But the Pritchard house had captured their interest. They all knew it was the home of Robby Pritchard, who had discovered the carnage down the street, and who had been the killer's best friend. But there was more.

There was all the angry shouting that had been taking place there, and that gaping hole in the side of the Pritchard house that had seemed to be as much a mystery to Mr. Pritchard that morning as it was to all of them. And those three strange words written in the circle on the front door. What language was that? Or were they names, perhaps? And what significance did they have on the front door? Who was that man who'd limped into the house without knocking earlier? And what about all the screaming they'd heard in there just a little while ago? Was there some connection between the Garry killings and the Pritchard family? Were the killings cult-related, perhaps? Were the boys involved in devil worship?

The reporters had caught the scent of a story they could milk, and they weren't going anywhere until they got some answers. They'd moved their cars and vans up the street and parked them in front of the Pritchard house, where they waited for someone to come out and talk to them, or for something to happen, anything at all.

When the front door opened, they rushed forward.

It was that limping man again. He came out onto the sidewalk and waved at them, smiling as they came forward. Before the barrage of questions could begin, he spoke.

"I'd like to have a word with all of you, if I might. It'll just take a moment."

They moved in close and waited for him to go on.

"I am Jeremy Quillerman, the Pritchards' pastor. Needless to say, they're very upset about what has happened to their friends. In fact, the entire neighborhood is grieving today. I encourage you to keep that in mind. I know it is your business to report the news, but ... there is no news here, I'm afraid. Only tragedy. The writing on the front door is simply vandalism. The nasty hole over there is best dealt with by a carpenter, not reporters. So, please folks...until something else comes up, why don't you go back to your places of employment and write your stories. The people here have suffered a great loss and a great shock. They're in no condition to answer questions now." He smiled again, nodded with a finality and said, "Thank you for your time." Then he turned and headed back into the house.

The reporters fired questions like bullets, shouting to be heard. He didn't even slow his limping pace. He went inside, closed the door and locked it.

They grumbled to one another as they turned and went back to their cars and vans.

* * * *

While Pastor Quillerman was outside, no one in the house moved from where they were when he left.

George was sitting at the dining room table with his head in his hands, eyes hidden from the dull, glaring light that shined in through the sliding glass door behind him.

Karen was leaning against the lip of the kitchen counter with Monroe in her arms, stroking the agitated cat and making soft, soothing noises.

Robby and Jen stood quietly in the living room, staring out at the reporters.

A bit earlier, Pastor Quillerman had explained to the family everything Robby already knew about Lorelle Dupree and, once again, Robby had been surprised that the pastor knew everything Ronald Prosky had known. Quillerman seemed to take it all in stride, as if this sort of thing happened all the time. Of course, it didn't. It couldn't. But Robby couldn't shake the feeling that it happened more often than he wanted to imagine and that more people were aware of creatures like Lorelle Dupree than he wanted to know.

According to the material Prosky had given Robby, Lilith had given birth to as many as a hundred infants an hour ... but for how many hours? How many were out there? The possibilities made Robby feel very small and vulnerable.

As Quillerman headed back up the walk, Robby whispered, "I told him everything, you know."

Jen's head snapped toward him. "You mean ... about us? Everything?"

"Everything."

Quillerman came inside and beckoned Jen and Robby to follow him into the kitchen.

"I spoke to them," he said, "but I doubt it will do any good. Once they've found a story, reporters are a little like ants and roaches – impossible to get rid of, because if one goes, there's always another to replace it. So, I guess we'll just have to do this in front of them."

Until that moment, Quillerman had gotten virtually no reaction from the family. There had been a few monosyllabic responses and odd facial expressions, but mostly they'd avoided his gaze and remained silent. But then:

"Do, uh...do what in front of them?" George asked from the table, lifting his head slowly. His face looked heavy, the skin sagged and drooped beneath his eyes and along his jawline.

"Deal with this problem we've been talking about here," Quillerman replied.

George stood. "Well, we haven't exactly been talking. You've been talking. And we've listened to your, um ... your story. Now I think you should go."

Quillerman's eye moved from George to Jen to Robby to Karen and back to George again. "You know," he said quietly, "you've been coming to church all these years and I've never been here to your house. I've never invited you to my house. I know pastors of other churches who know each and every member of their congregations well. They see them socially. They are considered friends of the family. Unfortunately, I am not made of the same cloth. Of my many faults, I'm afraid my greatest is the distance I tend to keep between myself and the members of my congregation. If I were closer to my congregation, perhaps I would have seen this coming. I might have been able to prevent your involvement. "

"Mr. Pritchard, what's happening here is not something you can dismiss. It will eat you alive if you let it. You've already allowed it into your home, then into your mind, and the next step is –"

"Pastor," Karen said, still cradling Monroe in her arms, "we appreciate your concern, but the idea of Lorelle Dupree being a ... a demon is –"

"Crazy? I suppose it does sound crazy. But the world is full of things that sound crazy. That doesn't make them any less real. But we have protected ourselves from them, shut them out so we aren't exposed to them. So much of what we do is just an effort to shut out all the things that seem crazy ... or scary. We've created religion, ritual, tradition ...

even the family is a protective measure, a way of insulating ourselves from the frightening darkness beyond the glow of our fires. I, of course, play a part in that insulation. Religion is one of the things people turn to for comfort and reassurance when they get a glimpse of the unknown. In the end, all we really have is each other. And that's why I'm here. Your neighbor knows this. She is pitting you against each other right now, and you will –"

"Get the fuck out of my house!" George roared, taking a couple of steps toward Quillerman.

Dead silence fell over the room as the pastor stared at him, a look of satisfaction on his face, then: "You see?" he whispered. "This is not how you normally behave, George." He looked around at all of them. "This is not how any of you behave. Can't you see what she's doing to you?"

George's fists were clenched and trembling at his sides. He opened his mouth to shout something again, but Robby spoke up quickly.

"Dad, you know it's true! She tore a hole in your bedroom wall. She flew through your bedroom wall! She chased me! She's not human, Dad, and you know it." He looked at Karen and Jen, too. "We all know it. So why don't we admit it and stop letting her do this to us!"

George stared at his son intensely for a long moment, then backed up slowly and lowered himself back into the chair. He leaned forward on the dining room table. His arms began to shake, just a little at first, but when he tried to speak they got worse.

"Well, whuh-what ... what do we, um ... wh-what're we supposed to ... I mean, what's –" He stopped suddenly, arms quaking so hard they rattled the table. He slapped a hand over his mouth, closed his eyes tightly and pressed his arms down on the table hard to stop the shaking. After sitting like that for a while with the others staring at him, he pulled his hand away and muttered, "What've we done?" Then, quickly: "I-I mean, no, no, I mean, what'll we do?"

Pastor Quillerman turned to Karen and, with nothing

more than a tilt of his head and the look in his eye, asked her if she agreed.

She looked away from him, rubbed her cheek against the top of Monroe's head then made a movement that might have been a conciliatory shrug.

Jen frowned, then nodded slowly.

Quillerman already knew how Robby felt, so he didn't bother asking.

"First," the pastor said, "you need each other. So whatever animosity you may feel toward each other right now, whatever feelings of anger or betrayal have been created by this situation – you need to let go of them. You need to forgive one another. And yourselves. She will use whatever she can to pull you apart. You've opened yourselves up to her and now she knows all she needs to know to finish her work in this house."

George asked hoarsely, "And ... what is that work?"

"Well, apparently she's already finished with the Garrys. And from the looks of things when I arrived here, she came close to finishing with you this morning. Murder and suicide are among the signatures of the succubus."

"Then what?" Robby said.

"First, we have to gain the support of everyone on this street who has been seduced by Lorelle Dupree. That won't be easy, especially with all those reporters out there, but we'll do our best –" He turned to Robby. " – won't we?"

Robby nodded.

"I have to drive over to the church to pick something up," Quillerman said. "It won't take long, but should you need me, I'll give you my cell number."

"What are you getting?" Robby asked.

"Something to make it a little easier to talk to your neighbors. "

Robby followed Pastor Quillerman to the door, where the man turned to him.

"You seem to have the best handle on all of this, Robby," he whispered. "Help them. They'll need it. I'll be right back."

He was gone.

Robby turned and started back toward the kitchen. The closer he got, the worse his feeling of dread became. What was he going to do? What could he say to them?

Karen was gone.

George was still seated at the table.

As Robby walked in, Jen started out.

"Where you going?" Robby whispered.

"My room. I-yum...I think I'll take a nap, maybe." She looked tired and a little confused as she left.

Robby went to the table, scooted a chair over and seated himself close to his dad. "You okay?" he asked.

He didn't answer for a while, then: "Yeah. Yeah, son, I'm fine."

"Where'd Mom go?"

"I don't know."

Robby stiffened before speaking again, bracing himself, knowing he might be making a mistake. "Don't you think maybe you should ... you know, go talk to her?"

George rubbed both hands over his face, slowly massaging his eyes, then stood. "Yeah. Maybe I should. Right now, though, I'm gonna do something about that hole in the bedroom wall." He walked away slowly as he muttered to himself: "Have to call a carpenter ... may be get that tarp outta the garage ... cover it with that for now ... "

Robby was alone.

* * * *

Outside, only a few of the reporters remained, and they were taking cover because the sky had become even darker and threatened more rain.

A thin, low mist permeated the neighborhood. It had appeared out of nowhere in seconds, swirling over the ground, seeping through shrubs, curling around the corners of houses and licking teasingly at the walls.

When the mist first moved in, a few dogs barked wildly up and down the street and a cat darted in several directions

– from yard to yard, from one side of the street to the other – before going up a tree, as if to get away from the mist.

Other than the animals, however, no one paid the mist any attention ... so no one noticed its swirling movement just beneath Jen Pritchard's bedroom window.

* * * *

Jen took the straight-back chair away from her dressing table, turned it around and straddled the back, leaning her chin on her wrists. She'd opened a package of Pop Rocks and put a few of the little pebble-like candies in her mouth. They fizzed and popped. She felt like she had a head full of Pop Rocks. Her thoughts exploded before she could complete them, then a new one would begin, only to end abruptly before another began to take shape.

What had they gotten into? Was it too late to get out?

When she thought of the things she'd been doing, she felt sick with self-hatred, as if Pastor Quillerman's arrival had been a glass of ice water thrown in her face that had startled her into hyper consciousness.

She wanted to go back to the day before Lorelle Dupree's arrival and do something that might have prevented all that had happened afterward. But what could she have done? There had to be something she could have done or said that might have strengthened the connection between herself, her brother and their parents, something that would have enabled them to turn away from Lorelle.

She tossed the half-empty bag of Pop Rocks on the dressing table and pushed the chair away as she stood, turned and –

– she threw herself backward with a choking sound, nearly swallowing some of the tiny candies whole and she stumbled and fell backward into the chair because –

– Lorelle was peering at her through her bedroom window. She smiled at Jen, lifted a hand and gave her a friendly wave.

"Hello, Jen," she said, her voice muffled by the glass.

"Is anything wrong in there? I noticed the reporters were paying a lot of attention to your house."

Jen hugged herself against a sudden chill. "Y-you know what's wrong," she said.

Lorelle frowned.

"Duh-don't...you?"

"I'm afraid not. Other than what happened down the street – those poor people, isn't that horrible? No, I don't know what's wrong. I'm worried about you."

Jen frowned, blinked. Could Robby have been wrong? Even Pastor Quillerman? Could it be that they'd just gotten involved with a disturbed woman who'd moved in across the street? When she thought about it now, what she'd done with Robby seemed like nothing more than a dark and fading dream. Had she really wandered around the house half-naked? Had she really touched her father's erection just that morning? The more she thought about it, the farther away it all seemed and the more she doubted Robby's and Pastor Quillerman's story that Lorelle was some kind of demon.

But she still wasn't certain.

"I knocked on the door," Lorelle said, "but no one answered. I began to wonder if everything was all right. By the way, what's that thing on your front door, that circle with three names in it?"

"You ... don't know?"

She shook her head. "It's not very attractive, if you want my opinion. You ought to wash it off."

Maybe she 'd like that, Jen thought.

"Why don't you come to the front door, Jen? It would be easier to talk."

"Well, I...I'm busy."

"You don't look busy. Come on, I'll meet you at the front door. You can come walk the dogs with me."

"I can't."

"Sure you can." She grinned.

"I-I don't think so."

Her grin melted. "Why, Jen? Are you ... embarrassed

maybe? Embarrassed about what happened between you and Robby?"

Jen gasped.

Real ... it happened ... it was real.

"You shouldn't be embarrassed, Jen. You certainly enjoyed it at the time ... didn't you? It can happen again, you know. It can happen again if you'll just meet me at the front door. We can wash away those silly names, then you and Robby can come over to my place –" The grin returned. " – and play."

Jen shuddered as she stood, moved behind the chair and latched a white-knuckle grip on its back.

"Wouldn't you like that, Jen?" Lorelle asked, moving her face closer to the glass.

Trembling, Jen closed her eyes and thought of Robby ... and her parents ...

* * * *

The staple gun made loud, sharp snapping noises as George stapled a dark green plastic tarpaulin over the hole in the bedroom wall. He felt weak and sluggish and worked slowly, pulling the plastic taut before each snap of the gun.

Before starting, he'd knocked on the door of the guest room assuming that was where Karen had gone. He'd knocked a second time before getting a response.

"Yes?"

"Uh ... are you, um, all right, Karen?" he'd asked.

A long silence, then: "Yes. I just want to be alone for a while."

He'd stood there for a long time, staring at the doorknob, tempted to try it and maybe go in and talk with her, but she didn't sound like she wanted to talk. And for a brief moment, that made him furious. His teeth ground together and he wanted to put his fist through the door, felt angry and strong enough to be able to poke his hand through the wood as if it were paper, then go into that bedroom and do the same thing to Karen, but –

– he'd caught himself and moved back away from the door, slowly relaxing his clenched fists and taking deep breaths. Then he'd gone to work in the bedroom.

The next time he squeezed the gun, he got a hollow clack. It was empty. He released the tarpaulin, leaned down for the box of staples on the floor, and removed another strip. Once he'd reloaded the staple gun, he stood up straight and reached for the drooping flap of plastic, but –

– George jerked his hand back as if it had been bitten and dropped the staple gun as his shock came out in a dry cough, because –

– Lorelle peered in through the opening left by the unstapled section of the tarpaulin and purred, "I could use a handyman, George." She wore a black leather teddy with perfectly round holes over her breasts through which her dark nipples stood erect. She wore no panties above her black fishnet stockings. "Would you like to be my handyman for a while, George?"

His mouth was suddenly filled with moist cotton. "Guh-get away ... from me," he breathed.

"That's not nice, George. Not after all the good times we've had. What do you say we do your favorite? You fuck me up the ass while I use the vibrator on my pussy. How does that sound, huh?"

"Nun ... no. No."

"No? I'm shocked, George. I'm hurt. Why no, all of a sudden? Have you ... ah, yes, I bet you've found someone else to do those things for you. Who could it be? Hmmm ... Karen? No, not Karen. She doesn't like cocks. She told me that, George. She said they were ugly. Even yours. All lumpy and stiff and stubby." She wrinkled her nose and went through a mock shudder. "Ooooh, no. Karen doesn't like that at all. She told me herself. No, Karen prefers ... other things."

George began to feel sick, partly because of what Lorelle was saying to him, and partly because, in spite of her words and in spite of what he knew about her – or thought he knew about her – he was getting an erection.

"So if it's not Karen who's replacing me, maybe it's ... Jen? She's young but ... very imaginative. Maybe Robby wasn't enough for her. Maybe his cock wasn't big enough. After all, father knows best, right?" She laughed as she licked a fingertip and ran it around one nipple, then squeezed. "But somehow, I don't think so. I think you still want me, George. You know nobody will give it to you like I did. You know that. And so does whatever's standing up beneath your robe." She laughed again, licked her finger Again and buried it for a moment in the patch of red hair between her legs as she closed her eyes and leaned her head back with pleasure. Then she lifted her hand to her face and ran the glistening finger back and forth beneath her nose. "Mrnmm, George," she said as she held her hand out toward him. "Want to smell? Want to taste? Nectar, George ... nectar. Smell it ... lick it ... suck it off my finger, George."

His lungs felt empty and his knees weak, and the pounding between his legs became more and more insistent until it drowned the throb of his head and he was about to step forward just one step, a short step, and take that finger in his mouth so he could suck off that sparkling fluid, but –

– he growled through clenched teeth, "No, I won't. Not again. I won't!" He swept the staple gun off the floor, slammed the loose section of the tarpaulin against the wall, and began stapling hard and fast as –

– Lorelle, just outside, continued to say softly, "Lick it, George, taste it again, come out and taste it, George –"

" – No, dammit," George rasped as he stapled.

"Come out and put your tongue in it, George ... put your tongue in it and roll it around ... put your cock in it, George, just slide it in ... "

He thought of Karen ... of Robby and Jen ... of Christmases and Thanksgivings ... school plays and recitals ... of Robby's birth ... he even thought of Laura.

Lorelle giggled as she dragged her fingernails slowly down the other side of the plastic.

* * * *

Karen lay on the bed in the guest room with the door closed and locked, stroking Monroe gently. The cat was curled up on her stomach, purring like an idling engine, as if he hadn't been less than an inch from bloody injury and most likely death only a short time ago.

"What am I going to do, Monroe?" Karen whispered.

The cat didn't even stir.

"What ... am I going ... to –"

There were three short taps on the window pane.

Karen's head jerked to the right and looked up at the rectangular window. The white shade was down and the light-blue curtains were half drawn.

Three more staccato taps.

She felt her heartbeat in her fingertips.

Monroe protested with a half-hearted meow when Karen sat up and lifted him off her. She swung her legs off the bed, stood and stared at the window.

More gentle tapping.

Karen could see a hazy, dark shape through the white shade. She stepped forward, reached out a trembling hand and almost jerked it back and hurried out of the room. Instead, she tugged on the shade. It snapped up with a clatter and –

– Karen stumbled backward with a gasp and whispered, "Lorelle!"

She was naked beneath a sheer black cloak that fluttered around her gracefully in the breeze. Her hands rested between her breasts where she held the cloak together. Lorelle's voice was dulled by the pane of glass, but Karen still heard her.

"I thought you were coming over, Karen," she said.

"Well, I ... I-I ... "

"I've been waiting for you."

Karen inhaled deeply and closed her eyes, then said in a trembling voice, "I'm suh-sorry, but I had to stay with ... I, um, I need to stay with my family."

"Why?"

Karen's eyes snapped open. "What?"

"What's holding you to your family, Karen? The children are old enough to take care of themselves. Robby's not even yours. And your husband ... well, things will never be the same with him, will they? He'll never do for you what a woman can do ... what I can do."

"Please stop," Karen said, turning her back to the window and crossing the room.

"He'll never make you feel the way you felt with me."

"Don't." Karen put her face in her hands, fighting the urge to turn and look at Lorelle, to drink her in with her eyes. "Please don't do this to me," Karen whispered.

"I'm not doing anything to you. But I want to. Look."

Karen didn't move.

"Please, Karen. Look."

She turned cautiously.

Lorelle had pulled the cloak away from her left breast and was fingering the small silver earring that hung from her pierced nipple.

"I wore it for you," she said as she placed a hand on the glass and moved closer, closer, until the earring chattered against the pane, until her breasts were pressed flat to the glass.

"Please ... go away," Karen breathed.

"You don't want me to go away. You want me to touch you ... "

"No, please ... "

" ... and lick you ... "

" ... go away ... "

" ... but I can't do any of those things until you come to me, Karen. Do you hear me?"

Karen closed her eyes.

"Come to me, Karen ... come to me ... "

Karen covered her face with her hands again and cried.

* * * *

Robby had not left the dining room table. He sat with his back to the sliding glass door, unaware of the mist blanketing the back lawn. He'd eaten nothing for breakfast or lunch and was beginning to feel a few pangs of hunger, but he couldn't bring himself to eat. Not yet. Somehow, the idea of food was not appealing, no matter how hungry he felt.

He didn't know how long it had been since Pastor Quillerman had left, but he wished the man would get back soon. How long would it be before Lorelle began trying to lure them over to her house again? To what lengths would she go? And what would she do to him?

Robby had seen her with her guard down, as she really was. He knew the truth about her and, unlike Ronald Prosky, he was still alive to share it with others.

What would she –

"Robby?"

He jumped to his feet so suddenly, he knocked the chair over. When he spun around, he saw Lorelle outside the glass door. She stood naked in a mist that surrounded her ankles and curled up the back of her body, its tendrils caressing her calves, hips and back.

She smiled and said, "Are you glad to see me?" Her eyes moved slowly down his body, then: "Or is that a gerbil in you pants?"

He looked down at himself and was surprised to see that he did, indeed, have an erection. He'd been too frightened to feel it growing. When he looked at her again, her fingers were snaking through the hair between her legs.

"Come on over, Robby," she said. "We'll have some fun."

He tried to speak but couldn't, so he just shook his head.

"Why not?"

"You know why not."

"Aaww, c'mon." She rattled four fingernails against the glass.

Her skin looked so smooth. The very sight of her stirred vivid memories – more like actual sensations – of the things they'd done together.

Her nails rattled, her tongue peeked out the corner of her mouth, her hand continued to move as she lifted one leg slightly. "Come over, Robby. Come over and play ... "

Robby spun around, eyes wide, placed both palms flat on the tabletop and breathed, "It won't work. I know what you are ... what you really are."

The glare from the clouded sky outside was swallowed up suddenly by a shadow that rose up from behind Robby.

The sound of Lorelle's nails tapping against the glass lost its delicacy and became loud and sharp, sounding dangerously close to breaking the glass.

A familiar voice – wet, thick and inhuman – said "Raaaawww-beee." The nails scratched over the glass with a horrible, shrill sound ... a grinding sound ...

"Go away!" he shouted, eyes tightly shut. "You're not here! We know what you are!"

"I'll suck your cock, Raaww-beee."

"Go away!"

"I'll suck your cock out by the roots, Raaww-beee."

The glare from outside returned. The shadow was gone. So was the horrible scratching against the glass. Robby opened his eyes and spun around. Lorelle had disappeared.

Walking unsteadily and taking deep, tremulous breaths, Robby went down the hall to help his dad cover the hole in the bedroom wall...

Chapter 19

A Voice Crying in the Neighborhood

IN the dreary light of the afternoon, a battered white pickup truck with an old silver camper shell on the back moved down Deerfield at a crawl. On the driver's door was written CHRISTIAN FELLOWSHIP NON-DENOMINATIONAL CHURCH, and attached to the top of the pickup was a large, gray, bell-shaped speaker.

In spite of the fact that the pickup was moving suspiciously slowly, no one paid it any attention, not even George and Robby, who were cleaning up the chunks of wood and glass scattered over the front lawn. The mist had grown patchy but still hovered and drifted over the ground in places. Both George and Robby thought it odd, having never seen such a mist in their neighborhood, but both had other things on their mind.

They'd agreed to ignore the reporters as if they weren't there, and they did. Questions were called, but George and Robby did not respond or even look at the reporters. They'd said little to each other since coming out to put another tarpaulin over the hole on the outside of the house, but they exchanged an occasional smile and moved around one another with much more ease than either of them had felt in the last few days.

Jen came outside wearing jeans and a sweater, hugging herself against the chill. "If you guys're hungry," she said timidly, never quite meeting their eyes, "Mom's got some stew on the stove. She's asleep in the guest room now, but if you want some, I'll get it for you. I know I'm hungry."

"Sure," George said. "That sounds good."

After Jen went back inside, a deep, resonant voice that seemed to come from everywhere at once suddenly called out, "Ladies and gentlemen, I am Pastor Jeremy Quillerman, and I'd like you to listen to me for a moment if you would."

George and Robby noticed the truck then. So did the reporters. They turned to the pickup, watched it a moment, then headed in that direction.

"What I have to say is in your best interest," Quillerman said.

After exchanging a couple of confused glances, George and Robby removed their heavy work gloves as they headed across the yard toward the pickup.

"You are all in great danger." Quillerman's voice resonated through the neighborhood. He stopped the pickup and rolled down his window when George and Robby approached.

"What are you doing?" George asked with a mixture of bewilderment and annoyance.

"I'm talking to your neighbors," he said with a smile. "I don't think it would be wise to go door-to-door because, for one thing, it would take too long and, for another, it wouldn't be safe. Think about the emotional climate in your own house, and about what happened just a couple of houses down. These people are on edge. But they need to hear what we know. That's the only way they're going to be able to resist her."

George winced, uncomfortable with the idea, then asked "In front of the reporters?"

He closed his eyes and nodded. "In front of the reporters."

"But ... what if somebody calls the police? I mean, you'd be disturbing the peace and –"

"I realize that, and it's a possibility, but the police aren't here now, and this needs to be done."

"Where did you get that?" Robby asked, nodding toward the horn on top of the pickup.

"It belongs to the church. We used to use it at Christmas

time. We'd drive around the neighborhoods playing carols while church members went door to door gathering food for the needy. Then the city passed a law prohibiting the horn, so we put it away. Till now."

"Shit, it is illegal," George said.

"Let me worry about that. You worry about your family."

Pastor Quillerman rolled up his window and the pickup began to move again.

"Well," George said softly as he watched the truck, his face long and pale, "that ought to wake your mother."

* * * *

The afternoon began its dreary descent into evening as the pickup crept up and down Deerfield. Pastor Quillerman spoke to the neighborhood about Lorelle Dupree without actually mentioning her name.

"You are all in great danger," he said, "and I think you know it. Many of you have recently become involved with a woman who lives on your street."

The reporters rushed toward the truck with their cameramen behind them, cameras hefted on their shoulders, but Quillerman only increased his speed a bit and drove by them, giving in to a small smirk as he watched them in his side view mirror, staring after him and frowning with frustration. Then he lifted the microphone and continued, his eyes darting all around him as he drove.

He'd noticed the mist when he arrived and he didn't like it. It didn't act like any mist he'd seen in the Redding area before – it moved around in an odd way and, unless he was mistaken, he'd seen it move independent of the breeze. He'd just driven across town and back and had seen no fog or mist anywhere – it did not stretch beyond Deerfield.

"Perhaps you've noticed a few changes in your household since you and perhaps other members of your family became involved with this woman," he went on. "You're beginning to feel hostile. You're quick to anger. Perhaps your entire family has been fighting bitterly, even violently."

As he continued, pale faces appeared in windows. A front door opened and a little boy appeared, watching the talking pickup with the same intense interest he might bestow upon an ice cream truck, but without the smile.

"These changes," Quillerman said, "these feelings, are all due to your involvement with this woman. She means you great harm and she is not – I repeat, she is not – human. That sounds preposterous, I know, but think about it a moment. I think deep down inside, where you put all the thoughts and desires and suspicions you want to keep from yourself, you know that it's true."

Quillerman drove back and forth as eyes watched, the sky darkened and the mist crept silently through the neighborhood...

Chapter 20

Into Temptation Again

THE kitchen floor creaked under Betty LaBianco's considerable weight as she searched for the jar of Skippy peanut butter. Ed had probably hidden it. That was the kind of stupid thing he'd been doing lately. Normally, she would ask him about it, but they weren't speaking to each other. Ed seemed to have other things on his mind, but that was just fine with Betty. She had other things on her mind.

Things like Lorelle Dupree. Betty hadn't been the same since Lorelle had first breathed in her ear, first touched her like Ed never had, never could.

Ed. What an idiot. It had taken her long enough to realize it, but better late than never. She'd been married to that buffoon for nearly thirty years and it had taken a neighbor to make her realize that those years had been wasted.

Sometimes – yes, she could admit it to herself – sometimes she just wanted to kill him.

The television was on in the living room and Ed was sprawled in front of it on the sofa, grumbling about the amplified voice that echoed through the chilly afternoon outside.

Betty squatted in front of the counter and opened one of the lower cupboards. No luck.

A draft was coming in from beneath the back door and she felt it on her bare feet, thinking vaguely that something needed to be done about it as she opened another cupboard.

Her back was to the door, so she didn't see the mist curling in beneath it, didn't see it rise and begin to take shape.

No Skippy. Damn. She closed the cupboard, stood and turned.

"Hello, Betty," Lorelle whispered.

Betty slapped a hand over her enormous breasts and leaned back against the counter. "Good Lord, you scared me. You ... you're ... " Lorelle was naked. Betty looked around, confused. "How'd you get in here ... like that?"

Lorelle ignored the question, stepped forward and placed a hand on Betty's round cheek. "Do you hear that voice outside?"

Betty nodded.

"That's the voice of a man who wants to hurt me. He's saying things about me that aren't true. Awful things. And he's saying them over a loudspeaker."

Betty's eyes were wide and her mouth curled into a small O as she stared dreamily at Lorelle. "Why?" she asked after a long time.

"Because he's jealous."

She slid her hand down Betty's flabby neck ...

"He's jealous of what we have, what I can give you."

... down her chest to one enormous, liquidy breast, which she caressed and cupped, rubbing her thumb over the nipple.

"He wants what we have. He'd snatch it up in a second. But he thinks it's wrong. He thinks it's bad. But we know better, don't we Betty?"

Betty nodded, her eyelids drooping heavily as Lorelle moved her hand down Betty's side, over rolls of fat and around to her back, where her fingers massaged firmly, then gently, firmly, gently.

"He's someone you know, Betty. You have to resist him if you want to see me anymore. You have to show everyone how wrong he is. You have to make him go, Betty. Him and the reporters. All of them. Do you understand, Betty? You have to make them go."

Betty nodded as Lorelle's face came closer and closer and

their lips finally touched. Lorelle's tongue slipped in and out of Betty's mouth and she sucked on Betty's lips.

The kiss was too much. Betty felt her strength giving out, felt her knees bending beneath her, then she lost consciousness as –

– Lorelle eased Betty to the floor in her arms effortlessly, then turned and went into the living room where she stepped in front of the television, smiled and said, "Hello, Ed."

* * * *

The mist eased through the neighborhood, shifting direction now and then. A single swirl moved over the surface of the mist like a small and lazy tornado. It went from the LaBianco house to Sheri MacNeil's, where it disappeared for a little while ...

... then across the lawn to the Weylands' houses ...

... and later, to the Parkers ...

... from house to house ...

... to house ...

Chapter 21

Observations

THE two remaining reporters and their crews stood watching the white pickup go back and forth, listening to the bizarre warnings coming over the loudspeaker. Finally, Alana Carson, the reporter from KCPM 24 in Chico, left her cameraman and assistant at the car and approached the van with KRCR 7, a Redding channel, painted on the side.

"Does this go on a lot around here?" Alana asked as she approached the young man standing beside the van. He was tall and thin with blond hair, in his late twenties.

"I don't think so," he said. "But then, I'm kind of new to the area. For all I know, people do this a lot here. Do you understand what he's saying?"

"I'm not sure. Do you know who he is? Are you familiar with his church?"

"No. But I'm going to get familiar with it."

"Any idea what woman he's talking about?"

He shook his head, then smiled at her and said, "By the way, I'm Steve Lang."

She introduced herself, shook his hand, then their attention returned to the pickup as it drove by them again, heading north.

"You must cling to all that is good within you," Quillerman said. "Turn to god, turn to your families, use your love for each other to resist whatever temptation this creature puts before you."

Steve said, "He sounds batshit crazy."

"Most likely," Alana muttered.

"In the book of James, we read, 'But each person is tempted when he is drawn away and enticed by his own desire. Then when the desire has conceived, it gives birth to sin, and sin, when it reaches maturity, produces death.'"

"But we don't have to be afraid of that temptation," the echoing voice went on, "because Peter has told us that 'the Lord can rescue you and me from –"

The pastor's voice gasped over the loudspeaker and the pickup screeched to a lurching stop because –

– an enormously fat woman in a teal and purple muumuu jogged into the street with surprising speed, her entire body jostling with every step – large, flabby breasts flailing up and down, rolls of fat around her neck and torso flopping – until she stepped directly in front of the pickup.

"Later," Alana said abruptly, waving to her cameraman to come over as Steve and his cameraman approached the pickup, where –

– the fat woman walked to Quillerman's door as he rolled down his window and gave her a broad smile, hoping for the best.

"I don't know what you think you're doing out here, Pastor Quillerman," she said in a nasally voice, "but I wish you'd stop. Somebody's liable to call the police on you for yelling through that thing."

"Hello, Betty," the pastor said pleasantly as he leaned his elbow on the edge of the open window. "I'm glad you came out. I'd like to speak with you about a –"

"What are you doing out here, anyway?" she asked, ignoring him. "I mean, driving up and down the street, talking nonsense through that damned speaker –"

"Excuse me, ma'am," Steve said as he came up behind her holding a microphone. His cameraman, Malcolm, stood behind him, camera operating. "Could I have a word with –"

Betty spun around and aimed her forefinger at Steve like a gun. "You just stay away from me with your microphones and cameras, young man. I'm not answering any of your questions and if you had any decency at all, you'd get out of here. There's been a tragedy in this neighborhood and nobody's in the mood for you bloodthirsty reporters." She spotted Alana heading toward her and pointed the finger at her, saying, "And that goes for you, too! You just stay away from me!" She lowered her arm and, as if they'd already gone, she turned back to Pastor Quillerman.

He was frowning at her, concerned. Her anger surprised him ... and so did her pale, sickly appearance. "Are you all right, Betty? You don't look well."

"I'm just fine. It's you I'm worried about, driving up and down out here, talking over that thing about ... what were you saying? Something about a ... what kind of a demon? Are you serious, Pastor?"

The pickup idled as Quillerman looked into Betty's eyes for a long time, then: "Do you know a woman named Lorelle Dupree?"

"Yes, I thought she was the one you were talking about."

"Why did you think that?"

"Well, because she's different. She's an artist. They're all different. But she's no demon, and I think you oughtta be ashamed of yourself for saying so."

"Do you know her well?"

She pulled her head back and blinked several times and her lips remained pursed for a long moment before she spoke again. "She comes over now and again. I go see her sometimes. And she's just as nice as –"

"Who's nice?" Ed LaBianco asked, suddenly standing beside his wife.

Betty was startled and stumbled over her words, then said, "Lorelle Dupree. Pastors' saying she's some kinda demon."

Quillerman turned his gaze to Ed and his frown grew deeper. "Are you feeling all right, Ed?" he asked.

"Oh, I, um –" He rubbed his hand over his long pasty face, smoothing out the deep wrinkles for a moment, wrinkles that hadn't been there when he'd last attended church. " – I guess I haven't been, you know, getting a lot of sleep lately."

"Any particular reason?" Quillerman asked, although he knew the answer.

"That's not important," Ed muttered, dismissing it with a wave, then rubbing his puffy eyes with a thumb and forefinger. "What brings you over here, Pastor?"

Before Quillerman could respond, Betty said, "He's been driving up and down the street here, spreading some nonsense about Lorelle being a demon, some kind of, oh, I don't know, a vampire, or something."

Ed gave the pastor a tired frown and said, "That doesn't sound very Christian." In contrast to his words, Ed's voice was pleading rather than chastising and his eyes seemed to hold more desperation than protest.

Quillerman said, "Betty, may I have a word with your husband, please?"

"Go right ahead." She folded the slabs of her arms across her breasts with effort.

"I mean alone."

Pastor Quillerman flinched hard at the hatred that flashed in Betty's eyes for a moment. Her upper lip curled a bit, stopping just short of a hateful sneer. Then she turned and headed back toward the house, shouting at the reporters who stood nearby.

"Ed, that's not like her," Quillerman said softly. "That's not like Betty at all."

"Well ... we've both been fighting the flu, I think. She's probably just, um ... " He averted his eyes as he ran a fingernail along his lower lip. "She's just not feeling well, that's all."

Quillerman gave his next words some careful thought before speaking. "Tell me, Ed, how well do you know Lorelle Dupree?"

Ed turned away even further then and became more fidgety, plucking at his face, rubbing his hand again and again over what hair he had left. "She's just a neighbor, you know. Hasn't really been here long enough to –"

"You know what I've been saying is true, don't you, Ed?"

More agitation and nervousness. He cleared his throat several times, looked around without Quillerman's eyes.

"Look, Pastor, I just, um, I don't think it's, you know, a good idea for you to be riding up and down the street and –"

"You know it's true, don't you?"

Ed closed his eyes for a long moment, licked his lips, then opened his eyes again and looked straight into Quillerman's. "Look, please, just go, all right? Just go and we won't –"

"I'm here to help you, Ed," Quillerman whispered. "Please, let me help you."

Ed's mouth worked, but nothing came out. He took a deep breath and prepared to speak again, but Quillerman beat him to it.

"She's evil, Ed. She's evil and you know it. I don't know what she's done to you, but you know, and you know that it's wrong. You know she's twisting you, corrupting you from the inside out, and you know that if you let it go on, you will be lost."

Ed's mouth continued to work, but he didn't speak. Tears glistened in his eyes and his hands shook as he placed them on the edge of the window. "Pastor," he whispered tremulously, "I ... I don't ... know what's ... happening to us."

"To you and Betty?"

He nodded.

Quillerman leaned closer to him. "It's her. Your neighbor. Lorelle Dupree. You know I'm right don't you, Ed?"

"I ... yes, I believe so."

"What you need to do now is –"

Something caught his eye. He faced front, peered through the windshield and saw Sheri MacNeil standing on the sidewalk in front of her house up the street. She wore sneakers, sweat pants and a heavy blue terrycloth robe. She stared at the pickup for a long time, took a few reluctant steps into the street, stopped and started again. Finally, she stuffed her hands into the baggy pockets of her robe and headed toward the pickup as Ed LaBianco bowed his head and cried silently, murmuring to himself.

"Pastor Quillerman?" Sheri asked, looking over Ed's shoulder. She was a tall woman, very pretty with short blonde hair. "Pastor, what're you doing?"

"Haven't you been listening?"

She nodded. "So has Chris. He's...scared. And I don't think you should be – I mean, maybe you shouldn't – it's not a good idea to –"

"Are you scared, too, Sheri?" he asked.

She stood very still for a while, then nodded slowly.

Quillerman was relieved and surprised to have gotten through to anyone so soon. But these were people he knew, people from his church. What about the others in the neighborhood who did not know him, who would think he was crazy and how, under the influence of the creature that called itself Lorelle Dupree, might react violently to his efforts?

He turned to Ed and Sheri and began speaking to them quietly as –

– the reporters watched.

Alana leaned toward Steve and said, "They look like they know him."

Steve said, "Worse yet, they look like they're taking him seriously."

They watched for a while until the blonde woman turned from the pickup, folded her arms against the cold and headed back up the street. Alana and Steve followed her without hesitation, flanked by their cameramen. They shouted at her simultaneously, Steve saying, "Excuse me, miss, could I ask you a few questions?" while Alana called, "Miss, what can you tell us about Pastor Quillerman? What connection does he have to the Garrys? Miss?"

The woman lifted a hand to hold them back and shouted over her shoulder, "Not right now, please, I don't want to talk." Then she went back into her house, where a small pale face peered out the front window, tiny hands pressed against the pane.

Alana and Steve and the two cameramen were left standing in the middle of Deerfield. Before they could turn back, the shrill, tangy voice of the fat woman in the Muumuu sounded again and they spun around to see her jogging down her front walk toward her husband.

Alana patted her cameraman's arm and said, "Get this, get this."

"But there's nothing happening," he said.

Alana and Steve went around the pickup and back up on the sidewalk where Malcolm and Will taped the fat woman as she pushed her husband aside and said, "Well? Are you gonna stop this nonsense, or not?"

Her husband put a hand on her shoulder and quietly spoke to her, but she pushed him away angrily, put her fists to her enormous hips and leaned into the window, pushing her face close to Pastor Quillerman's. "People are gonna start calling the police, you know! People don't like to hear this kinda crap spouted at their front door!"

Her husband stepped forward again, took her arm and said, "Listen to me, Betty, he's –"

"Get away from me and let me speak!"

In a voice that contradicted his meek appearance, he shouted, "Dammit, Betty, you know he's right."

She stared at him in shock, her jaw slack, arms limp at her sides. Finally: "What did you say?"

"He's right. We both know he's right."

Neither of them moved for a long moment. The vapors of their breaths mingled in a small cloud before their faces.

"Why don't the two of you go inside and talk about this," Pastor Quillerman said softly? When they turned to him, he smiled and nodded encouragingly. "Please, go inside. We'll get together later."

"Thank you," the man said, then took his wife's hand. They turned and did as the pastor had said, ignoring Alana and Steve and the cameras as they passed. The man looked almost sick with sadness, while the woman seemed barely able to hold in her anger.

The reporters dove toward the pickup and Quiller man's open window, but he was already rolling it up. He put the pickup into gear and drove away slowly, his voice sounding over the loudspeaker once again.

"Dammit," Steve muttered, looking at his watch. "We're gonna have to go. We've got a deadline."

"You're leaving?" Alana asked, surprised.

"I think the only story here has already been reported," he said, nodding toward the Garry house.

"Weren't you listening? Those people actually believed him. They think their neighbor is a demon."

Steve grinned. "Gullible people aren't exactly news. This town's got more churches than gas stations." He turned to Malcolm and said, "We've a gotta get going." Then to Alana: "Nice meeting you." They went to their van.

"Let's stick around a while, Will," Alana said. "I've got a feeling this is gonna get weird."

She was right.

Chapter 22

The Mist

GEORGE and Robby Pritchard stood at their living room window watching Pastor Quiller man's pickup drive back and forth. Jen was seated in her dad's recliner behind them. She'd served them some stew earlier and the bowls were still on the coffee table. None of them had spoken for a while.

They'd watched Mr. and Mrs. LaBianco and then Sheri MacNeil approach the pickup, and they'd watched the reporters standing by, waiting patiently for a few crumbs. Occasionally they heard the voices of people shouting at Pastor Quillerman from their porches. They called him foul names and told him to keep his opinions and his religion to himself. But Quillerman ignored them and continued to warning of the danger they were in, appealing to the goodness in them, the goodness not yet stolen away by their new neighbor.

Across the street and one house to the north, Mr. and Mrs. Weyland came out to the sidewalk, both wearing bathrobes. Mrs. Weyland had carried a stained brown paper bag and her husband a plastic green garbage bag. When Pastor Quillerman drove by, they reached into their bags and began to throw garbage at him – cans, cartons, boxes and old slimy fruits and vegetables that made a thick wet mess on the pickup's hood and windshield. As they threw garbage, they shouted at him to go away before they shot out his tires and removed him bodily from the neighborhood themselves. Pastor Quillerman spoke to them calmly through the loudspeaker, imploring them to take a look at themselves, to think about what they were doing and why, and to think about what kind of people they'd been just a few days ago, before they'd met their new neighbor.

And through it all, the odd mist had remained.

Once things had calmed down a little and the only action outside was Pastor Quillerman's slow and monotonous trips up and down the street, Robby paid close attention to the mist. It moved slowly, sometimes changing direction abruptly, and occasionally a smoky tendril or two of the mist would rise fluidly above the restless surface, reminding Robby of Lorelle standing naked outside the glass door while the mist crawled up her body. He closed his eyes a moment and gave his head a couple of hard shakes. He didn't want to think of her.

The afternoon darkened with the approach of evening. The streetlights on Deerfield came on as the clouds went from murky gray to a mottled charcoal. Quillerman turned on the pickup's headlights and their beams gave an even eerier quality to the mist. Robby watched as it moved with what almost appeared to be a life of its own ... a purpose. His eyes scanned the mist from left to right until he spotted something strange at the base of a power pole on the opposite side of the street between the LaBianco house and the Parkers'. Robby squinted and leaned forward a bit, not quite sure of what he was seeing. A tentacle of mist seemed to be winding its way slowly up the pole.

Robby reached over, tapped his George's arm and said, "Dad? You ever seen mist do anything like this before?"

George looked out the window with heavy, preoccupied eyes. "Not around here," he drawled flatly.

"Isn't it kinda weird?"

"I don't know," he shrugged. "Not really."

"I mean that." Robby pointed at the power pole.

The mist, winding steadily up the pole like a snake, had nearly reached the top. Once it did, it moved quickly and engulfed the gray-metal transformer in a small cloud.

George said, "What in the hell is —"

Before he finished his sentence, there was an explosion of sparks that rained down on the ground and –

– the streetlights went dark at the same moment that –

– the light behind every window on Deerfield went out and –

– the Pritchard house became dark and the refrigerator's hum fell silent and –

– the mist that had climbed up the power pole dissolved quickly as the sparks that fell down around it hit the ground and bounced and rolled like glowing marbles.

"What the hell was that?" Jen asked, her voice weak and panicky.

"I-I'm not sure," George said, putting a hand on her shoulder, "but why don't you go get the flashlights out of the tool drawer in the kitchen."

She nodded and left the room. George moved to a phone, put the receiver to his ear a moment, then replaced it, saying, "Dead."

Robby watched the reporter outside. She'd been sitting on the hood of her car with the cameraman standing beside her when the transformer exploded. She had fallen from the car and landed in a protective crouch while the man had spun around, leaned through the car's open window and grabbed his camera. But Robby knew they hadn't seen the mist climbing that power pole as he had.

"Mr. Prosky told me she could move around as a mist," Robby said quietly.

"You mean Lorelle?"

Robby nodded. "He said he'd seen her do it."

George took a moment to digest that bit of information, then pressed both hands over his face and rubbed them up and down, sighing. "Boy oh boy oh boy."

Pastor Quiller man's pickup appeared again, heading south on Deerfield, but it was going quite a bit faster than before until –

– it pulled over to the curb and screeched to a halt and Pastor Quillerman got out, hobbled around the pickup and stopped to look about him frantically at the mist because –

– it was swirling rapidly over the ground pulling away from houses and tree trunks and shrubbery and fences, pulling away quickly as if it were being sucked away, and –

– Pastor Quillerman staggered in a tight circle as he watched the mist rushing away around him, his eyes and mouth open wide with surprise and confusion as his head jerked around in a frightened, bird-like manner because – – the mist was rushing into Lorelle Dupree's house as if the house were a giant vacuum cleaner, and –

– Pastor Quiller man spun around and looked at their window, then hurried up the walk toward the front door, his limp making him zigzag all the way to the porch steps.

George rushed to the front door and opened it just as Pastor Quiller man stumbled through the doorway saying breathlessly, "It was her ... the mist ... she was in it ... she-she was the mist!" He leaned against the wall and pressed a hand to his chest as he tried to catch his breath.

"You okay?" George asked.

"Can I get you something?" Robby asked.

Jen appeared with three heavy-duty Maglite flashlights and handed one to George, one to Robby, and kept one for herself. With all three lights shining, George took Pastor Quillerman's elbow and led him into the living room. Once the pastor was on the sofa, Jen sat beside him, George across from him in the recliner, and Robby remained standing.

"I should have known," Pastor Quiller man said, his voice dry and hoarse. He shook his head with frustration. "I knew there was something wrong with that mist. Why didn't it occur to me?"

"No, Pastor Quiller man, I should have known," Robby said. "Ronald Prosky told me. I just ... forgot, I guess, with everything else on my mind I –"

"Don't worry about it, son," Quiller man said. "It's too late now."

"But she's been out there all this time, probably going from house to house. She came to me at the glass door in the dining room. She came out of that damned mist, I should've known."

"She came to my bedroom window," Jen said softly.

George nodded, saying, "She came to me while I was trying to fix the hole in the bedroom wall."

Quiller man said, "She might have gotten into some of the other houses, but she couldn't get in here because of the names on the front door." He looked around at the three of them quickly. "The first thing we have to do is make sure she doesn't get into any more houses. We have to keep her from swaying these people. We need to...trap her somehow. With her out of the way, maybe we can talk some sense into everyone else on this street."

"How?" George asked.

Quiller man closed his eyes and sighed hopelessly.

"What about the three names?" Robby asked. They all turned to him. "I mean the three angels' names on the door. If they'll keep her out of here, maybe they'll keep her in over there."

"But you said she burst out of here while Prosky was writing the names on the door," George said. "What would keep her from doing the same thing over there?"

Robby chewed on his lower lip a moment, then said, "She rushed out of here before Prosky finished writing the names. He hadn't completed the circle around them yet. Maybe if he had, she wouldn't have been able to get out. I think I can do it fast enough – as long as it doesn't have to be done in charcoal. " He gave Quiller man a questioning look.

"I'm not sure if it makes any difference," the pastor said with a shrug. "I was not familiar with that particular method."

"I could use, um ... well, a Magic Marker, maybe," Robby said. "We've got some around here somewhere."

"Tool drawer in the kitchen," Jen said, as she stood and headed into the kitchen, following the beam of her flashlight.

"Can you write that fast, Robby?" George asked.

"I can try."

"You'll have to do more than try."

"He will," Pastor Quiller man said with calm certainty.

* * * *

The neighborhood was tomb silent. With the streetlights out of working order and all the windows dark, Deerfield was blacker than Robby had ever seen it before.

He had practiced writing the three angels' names and circling them with a Magic Marker several times on a yellow legal pad until the movements of his hand and wrist became automatic and fluid. Pastor Quiller man had said a prayer, and at his dad's insistence, Robby had gone out the back door and rounded the house cautiously, just in case someone had been watching the front door.

With a flashlight tucked beneath his arm and a Magic Marker in a pocket of his black jacket, Robby walked along the tall wooden fences that separated their yard from the next. When he reached the sidewalk, he walked a few yards north before crossing the street, then moved south toward Lorelle's house.

The reporter's car was still parked at the curb several yards past Lorelle's house but he couldn't see the woman or her cameraman. He hoped they wouldn't see him.

His heart pounded in his throat and, in spite of the cold, he felt sweaty, as if he'd run a great distance. He rounded a corner of sharply trimmed shrubs and stepped onto Lorelle's lawn, stopping for a moment to stare at the front door. He couldn't see the door itself, only a vaguely rectangular opening that was darker than black. The door could be open for all he knew. Lorelle could be standing in that blackness watching ... waiting for him ... Lorelle or her dogs.

He realized he'd been holding his breath and let it out suddenly in a swirling vapor, then started across the lawn as −

* * * *

– Pastor Quillerman knelt on one knee by the sofa, praying, while George and Jen stood at the front window. The flashlights were out and the house was dark.

"I can't see him," Jen said.

George pointed. "There he is, on her lawn."

Pastor Quillerman prayed quietly at the sofa, then stopped abruptly and remained silent for a long moment, until George and Jen turned toward his vague shape in the darkness.

"Where is Karen?" the pastor asked.

"She's in the guest bedr –" George froze. "Oh, God," he breathed, flicking the flashlight on and rushing out of the room and down the hall. Jen and Pastor Quillerman followed him. He pounded on the door several times and shouted, "Karen! Karen, what're you doing? Are you awake?"

They listened silently, but there was no response.

George tried the doorknob, but it was locked. They pounded the door and called her again.

Nothing.

Swearing under his breath, George spun around and rushed into the master bedroom, leaving Jen and Pastor Quillerman in the dark hall.

* * * *

Robby walked carefully on the balls of his feet up the front steps of Lorelle Dupree's house, taking the Magic Marker from his jacket pocket. He took the cap off, put it in his pocket and stood before the door in complete darkness.

He listened closely for any sounds and when he heard nothing, he took the flashlight in hand, turned it on and lifted the pen. He paused, took a deep breath which he let out slowly, then began to write as fast as he could.

* * * *

Jen and Pastor Quillerman watched the darting flashlight beam in the master bedroom as George pulled out a dresser drawer, shuffled through its contents, slammed it, then opened another. He finally returned with a key, which he slipped into the guest room lock and turned. He pushed the door open, calling, "Karen? Hon?" and shined the flashlight into the room.

The window was open and the room was empty.

Karen was gone.

"Oh, god," Quillerman whispered.

* * * *

Robby's hand raced through the letters of the last angel's name as his heart beat faster and his throat grew tight. The instant he finished the last name, his hand swept quickly around all three, enclosing them in a circle as –

– a sound erupted from inside the house that was worse than anything Robby had ever heard, a screaming sound more monstrous and inhuman than he thought possible, and it grew louder and louder, impossibly loud, until –

– every window in Lorelle's house exploded outward and shards of broken glass cascaded over the lawn and sidewalk.

* * * *

George and Jen and Pastor Quillerman stood frozen in the doorway of the guest room, their eyes wide as they listened to the horrible sound from across the street. George broke away from them muttering, "Karen, oh my god, Karen," and ran down the hall.

* * * *

Robby staggered backward down the porch steps and the flashlight beam swept over Lorelle's marked door as it bulged outward until it splintered in the middle, and –

– the sound only grew louder, until Robby could feel it

slicing through his bones as he ran across the lawn, glass
crunching under his feet, until a familiar voice shouted –

–"Robby!"

The voice caught him so completely by surprise that
his legs failed him and he tumbled to the ground, rolling
over jagged pieces of glass that cut through his clothes and
skin. He rolled over, sat up, faced the house and aimed the
flashlight in the direction of the voice, hoping it was not the
voice he thought he'd heard.

The beam fell on his mother. She stood on the other side
of a broken rectangular window a few feet to the left of the
front door. She was naked and her skin was an unhealthy
white in the flashlight's beam. Shadow figures moved behind
her in the dark.

"Robby!" she shouted. "What have you done, Robby?"

"M-Muh-Mom?"

The mind-numbing scream continued.

"Damn you, Robby, damn you!" she shouted, her arms
stiff at her sides, fists clenched, her whole body trembling.
Her breasts swayed as she shouted at him.

Robby scrambled to his feet, ignoring his cuts, and began
to walk backward as he screamed at her, "What are you
doing in there!"

"You'll pay for this, you little bastard, you'll pay!" The
hatred in her face was so intense that it sickened Robby.

The horrible sound stopped.

The shadowy figures behind his mom moved away, then
even she disappeared into the darkness as Lorelle Dupree's
thick, distorted voice said, "That wasn't very nice, Raaww-
beeee."

He lowered the flashlight because he didn't want to see
it, not again, but even without light, he could see those eyes
shimmering in the darkness and he turned and ran across
the sidewalk and into the street, dropping the flashlight
along the way, but moving ahead blindly, anyway. Getting
away from that house and what he knew was inside was
more important than the flashlight.

"Eat you, Raaaww-beeee!" the Lorelle-creature roared. "I'm going to eat you alive!"

He tried to listen only to his breathing and his dangerously rapid heartbeat as he ran across the street, trying to ignore the creature's voice, but –

– there was another figure moving toward him in the dark and Robby felt panic closing his throat and he was about to scream when –

– his dad turned on his flashlight and said, "Robby, you okay?"

"Yuh-yeah." He took a moment to catch his breath as his dad put an arm around him to hold him up. "Mom's over there, Dad, sh-she's in the house ... with that thuh-thing."

George looked at Lorelle's house and said with almost childlike helplessness, "What're we gonna do, Robby? What're we gonna do to get her back?"

"I, uh ... I don't think she wants to come back, Dad."

"Oh, god. What ... what have we done?"

They embraced and stood there at the edge of the street until Pastor Quillerman came out and let them back into the house.

* * * *

Alana Carson said "What the hell was that?"

"I don't know," Will replied softly, "but it didn't sound fun."

They'd been sitting in the car debating whether or not to get a bite to eat and find a restroom when it happened. Now their hunger and bladders were forgotten.

"Look," Will said, "if you wanna stay here and do some kind of report on this – whatever this is – that's fine, but I want out, okay? I'm just gonna quietly back out of this one. You can keep the car if you want and I'll walk into town from here."

"'I need you Will."

"No you don't. Keep the camera, too. It's easy to use."

"You'll lose your job."

"Fine. Let 'em fire me. There's some really weird shit going on here and I don't want to look into it any more than we have. Whatever made that sound is not friendly, and it's in that house right over there."

"I don't understand why no one is calling the police," Alana said, looking around at the other houses.

"Because there's something wrong with this whole fucking neighborhood. Something's not right about this place, about these people. Can't you feel it?"

Alana turned toward him in the seat. "In that case, this story could really do something for us."

"Like what? Get us killed?"

"No, I mean for our reputations, our careers. Look around. You see any other reporters here? Nope. We're it. We could be sitting on a gold mine here. Now grab that camera and let's go get some –"

"No."

She sighed. "Tell you what, Will, if you stick with me, I might just break my own rule."

"What rule?"

"My rule about not fooling around with co-workers."

"Oh that one. That was weeks ago. I expected you to say that. Just thought I'd give it a shot."

"C'mon, Will." She took his hand. "Please."

He thought about it a while, then growled, "Shit," and opened the car door.

* * * *

Pastor Quillerman stayed on the front porch while George and Robby went inside and closed the door behind them.

Quillerman stared across the street at Lorelle's house, reached into his pocket and jingled his keys as he murmured, "Now we can get something done."

He went down the porch steps and headed for his pickup.

Chapter 23

In the Street

INSIDE, Jen followed George and Robby to the living room where they fell heavily onto the sofa. They sat there silently for a long while with Jen staring at them, frightened.

"What wrong?" she whispered finally. When they didn't reply, she moved toward them and, with panic in her voice, asked, "What's happened? Where's Mom? Dad? Where is she?"

George stared at her with empty, frightened eyes.

The pickup started outside.

George turned toward the window slowly, stood and looked outside.

The pickup's headlights cut through the neighborhood's blackness like swords. It pulled away from the curb slowly, easing all the way up the street and then turning around before Pastor Quillerman finally spoke into the loudspeaker.

"I know that the creature of which I spoke earlier has visited you today," he said. "I know that she has tried to warn you about me, probably instructed you to get rid of me. But I am still here. I hope you will listen to me and I hope you will think carefully about what I have to say."

The pickup reached the end of the street and turned around again.

* * * *

Alana said, "I'm gonna go stand in front of the damned thing."

"Didn't do any good before," Will said.

"I won't move. I'll jump on the hood if I have to."

"I suppose you want it on tape."

"Of course. What good is it if we don't get it on tape?"
She stepped off the sidewalk and into the street.

* * * *

Pastor Quillerman lifted his foot off the accelerator
and the pickup slowed to a stop. He stared at the woman
standing before the pickup as he continued to talk into the
microphone.

"Come out, please. Come out and talk with me. Let's
all talk together. I think if you listened to one another, if
you simply looked at one another, you would realize what's
been happening around you. You would realize what this
woman – this creature – has done to your neighbors, and to
you. So please come out here and let's talk together."

The reporter shouted, "I'd like to talk to you, Pastor."

"You have my word that I am not here to proselytize or
preach," he went on, ignoring her. "I am not here to recruit
members for my church. I am only here to help people who
I know are in trouble. You are all in trouble here, and I beg
you to make it stop. Please come out here, all of you, and
talk. Please."

The reporter waved her cameraman over and he stood
before the pickup while she went to Pastor Quillerman's
window. She rapped her knuckles on the glass and said.
"What woman are you talking about? What has she done?"

"I'm sorry," he said, "but I can't talk right now."

Her shoulders sagged with frustration and she stared at
him.

Pastor Quillerman lifted the microphone again, opened
his mouth, but said nothing because –

– there was an odd rumbling sound coming from the
darkness to the left. The woman heard it, too, and turned,
as Quillerman did, in the direction of the sound.

Quillerman could see nothing yet, but the sound grew

louder. He started to roll down the window so he could hear better, but –

– the man standing in front of the pickup shouted, "Oh, fuck!" and ran to Quillerman's right, into the darkness, hugging his camera to his chest, as –

– an enormous malamute ran into the glow of the headlights and faced the pickup, black lips pulled back over long glistening fangs, crouched low and ready to pounce. But the sound the creature made was not the sound of a mere dog. It was a much bigger, deeper sound than that of any dog Quillerman had ever encountered, and –

– its eyes glowed.

It snapped at the air, clacking its fangs together.

The reporter standing beside the pickup screamed and slammed herself against the door.

The dog inched closer to the pickup as its entire body shuddered. Two long black bonelike limbs suddenly shot upward from its shoulders, spread and unfolded into broad, bat-like wings. With one sudden movement of the wings, the creature was on the hood of the pickup, its face little more than an inch from the windshield. Its growl grew louder as its lips pulled back even farther ... and farther ... until they peeled away to reveal black, ripply skin beneath.

Pastor Quillerman lifted the microphone to his mouth and shouted, "In the name of god the father and his son Jesus Christ and all that is holy, I command you to leave this place!"

The creature rose up on its hind legs, swept its wings madly up and down and released a cry that made Quillerman's eyes tear up and his bowels tremble. When it dropped back down on all fours, any resemblance to a dog was gone. Its body trembled and a thick white foam dribbled from its stubby black snout. It snapped at the windshield and its fangs nicked the glass, then it looked Quillerman in the eyes and its glistening black lips curled into a grotesque mutation of a grin.

"Whatsamatter, Quillerman?" the creature asked in a gleeful, retching voice that was neither male nor female.

"Don'tcha wanna join your wife and sons? Don'tcha wanna join your wife, the dyke, and your cocksucking sons?"

Quillerman's face twisted in horror and he clenched his eyes shut, trying to block the flood of memories that he had avoided for years. The last time he'd seen his family they were all dead by his oldest son's hand – his wife on the bed, his boys lying in a hideous, bloody embrace with their eyes open and their skin the color of dirty snow, and –

– Quiller man whispered to himself, "No, no, that's over, it's behind me and –" He lifted the microphone to his mouth. " – and I command you to leave this place in the name of Jesus Christ!"

Two things happened at once: the creature vomited explosively, shooting a thick black substance on the windshield, and it shot backward off the hood of the pickup, shrieking. It landed in a clumsy heap on the pavement, several feet in front of the pickup.

"In the name of –" Quiller man began again, but the creature flapped its wings and rose from the ground, hovering for a moment as it stared straight into Quillerman's eyes, then released a cry so full of hatred it made Quillerman briefly nauseated.

It was gone in seconds.

Quillerman couldn't move for a while. One hand clutched the steering wheel, the other clutched the microphone and all his knuckles were white and fingers were numb. Suddenly, as if a spell had been broken, his hands and arms relaxed and he looked out the window to his left. At first, he thought the reporter had gone, but then he saw the top of her head rising slowly. She had ducked down beside the pickup. Her eyes were wide, face pale, and she stared at him as if she didn't know where she was.

Quillerman got out of the pickup and asked, "Are you all right, Miss?"

"What ... the fuck ... was that?" she asked, but there was more amazement in her voice than fear. Quillerman was quite amazed to see that she seemed about to burst into a grin.

Before Quillerman could reply, the cameraman staggered

around the pickup and joined them. The woman grabbed his lapels and shook him, saying, "Did you see that? I mean, did you see that? Did you get it? Oh, please, Will, tell me you got that on tape, tell me you got it!"

He stared at her a moment, then said in a barely level voice that rose as he spoke, "I didn't get it on tape because I was too busy shitting my pants! Now do you believe me? Now can we leave?"

"You go right ahead if you want, Will, but if you put a hook in my tongue you couldn't drag me away from this story. Just leave your camera."

"I think he's right," Quillerman said. "You'd better go. It wouldn't be a good idea to stay here any –"

Something caught his eye and he looked up the street.

Flashlight beams were cutting through the darkness on both sides of the street.

People were coming out of their houses and walking slowly toward the pickup. First, a man and woman. Then a child. Two teenagers with a woman. And there were others. Their steps were uneven and some were limping, but they were coming. Quillerman whispered, "Good. Good." He stepped around the reporter and went to meet them.

* * * *

Jen gripped George's arm and said, "Daddy, what's happened to Mom? Why won't you tell me?"

He'd been watching out the window silently, unable to respond to Jen's questions about Karen. What could he tell her? That Mom had decided she preferred to be with the new neighbor?

"She's over at Lorelle's," Robby finally said.

Jen stared at him in silent horror, shaking her head. "No," she whispered. "We have to get her. Did you hear me? We have to get her, Daddy!"

George put his arm around her and said, "We're going to try, honey." To Robby: "I'm going outside to talk with Pastor Quillerman."

"I'll come with you," Robby said.

Jen said "Me, too."

George looked from Robby to Jen and was about to protest and tell them to stay in the house. But he saw their determination and said nothing. They followed him out.

As they headed down the front walk, they saw the others nearing Quillerman from both directions, coming out of the darkness in small groups, some with flashlights, a couple carrying kerosene lanterns with golden light that flickered over shadowy faces.

"Hello, George," Pastor Quillerman said quietly as George approached.

"What's going on?" George asked.

"My prayers have been answered. They're coming to talk. I think we might make some progress now."

Footsteps scritched to a halt on the pavement as people gathered around the pickup. Flashlight beams crisscrossed in the darkness and the people behind them were reduced to murky, faceless shadows.

George squinted against the lights and searched for a familiar face or figure, but could not make out enough details in the dark to recognize anyone.

"My husband is gone," a woman said in a voice soggy with tears.

"Our daughter is missing," a man said.

A woman beside him added, "One minute she was in the house and the next she was gone."

A man stammered, "I truh-tried to ... to suh-strangle my w-wife today and ... and I –" His words dissolved into sobs.

"It's all right, honey," a woman whispered reassuringly, "that's over now."

Others spoke up and their words overlapped:

"I can't find my wife."

"What has that woman done to us?"

"We had a fight with our son today and I-I ... hit him ... for the first time ever, and now he's disappeared." "We're coming apart, our whole family is just coming apart."

"My husband said he'd kill me if I came out here. I had to sneak out of the house."

Pastor Quillerman raised his arms to quiet them down. "I know what you're going through," he said. "I understand your fear and your feelings of guilt. I realize those of you with loved ones missing are especially upset right now. But please listen to me for just a few minutes."

George listened as Quillerman told them the truth about Lorelle Dupree. He told them everything that Robby had told George that morning, all the things that George wouldn't listen to then. They listened silently as Quillerman spoke in his best pulpit voice. Then:

"Thanks to young Robby here, we think she's trapped in her own house right now." He stepped over to Robby's side and put an arm around his shoulders. "Unfortunately, some of your family members are in there with her. They are there of their own free will, just as many of you gave in to her of your own free will. But you might be able to change that. With words of encouragement to your sons and daughters and spouses, you might be able to draw them out of her house. If we all resist her, reject her, there will be nothing to keep her here. She will have no choice but to go."

"Why can't we kill the bitch?" Mr. LaBianco asked.

Quillerman hesitated. "To be honest, I don't know how to kill her."

"She seduced my husband!" a woman shouted. "In just a few days, that bitch destroyed my marriage!"

"Please!" Quillerman said, raising his arms again. "I know you're angry and you have every reason to be, but you must let go of that anger. It will only weaken you. It demeans you, and that is precisely what she wants. She feeds on it. It's important to let go of that anger and hatred. We're all human, we are weak. We must pray to god for –"

"I don't pray," a man said coldly.

"Yes, I understand that some of you may not have any religious beliefs. Perhaps many of you. But you can still let go of the anger and hatred you feel toward her. You can –"

"I'm not so sure I believe what you say about her," another man said.

Quillerman turned to George in desperation.

George's mouth opened and closed as he searched frantically for something to say.

"Some of you probably know George Pritchard, here," Quillerman said. "He has been going through many of the same things you have." He looked at George again, nodding encouragingly.

George said, "My family and I ... well, like all of you, I'm sure ... we got involved with Lorelle and we became uh... my wife Karen is, um, she's over their right now, and –"

"I don't give a damn, Pritchard," Mr. Weyland barked. "All I want to know is how to get my daughter out of there and how to get rid of that cunt."

Quillerman sighed. "Please listen to yourself. That kind of attitude is what she wants! You must have compassion for your neighbors, think of the pain they're going through, too, and don't –"

"I'm thinking of my husband right now," a woman said.

A man shouted, "And we're thinking of our son!"

"I thought you wanted to help us," another man said. "You're a man of god. Wouldn't god want us to stop that slut?"

"Yeah!" Mrs. LaBianco shouted. "Christ kicked the moneychangers out of the temple, why shouldn't we kick that twat off our block?"

"How the hell're we supposed to do that?" Mr. Parker asked.

"Drag her out by the hair if we have to!" Mrs. LaBianco replied.

"No, no, please listen!" Pastor Quillerman shouted.

"We are listening," Mr. Weyland growled, "But you're not telling us anything!"

"I'm trying to tell you something," Quillerman said, his voice lower now, more calm than before. "I have been through the exact same thing you're going through! I wish someone had come along and tried to help –" His voice

broke and he cleared his throat, then lowered his voice a bit.
" – tried to help my family. But no one did. So I haven't had
a family for many years, thanks to a creature just like the
one in there," he said, pointing at Lorelle's house. "But that
doesn't have to happen to you."

"It's already happened to us!" a woman shouted. George
recognized the voice as that of Trish Mason. She and her
husband lived at the end of the street with their three kids.
"My husband is gone and I want to get him back before it's
too late. You're not telling me how to get him back."

"He has to make that choice himself," Quillerman
answered.

"What if we make the choice for them?" Weyland asked.

"Fine," Quillerman said. "Then why aren't you storming
the place? Why aren't you bursting in there and rescuing
those people? I think it's because deep down inside, even if
you don't admit it to yourself, you're afraid of Lorelle Dupree.
But I'm trying to tell you that you don't need to be afraid of
her! You have a much greater power at your disposal. Your
love for your sons and daughters and husbands and wives
could bring them back to you if you'd just let it. But you
mustn't give in to the dark, angry part of yourselves that
she's trying so hard to bring out! She wants you to –"

"He's a madman!" a woman's voice shouted from a
distance.

Everyone turned and shined their flashlights in that
direction.

Lorelle stood in the same window in which Robby had
seen Karen earlier. She wore a red robe open just enough to
bare a narrow strip of pale flesh down the front.

"Don't listen to him," she said. "He's a liar. A crazy liar!
He'd be in a mental hospital if he didn't have his pulpit to
hide behind!"

"Don't listen to her!" Pastor Quillerman shouted, raising
his arms high. "Wear the armor of righteousness! Fend off
the arrows of evil!"

"Listen to his holier-than-thou talk!" Lorelle shouted at

them. "Have I talked to any of you that way? Have I done anything to any of you? I've done nothing!"

The crowd was silent. No one responded, but looks were exchanged, brows creased.

"If I've done anything at all, I've given you pleasure. You know that's true, each one of you. You know in your hearts that this lunatic is lying to you. And as for your friends and loved ones who are here with me ... they are here because they want to be. You may not like it, but they are here by choice. " Over her shoulder: "Isn't that right?"

A chorus of voices rose in agreement from the darkness behind Lorelle.

George put his arms around Robby and Jen and said, "Go back to the house."

"That was Mom's voice!" Jen shouted, pulling away from him. "I heard her!" She took several steps toward Lorelle's house as she shouted, "Mom! Come home! Please come home! Mom?"

Silence. Everyone stared at the window, at Lorelle.

"I don't want to!" Karen shouted.

A whimper escaped Jen as she spun around and faced George. He embraced her and whispered in her ear, "Please, honey, please go back to the house now."

Before she could do as he had said, a frightened man's voice called, "Carl? Carl, your mom and I want you to come home now. We're sorry for what happened earlier and we'll –"

"Fuck off!" a young male voice shouted back.

"Marlene?" a man shouted. "Marlene? Hon? Please come out of –"

From behind Lorelle, a woman giggled drunkenly and the man who had called for Marlene whispered, "Oh, my God."

Lorelle said, "I don't care what he says – these people have chosen to be here and no matter what you do, they won't leave until they choose to leave. They don't want to come back to you right now." She paused, then: "Of course ... you could always come join us."

"No!" Quillerman roared, raising a hand in the air. "If you go in there with them, you'll all be lost!"

Laughter came from Lorelle's house. When they turned toward it again, she was gone and the window was black once again ... but undefinable shapes moved in that blackness and laughter rang out now and then as if a party were going on, as if toasts were being made and jokes were being told...

"If they don't want to be with us," Mr. Weyland said, "why should we go in there and get them"

Everyone spoke at once and their voice blended into an incoherent babble, but the tone was unmistakably one of angry agreement.

"Wait a minute, please!" Pastor Quillerman shouted. "You're not hearing me!"

"We hear you fine!" someone sneered. "You're just not worth listening to!"

"Wait, please, aren't there any Christians here?" Quillerman asked.

Several voices rose affirmatively.

"But," Mrs. LaBianco said, "being a Christian doesn't mean I have to sit still for that woman, that-that ... whore in there! She doesn't have any of my family with her, but I've been married for thirty-one years and I don't take kindly to some bitch coming into my life and screwing up my marriage!"

"But you allowed her to!" Quillerman said.

"Yeah," a woman replied angrily, "just like my husband is probably allowing that slut to do god knows what with him in there right now!"

Quillerman spread his arms and cried, "But most of you here allowed her to do these things! How can you pass judgment on –"

A heavy black flashlight flew out of the darkness and struck Pastor Quillerman with a sharp crack across the bridge of his nose. He fell back against the pickup and released a whimpering sigh as he slid limply to the ground.

George and Robby knelt beside him and George shouted

at the crowd, "He was just trying to help you! Why did you do that?"

Quillerman, stunned and bleeding, rolled his head back and forth slowly as he groaned.

No one responded to George's question. They simply stared at the fallen pastor, moving their flashlight beams over him as they whispered and hissed to one another conspiratorially.

"That's probably going to need stitches," George muttered.

Robby whispered, "Dad, I don't like this. I'm scared. These people are getting ... well, mean."

"I know." George looked around at them, snapping at one another and arguing. He tried to make out what they were saying.

" – should've listened to the pastor."

"I've been a Christian all my life, I don't need some lunatic telling me –"

" – say we just go over there and bring them out."

"Hey, I've got a can of Kerosene in the garage," Weyland said, "we can take it over there, empty it on her house and –

" – but what about all the others in the house with –"

"Fuck 'em if they want to be with her. What was that the old guy said? Something about wearing the armor of righteousness? Well, there's nothing righteous about anybody who wants to be with her!"

"My god," George breathed, closing his eyes. "This is insane, completely insane."

"Dad, what should we do?" Robby hissed. "Mom's in there, and these people are talking about burning the place down!"

George turned to the pastor, who was trying to sit up. He took a handkerchief from his back pocket and handed it to Quillerman, then asked, "You gonna be okay, Pastor?"

Quillerman nodded and waved him away with one shaky hand while pressing the handkerchief to his bleeding nose with the other.

George stood and looked around until he spotted Jen. She was standing in the middle of the street, staring at Lorelle's house. Quiet sobs shook her shoulders. George gripped Robby's arm and said, "I want you to get your sister, go into the house and wait there, okay?"

Robby nodded.

"Don't come out unless I call you and don't let anyone else but me into the house, got it?"

Another nod.

George patted Robby's back and the boy hurried to his sister and led her out of the street toward the house. Once they were inside, George looked around again, this time looking for nothing in particular ... except, perhaps, for something to say to them, something that might get through to them. He spotted Alana and got an idea.

After jumping up on the pickup's hood, George shouted. "Hey, everybody, listen to me."

Silence. Shadowed faces looked up at him.

"What you're thinking of doing," he said, "is wrong. I understand how you feel, but it won't work. See these people over here?" He pointed at Alana and Will. "Well, they're reporters and they've got a television camera. If you torch that house with these people inside, it'll be on videotape. You'll be on videotape."

Alana stepped forward and said loudly, "The camera is rolling now. We have all of this on tape. Would anyone care to comment?"

There was a sudden stir as Mrs. LaBianco plowed through the crowd growling, "Aaarre yooouu stiilll heeere?" She shot out of the crowd with both enormous, flabby arms outstretched and –

– Alana screamed as Mrs. LaBianco threw herself on her and –

– that was the beginning of the bloodshed.

Chapter 24

Mob

WITH no moon or stars in the thickly clouded sky, the neighborhood was shrouded in a darkness so dense it appeared artificial, as if the entire neighborhood were nothing more than a set on a Hollywood sound stage with false fronts and rolled-out lawns, plastic hedges and empty car bodies parked in the driveways. The scene was made even more surreal by the small crown of people standing in the street, sending up a loud chorus of approval as Betty LaBianco threw herself on Alana Carson, knocked her to the pavement and began to beat her relentlessly with fleshy white fists.

Alana's screams rose above the voices of the neighborhood's residents as she kicked and hit at the fat woman who straddled her and pummeled her face and chest.

Will lowered his camera immediately, rushed forward, hooked his left arm around Betty's neck and began heaving backward to pull her off Alana, shouting, "Help me, somebody help me!"

George was already on his way. He grabbed one of Betty's arms and pulled along with Will, but she continued to hit Alana with her free fist, now slick with blood, and growled through clenched teeth, "Fucking reporters can't find your keep your fucking noses out of –"

She stopped long enough to swing her fist up and punch George in the groin.

He doubled over and hit the ground hard with both hands clutching his groin. He gagged as he rolled over the pavement, his eyes stinging with tears, stomach burning as if it were tearing open.

"Stop, Betty!" Pastor Quillerman shouted in a hoarse voice. "Please stop, Betty!" He struggled to get to his feet, but the spinning in his head kept sending him back to the ground. Frustrated, his face streaked with blood, Quillerman looked up to see four men break away from the crowd and rush toward the scuffle. Quillerman leaned back against the pickup, relieved that the reporter was going to get some help, but –

– each of the four men took hold of Will, pulled him off of Betty and slammed him to the ground. His camera crunched and chittered as it slid over the pavement, scattering broken pieces in every direction. The men hunched over Will and began to beat him with their fists and their flashlights, to kick him and stomp him.

As he kicked Will, Mr. Weyland spat, "Fucking reporters've ruined this whole fucking country is what they've done!"

George rose to his hands and knees, teeth still clenched so hard that his jaw throbbed. He recognized Weyland's voice, although it sounded distorted and foul, and he looked up to see the men hammering their fists and kicking wildly. As he watched helplessly, the deep burning ache that radiated from his testicles into his abdomen was joined by a sickening fear that crept all the way up into his throat. Something was happening around him. The texture of the night was changing. The very air was suddenly charged with a malignant electricity that stiffened the hairs on the back of George's neck and made his skin crawl. Groaning at his pain and nausea, he got up and staggered to find his balance as –

– Betty LaBianco rolled off of Alana Carson's still, sprawled body and stood. Her muumuu was stiff and dark now, and glistened wetly in the glow of the flashlights and lanterns. She slapped her blood-slicked hands together as if she were dusting them off and turned to the four men as –

– they stood and backed away from their victim, whose

blood was splattered all over them and was spreading over the pavement in a growing pool. They exchanged looks with one another, then with Betty, then they turned to the crowd.

"Okay," Weyland said, "let's go get the cunt who started all this!"

"Wait!" a man shouted. "Our son is in that house!"

"Then you've already lost him," Weyland replied.

Quillerman cried, "No, that's not true!"

Weyland turned to Quillerman and began walking toward him slowly.

"Those people are not lost" Quillerman went on. "But you will be if you do this! You're allowing her to bring out the worst in you, the evil in you!"

Weyland towered over the pastor, fists clenched, and said in a low, gravelly voice, "We're doing god's work –" He spat the last word. " – pastor!" Then he pulled his foot back and kicked Pastor Quillerman in the face.

Blood spurted from the pastor's nose and mouth as his head snapped back and cracked against the side of the pickup. He slid sideways until he hit the ground, unconscious.

Weyland turned as George stumbled in front of him and gripped his shoulder. "I'm telling you," he said, "Don't do this! My wife is in that house! And your daughter's –"

"My daughter's chosen to be in there," Weyland growled, pushing George away from him. "And as far as I'm concerned, that means my daughter's just as much a godless whore as that bitch she's with, who just might be a murderer if she had anything to do with what happened to the Garrys, and I don't know about you but I think she did!"

"Then call the police."

Weyland laughed, then turned to the crowd and shouted, "Shall we call the police or take care of this bitch ourselves?"

Their voices rose in an incoherent but unmistakably positive cry. The cry became a long, wild cheer, flashlights were clenched in fists and punched straight up into the air. The crowd began to move as a single entity away from the pickup toward Lorelle's house, all except for Weyland, who turned and jogged toward his own house.

George watched him go, then looked at Pastor Quillerman who was still unconscious on the ground. He turned to the moving crowd, felt suddenly alone and isolated and weary enough to lie down and close his eyes. Shut everything out, forget all of it, including his wife and children. But he couldn't, wouldn't, and hurried after the crowd instead. His pain had faded little and he still limped, but the knowledge that Karen was in that house and was in danger – along with everyone else who had joined Lorelle there – strengthened him and helped deaden the pain.

He followed, a small distance behind the crowd, but didn't worry about his lack of speed because he knew he'd catch up soon enough. But the prospect of catching up with them was not a comforting one because –

– George's neighbors, young and old, had become a tribe of screaming, snarling savages, more animal than human, with veins that flowed with cold, black hatred. Their eyes seemed to show more white than pupil and their lips were torn back over their teeth in hellish, skull-like grins as they ran toward Lorelle's house like a group of mad schoolchildren running for a playground at recess.

George ran after them.

* * * *

Robby stood at the window and watched it all. Jen stood beside him, clinging to his arm as if for life. He could feel her heart pounding against his elbow. They still wore their jackets.

"What're they doing?" she asked, her voice weak with fright.

Robby didn't answer. He wasn't sure he wanted to know.

"Look," Jen said, pointing at a single figure running across the street, well behind their father.

"Mr. Weyland."

"He's ... carrying something."

Chips of ice rolled through Robby's veins when he recognized the object Mr. Weyland was carrying. He pulled away from Jen and hurried toward the door. When she followed him, he spun around and said, "Stay here."

"I'm not staying here by myself."

"But what if Mom comes back and nobody's here?"

Her shoulders sagged and she looked at him sadly as she shook her head and said, "Robby, you know Mom's not coming back on her own. Lorelle won't let her. Lorelle's got her, or Mom wouldn't be over there in the first place."

He couldn't argue with her because he knew she was right, so he didn't protest when she followed him out the front door.

* * * *

George watched the crowd attack Lorelle's house. Broken glass crunched under stomping feet. The gardenia bushes in front of the house were trampled and the rectangular black mailbox on the wall by the front door was ripped off and thrown down the porch steps. The front door was pounded and kicked and angry voices clashed together as they shouted for their children, spouses and, loudest of all, for Lorelle.

Flashlight beams crossed like swords as they cut through the darkness. Occasionally, light flashed into one of the broken windows and fell on pale bare flesh and long grinning faces. Mocking laughter came from inside the house.

George spun around to see Weyland moving toward the house with a blue ten-gallon polyurethane kerosene can, its cap dangling by a thin chain from the two-inch spout.

"No, stop!" George shouted, throwing himself toward the man.

Weyland lifted the can before him and George slammed into it. The fluid splashed sloshed inside and splashed up out of the spout, slapping onto George's left cheek and shoulder, dribbling down his neck and stinging his skin. George staggered backward, coughing and sputtering.

Weyland grinned. "You want some more, Pritchard?"

"Please ... please don't."

"Then stop me!" He stepped around George, shouting into the crowd, "Okay, who's gotta light?"

George winced at the biting odor and sting of the kerosene that had spilled on him, but –

– it did not smell like kerosene.

George ran after Weyland, shouting his name. He grabbed the man's arm and spun him around. "That's gasoline, you idiot!" he snapped. "You're gonna kill yoursel –"

Weyland's fist struck George's jaw, clacked his teeth together and knocked him to the glass-strewn lawn. Turning his back on George, Weyland was swallowed by the crowd.

George sat up slowly, rubbing his jaw. How could Weyland not know that the can carried gasoline and not kerosene? Perhaps he knew, but wasn't aware of the difference between the two – that, unlike kerosene, gasoline fumes were flammable and could detonate the very air around a fire. But George doubted that. He didn't have time to figure out why Weyland would endanger his own life and the lives of everyone outside Lorelle's house. He had to get Karen. He stood and rushed back to the window, crying, "Karen, where are you? Karen come out here noowww!"

She popped up from beneath the window, naked and grinning, and said "Boo!" Her eyes were half-closed and she laughed drunkenly at her little joke as she swayed back and forth.

"Karen, get out of there now!"

"But I don't have a thing to wear," she giggled. She waved a hand back and forth in front of her face and wrinkled her nose. "You stink."

"Karen, you've got to get out of there! They're gonna torch this place and everyone in it and –"

"It won't matter," said a voice from behind her.

George moved the flashlight until its beam fell on Lorelle. She was naked ... and beautiful. Her former pale, sickly appearance was gone. She had a healthy, lustful glow.

"Nothing really matters anymore, does it, George?" she asked.

Or had she spoken at all? Suddenly, George was uncertain if the words had come from her or had floated silently through his head.

"Your family is no more, George," Lorelle went on – definitely out loud now – in a low, throaty voice. "It's finished. You've lost your wife – or should I say you've lost another wife – and your children will inevitably follow when they see what a failure you were in saving their mother."

The furious voices around him, the sounds of the front door cracking under the battering it was getting from the savage crowd, and the thick crunch of chunks of the house being broken away all faded as George listened to Lorelle. His pain was forgotten and he felt a growing tightness in his pants which, after a few hazy moments, he realized was due to his arousal at the very sound of Lorelle's voice.

"Why don't you come inside, George?" she purred, her voice the only sound in the world. "Come inside ... relax ... with your wife ... and me ... the three of us, George ... together ... "

It wouldn't be too difficult to climb through the window. He'd just have to avoid the spikes of glass stuck up in places. Then he'd be inside ... he'd be a part of the comforting darkness that surrounded Lorelle and Karen ... and all of the horrible things that had been happening would be over ... all the confusion and anxiety and anger and pain would end ... but –

– he smelled the gasoline again and jerked his head back with a gasp as the mad voices and sounds of destruction rushed in on him once again. He turned from Lorelle to Karen again, held out his hand and pleaded with her, "Come with me, Karen, please, the kids need you, I need you, please Karen, I love you and I'm not gonna leave you here, now come out the window right now Karen, right now right –

He stopped because he saw her eyes brighten for a moment. They opened wider and the dull, drunken look left them and she looked at the pieces of glass sticking up along the bottom of the window and said, "But I ... I'll cut m-myself." Her voice was weak but clear and, suddenly, afraid.

George saw that as a good sign and moved forward quickly using the butt of his flashlight to knock the pieces of glass out of the way.

He put an arm on the ledge and prepared to hoist himself up through the window so he could bring Karen out, but –

– Lorelle grinned and hissed, "Yes, George, come in. Come inside with us."

He froze, watching her as she took a few steps to stand behind Karen. She wrapped both arms around Karen's midriff, placed one hand over her groin, the other over one breast, and smiled at George over Karen's shoulder. But that wasn't the worst of it.

Karen smiled, too, then threw back her head and laughed hard.

George slid away from the window, horrified and sick. He felt as if the center of him had been hollowed out. In a heartbeat, all the events of the past days ran through his memory and he thought about what he'd done to Karen, about his infidelity and cruelty, his hateful thoughts toward her, and he felt crippled with regret. Suddenly, it didn't matter that Karen had been guilty of some of the same things. In fact, it didn't even occur to George.

"Please, Karen," he said, his throat thick with gathering tears. "I'm sorry for the things I've done and I promise that if you just come with me, I'll make up for all of it. We'll be fine. I swear. Please, we need you, honey, we –"

"I couldn't bear to look at your ugly cock one more time," she sneered.

George's words crumbled into a small, pathetic sound in his throat as he stared in open-mouthed horror at his wife.

"Dad! Dad!"

He heard Robby's voice but didn't turn. He couldn't. He knew he was looking at Karen for the last time ... and she was laughing.

The smell of gasoline was thick in the air and George

glanced to his right and saw Weyland walking toward him along the front of the house, splashing gasoline onto the front wall.

"Dad," Robby shouted, grabbing George's arm, "we've gotta get outta –"

"Mom!" Jen cried, hurrying past George toward the window, but –

– George swung an arm out and pulled her to him.

"Let me go!" she snapped. "Mom! Mommy, what're you doing in there, you've gotta come out right now you've gotta –"

All three of them were shoved out of the way by arms that snaked out of the small mob like tentacles. George and Robby fell to the ground, but Jen just stumbled backward, still calling for her mother.

"Everybody back!" Weyland shouted.

Lorelle began to laugh and her laughter rose above the manic voices.

The crowd backed away from the house and George got to his feet with Robby. "Run back to the house!" he shouted.

Robby hesitated.

"I said run!" Once the boy was running, George looked for Jen. She had disappeared in the crowd. He spotted her shouldering her way through to get to the house, still calling for Karen, who was now gone. The window was dark and empty. "Jen! Jennifer!" he screamed.

She ignored him.

George drove forward, knocking people aside, and wrapped his arms around her from behind. He lifted her from the ground and turned to carry her away from the house when –

– someone threw a lighted kerosene lantern at Lorelle's house and –

– the lantern smacked against the wall beneath a window as –

– George dragged Jen away from the house, shoving people aside again, horrified to see that they were grinning in anticipation, and Jen began to shriek as –

– a bone-cracking whump lit the night a bright orange and what sounded like the screams of hell rose around them as –

– the crowd of people was blown apart by a powerful rushing wall of burning air. Bodies burst into flames as they were thrown to the ground. George realized he was screaming, too, as he and Jen went down because –

– flames had burst from the left side of his face and his shoulder, and the sound of his own skin sizzling drowned out the cries of the burning people around him. He pushed his face into the damp grass beneath him and rolled his head back and forth, still screaming, but the searing pain that spread over his jaw and neck and over his shoulder as the fire burned quickly through his jacket was unbearable and his mind shut down. George lost consciousness.

* * * *

Robby had run when his dad told him to, but not all the way back to the house. He stopped in the street by the white pickup where Pastor Quillerman was pulling himself laboriously, painfully to his feet. Robby turned and faced Lorelle's house, walking backward the last few feet as he watched the crowd. He spotted his dad and Jen and kept his eyes locked on them.

"Whuh-what's happening?" Pastor Quillerman croaked. His face was dark with blood, his mustache caked with it, and the flesh around his glass eye was swollen and dark. But he seemed to have little interest in his own injuries.

Robby wasn't sure what to say at first, then answered as simply and accurately as he could; "They've all gone crazy."

"Yes," Quillerman said. "That's what she wanted."

Robby watched his dad drag his sister away from the house and through the crowd, but his attention was caught by the kerosene lantern that was thrown into the air. He cried out when the flames went up.

For a moment the air caught fire and –

– bodies flew with arms and legs splayed and –

– Robby was running before he even realized he'd moved, screaming for Dad before he knew he'd made a sound, because Dad had fallen to the ground with his face and shoulder in flames.

Jen knelt beside him, screaming, trying to help but too confused to do any good.

Robby tore his jacket off as he ran to Dad with the jacket held out before him. In seconds, he'd smothered the flames, but he could not smother the nauseating, clinging stench of burning flesh. He made shrill, childlike sounds as he snuffed out the fire. When he was finished, he was afraid to lift the jacket away from his dad's face.

Jen screamed, "Daddy Daddy Daddy Daddy," over and over again, but stopped when Robby pulled his jacket away and revealed what was left of their dad's face. His right eye was open wide, but the left was buried in blackened, glistening meat.

Robby lifted his head to shout for help and tell someone to call an ambulance, but his throat was hot and sore and his voice was nothing but a hoarse croak.. Sobbing, he turned toward Lorelle's house.

It was an inferno. Bodies were scattered on the lawn, some burning, some smoking, while some were up and about; others simply lay there on the grass. Voices screamed and shouted hysterically and at least one rose in maniacal laughter.

The house had been swallowed by roaring flames. Robby stared at it, feeling sick. His mother had been in there. Worse yet, she'd chosen to be in there.

The roar of the flames grew louder suddenly, and for a moment the fire grew brighter. With a sound like thunder, flames gathered and shot high into the air, writhing and expanding to take the shape of a flaming head and the form of a female body of fire and –

– there was a low rumbling sound that Robby could feel in the ground beneath him and the head lifted and a mouth opened and –

– it was gone in a pillar of black smoke and the fire burned as before.

"She'll go somewhere else."

Robby looked around to see Pastor Quillerman standing over him, staring at the fire.

"She'll go somewhere else and do it all over again. Just like all the others like her. And it gets easier for them every day." He knelt between Robby and Jen, whose face was buried in her hands as she cried. He frowned at George. "He needs to get to a hospital. I called 911. The ambulances will be here soon." He looked at Robby and Jen and asked softly, "Are you two all right? You aren't hurt, are you?"

Robby shook his head.

Jen sobbed into her palms. "Is he dead?"

Quillerman put an arm around her. "No, sweetheart, he's not dead."

She pulled her hands away. "He'll be scarred. Bad."

Squeezing her to him, Quillerman said, "All of us will be."

Robby spread his jacket over his trembling father as the screams and cries went on in the glow of the roaring fire.

About the Author

Ray Garton is the author of sixty books, including horror novels such as the Bram Stoker Award–nominated *Live Girls*, *Crucifax*, *Lot Lizards*, and *The Loveliest Dead*; thrillers like *Sex and Violence in Hollywood*, *Murder Was My Alibi*, and *Trade Secrets*; and seven short story collections. He has also written several movie and TV tie-ins and a number of young adult novels under the name Joseph Locke. In 2006, he received the Grand Master of Horror Award. He lives in northern California with his wife.

CPSIA information can be obtained at www.ICGtesting.com
Printed in the USA
LVOW11s1519151115

462668LV00002B/92/P